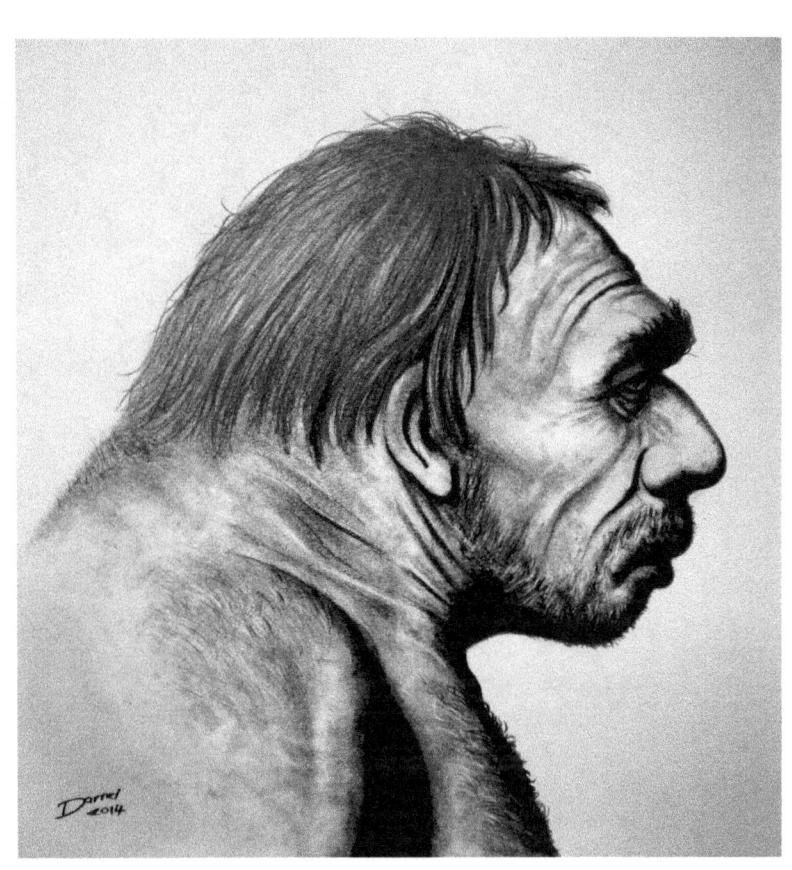

Contents

FOREWORD_____001

ACADEMIC TALENT_____003

ABOMINATION_____015

THE NEANDERTHAL SOLUTION_____031

A NEANDERTHAL IN BOHEMIA_____039

THE DISTANT APE_____053

ARC_____061

THE MODERN WOMAN_____077

ENGINEANDERTHALS_____093

THE UPHILL CLIMATE_____107

THE LUCKY ONES_____117

RIGHTS_____131

BORN ON A MONDAY_____145

A HARD MEAL_____151

THE PAST THAT YOU DON'T KNOW, CONTAINING
ALIENS_____159

FIRST MAN, LAST TRIBE_____175

EXPERT HELP_____187

A BRIEF HISTORY OF NEANDERTHALS IN
SPECULATIVE FICTION_____195

CONTRIBUTORS_____201

FOREWORD

Chris Amies

The 17th century hymn-writer Joachim Neander was so inspired by the valley near Dusseldorf where he lived most of his short life that two centuries later it was renamed after him: Neanderthal. And it was here in 1856 that curious heavy-set human remains were discovered. Others like it had been found previously in Belgium and Gibraltar and put aside as 'some kind of early human' but by the mid-1850s the scientific climate was such that the new discoveries were pounced on with glee.

We're most of us familiar with the Neanderthal look: sturdy, big-browed, the 'other' but still definitely human. Remains have been found across Europe from the Atlantic seaboard to the Urals, but nowhere else. The earliest, the Mousterian stone-tool culture, places Neanderthals in southern Europe about 300,000 years ago. And after about 30,000 years ago, there are no more. *Homo sapiens* neanderthalensis gives way to modern humans. The Neanderthal with their cold weather adaptations (brow ridges, big noses) may simply have been less adaptable to life in different environments. Current thinking is that they interbred with other human subspecies and the specific features died out; or mostly so. Red hair and white skin may well be Neanderthal characteristics; in which case they aren't as vanished as we would care to believe.

And given the 99.7% DNA correlation with modern humans (chimps are around 99%), would it be more than a tweak of the tail to bring them back? That is the idea behind the stories in this book. Here you will find tales of Neanderthals adapted to space flight or to mountain climbing; of the likely social status of 'designer' not-quite-humans; of thawed-out icemen finding a world much changed. How would we react to be sharing the world with Neanderthals all over again? Would we share it or would their future be silence?

ACADEMIC TALENT

Eric Stein

I answered the front door and met Carol with a warm hug. Then I shook the professor's hand. He nodded stiffly, forced a smile and asked how I was doing.

We made our way to the living room. He was taking in the scene, just like he always did. His expression was stony and his eyes lingered for an extra second over the new piece of artwork I'd hung in the entryway, and then over the gin and tonic I had left on the coffee table and then on the basketball game I'd been watching on the new flat-screen.

For a moment, I wished I'd ditched the drink and turned off the game before I answered the door. But then I thought, "Fuck it. I'm a man too, not his fucking museum exhibit, and if he doesn't like that then..."

I took a deep breath and offered to make him a drink. In the end of course, I knew that the improvement in my situation was mostly his doing. (Just as his good fortune was mostly because of me.) Carol was always talking about 'meeting the public's expectations,' and like it or not, the professor was the most important member of my public.

"Why that's very gracious of you, Grnntl, but not today. Thank you," he answered. The professor never accepted my hospitality.

"Ooh. I'll have a vodka and cranberry," Carol said. "I love what you've done with the place, G. The wet bar is an especially nice touch."

"Why thank you, Carol. Would you like the full tour? Wait till you see the new flooring I had put in in the main bathroom."

"I think we can pass on the tour for now, Grnntl," the professor said. The muscles in his neck were taut. "But that does sound very tasteful. Certainly very generous of the University, don't you think?"

The professor was wearing khaki pants, a sweater vest over a light button-down shirt open at the collar and tennis shoes, his uniform for our "casual" and "social" visits.

The professor appeared to be in his early sixties. The line of his grey hair started a couple inches above his forehead, accentuating the hard features of his face and his wiry neck.

He had more hair in the old videos I had seen but he had looked just as hard as he shouted back at the religious fanatics who used to demonstrate outside of his speaking engagements. Sometimes they would infiltrate his classes, pretending to be students and standing up in the middle of his lecture and shouting Old Testament verses. On a few occasions, they held multi-day vigils, making camp outside of his laboratory.

The professor held doctorates in both anthropology and genetic engineering. He had spent decades trying to make one of us, using DNA from old bones and such. He supposedly had gotten pretty close to succeeding.

In the end, though, that turned out to be much more effort than was necessary. Now, no one ever accused the professor of "playing God," whatever that means.

Before I answered him, I looked down into my drink and swirled it a little. I liked the sounds of the ice clinking against the glass.

"Well I certainly am grateful to the university and its donors," I said. "But you know, professor: many in the donor community view this sort of expense as a long-term investment."

He was silent for a moment before he answered.

"Is that so, Grnntl?"

"They do, in fact. The Chancellor and I were discussing this just the other day. He had invited me next door to see his new kitchen. You should see the countertops, Carol. Dark granite. To die for! He was saying that the competition for academic talent is so fierce these days. The college just has to do whatever it can to compete."

The professor stared at me blankly for several seconds.

"Academic talent?" he finally asked.

"Well," Carol said, sitting up straight and clapping her hands together. "That reminds me of the business we're here to discuss."

Carol then folded her hands in her lap and flashed that warm smile of hers. Carol smiled a lot. She would mingle at a reception, with a drink in her left hand, smiling at members of the press and foundation board members. She always remembered their names, no matter what city we were in or how long it had been since she had met the person before. She would smile and lightly touch their shoulder with her right hand and laugh as they discussed their family, or their latest academic honour or the good work their foundation was doing.

She was in her mid-thirties with short, dark hair that always looked like it had just been trimmed and styled. Unlike the professor she was clearly dressed for business, in heels and a pressed mid-length skirt. Carol always seemed to be dressed for business, whether the occasion was official or not. For Carol, nearly all business was social and most social occasions were really about business.

She wasn't an unattractive woman, despite the flat forehead and relative hairlessness. But I never thought of Carol as a potential mate. She was too important to me as a friend, one of few people who I believed really empathised with my situation.

That figured. Carol considered empathy to be her profession. Most people didn't think of Public Relations consultants that way, she had once told me, but that's really a PR person's main imperative. A Public Relations professional has to empathise with all the stakeholders in a public situation: the client, the press and the public.

"What can I do for you, Carol?" I asked her. "Are we taking this show on the road again?"

"We certainly are, G, and this is a very special trip." She turned and beamed at the professor. "Oliver, I have to say, I am so happy for you and so proud. I'm honoured just to be associated with this. Tell G. I'm sure he'll feel the same way."

The professor seemed to relax a little, almost but not quite smiling.

"I've been selected for a Lifetime Achievement Award from the International Academy of Anthropologists," he said.

"Hey! That's great, Oliver. Congratulations! Are you sure you wouldn't like a drink to celebrate?"

This was definitely a big deal. For myself as well as the professor. I thought about the media possibilities.

They seemed pretty good, but I couldn't see a way we could capitalise on this thing without giving the professor a lot of space in the spotlight. Unfortunately, that would reduce the upside. We would mostly be limited to public television and interviews with the more pointy-headed print media outlets. The professor was awkward and humourless. He refused to do the media training that Carol had arranged for him. So there would be no "Letterman" or "Good Morning America" on this occasion.

"So G," Carol said. "There will be a banquet and reception at Harvard. Oliver, of course, will be giving a speech on his work. And there will be a separate presentation where we would like you to share the stage with Oliver. You could be available to talk about Oliver's work from your perspective."

"You know you can count on me, Carol. Especially on this occasion. Wow. Really, congratulations Oliver."

"Yes, thank you Grnntl. Now... the logistics..." The professor paused for a moment and his eyes dropped toward my coffee table.

Here it comes, I thought.

The professor looked back up again and his eyes narrowed.

"The Harvard anthropology department has graciously arranged to make accommodations available for you," he said. "For this occasion, I would very much like you to accept this offer."

"Whoa. I don't know about that, Oliver," I said. I shook my head but I tried to keep smiling. I really didn't mean to be difficult. "That's going to be student housing. Really not very comfortable. You know, I'd kind of prefer to stay at the Boston Harbour Hotel. That's where I stayed on our last swing through Cambridge. It was really nice. The spa was excellent and I had this suite with a really spectacular view of the water. Carol, do you think we could get me that same suite?"

She looked at her shoes and shifted.

"Grnntl," the professor said. "I think it's important that you understand: this is a very important event, particularly to the scientific community."

He sighed. "Grnntl. You have learned a truly amazing amount in a short amount of time. But there are still things that you don't understand. Ways that you must behave."

"Oh, I understand, Professor." I tapped my forehead with my finger. "You said it yourself in our first research paper: 'We knew that the Neanderthal's larger cranium may have indicated a larger brain, but we never could have anticipated just how great an advantage this would afford him in many cognitive skills.'"

The professor blinked a couple of times. I felt giddy every time I had the opportunity to quote that line back to him.

I had first blown them away by picking up their language so quickly. Then they were all amazed by the development of what they called my 'social acuity.' The cute post-doc Courtney wanted to do a full study on it, but the doctor deemed the concept too 'fuzzy' and 'subjective.' When he told us this, Courtney and I exchanged glances and stifled our laughter. We joked for weeks about the professor's social acuity and it being fuzzy.

"Here is the thing, Grnntl," he said. "Just this once, could you please stay out of the night clubs?"

There was no way. The 'Caveman Night' they had had at that place on Boylston Street the last time we were in town was just about the best time I'd ever had.

"Now, Oliver, we've talked about this," I sighed. "I feel that when you make these requests, you're failing to respect my dignity and autonomy as a fellow human being."

There was one vein near the professor's left temple that seemed to bulge and grow more prominent at times like this. And the left corner of his mouth started to subtly twitch.

"Grnntl." He was speaking slowly now. "It is you who is failing to respect your dignity. And the dignity of what we are trying to accomplish here."

"What should I do, Professor? Should I show up to the banquet in a loin cloth and carry a spear? Should I grow out my hair and beard and stop washing it? Give it that three-day-hunting-party-in-pursuit-of-a-woolly-mammoth look?"

"That isn't necessary, Grnntl," he said through gritted teeth. "But it might look less ridiculous than your gold chains and your tattoo and some of the other choices you've..."

"Okay, gentlemen," Carol interrupted. "Now, this will be next month, the week of the seventeenth. I would like to fly in on Tuesday. That will give us time for plenty of media availability before the event on Friday. Now we have requests so far from the Boston Globe, CNN, NPR..."

"Excuse me, Carol."

"Yes, G?"

"Have you, by chance, checked on whether the Celtics are at home that week?"

I knew that she had. Carol was reliable like that.

"Well ... as a matter of fact, I do happen to know that they will be playing at home on Thursday night."

"Grnntl?" the professor said. "Is it really necessary for you to be on national television again, courtside at another basketball game?"

"Well, I suppose I could consider missing one. Carol, do we know who the Celtics are playing?"

Carol had a slight grin on her face and actually seemed to be blushing. She paused for a moment before she spoke.

"Well, G... I think the Lakers are going to be in town."

"The Lakers? Oh, you know I won't be missing that! Tickets! Carol, have you looked into tickets?"

She glanced sideways at the professor.

"As a matter of fact, G, we already have tickets."

"Oh for Christ's sake, Carol!" The professor pounded his fist on the arm of the leather couch. "Do you have to encourage this? One more time, a day for our accomplishments and the news will be dominated by images of him yelling like an idiot!"

"Actually, Oliver, Mr. Weathers bought the tickets for Grnntl. He said that they're a gift on behalf of the Foundation board for all of the work he's done."

The professor seethed for a moment before he spoke.

"Grnntl. If you have no respect for me, do you at least have any concern about your own dignity? Or your tribe's? Or for the field of anthropology? We give you all of the freedom and respect of a member of the human race and you repay me with..."

We were interrupted by the sound of shattering glass from down the hall. It must have been the sliding glass door between my bedroom and the breakfast patio, I thought. I started to stand when a young woman appeared in the hallway and levelled a gun at all three of us.

"Don't move, you fascists!" she screamed as she came out into the living room and walked sideways to her right along the wall.

A man emerged from the hallway after her, also armed and moved to the left so that the two of them were surrounding us.

The young woman wore a flannel shirt, ripped jeans and sandals. She wore her strawberry blonde hair in dreadlocks.

I know that the *Homo sapiens* associate dreadlocks with earthiness and closeness to nature, but they only made me think of my old mate back with the tribe. She was earthy and close to nature, I guess. She was a good kid but I hadn't thought of her much since they sent me away to the *Homo sapiens*. When I did, I mostly wondered what she would have made of all this. Would she like basketball and nightclubbing? Probably not. She would probably have found something totally different. So many choices.

The man was in his late thirties or early forties. He wore a tie-dyed shirt, jeans and beat up Converse sneakers. He was bald and had an enormous brown beard, bigger and nappier than my father's.

Both of them were wide-eyed and breathing heavily and the guns in their hands were shaking.

The woman yelled at the man to tie up "the two fascists."

"Oh, God!" I heard myself yelling. "Please don't hurt them!"

I was hyperventilating. I tried to imagine my life without my adviser and my sponsor; my mind saw nothing but blackness. Where would I go and what would I do?

Then I remembered a time back with the tribe. We had crept up on a doe grazing obliviously in an open glen. I steadied my spear, concentrated and let fly. The spear clattered against a boulder on the ground several feet to its right. Grntl laughed harshly as he bounded past me after the deer. Why don't you go back to the village and gather roots and berries with the women, Tsgrx hissed at me.

The man worked with duct tape to restrain the professor and Carol. His hands shook and he kept looking away from his work, furtively checking entryways and windows.

The woman was stroking my hair and speaking to me softly in a high-pitched voice like she was speaking to a baby she was trying to calm or a pet rabbit that she didn't want to startle.

"Oh, don't worry. We'll take you away from these evil fascists. Yes, we're going to take you, home, yes we will.." She continued in a quietly hissing stream of words as if I might start crying if she stopped.

The bearded guy finished restraining the professor and Carol.

"Okay," he said with intensity to the dreadlocked girl.

"Are you sure?" she snapped back. "If they get out it'll be all fucked up!"

"Yeah, yeah. I'm sure!" Bearded guy's voice was shaky and his eyes darted back and forth between the professor, Carol and dreadlock woman.

She turned to the professor and Carol and started screaming at them and gesturing with her gun. She told them not to dare try to escape for at least four hours. If they screwed this up, she would be back, she said. She called them fascists and said she would end their 'imperialism over the natural world.'

She and the bearded guy each took hold gently of one of my arms and walked me out the front door. A dark green, heavily dented early-model Toyota Corolla was parked at the curb in front of my house. The back bumper and hatchback door were plastered with bumper stickers in a wide variety of bright colours, most of them calling for "saving" one thing or another.

I recognised one of the stickers as the logo of FAHS — Free Archaic Human Species. At most of the professor's public appearances, there were usually four or five FAHS members hanging around outside the lecture hall, carrying signs and pressing fliers into people's hands.

Carol had warned us that we should stay alert when they were around. She said they were an offshoot of one of the radical animal rights groups who occasionally placed pipe bombs outside the offices of scientists who used animals in their research.

But the professor and I had both found FAHS comical. It was one of the few things we completely agreed on, although we each had our separate reasons. The professor was amused by how unthreatening they seemed, relative to the religious groups who obsessed over his work back in the days of his genetic engineering projects. I on the other hand would read their fliers and laugh hysterically over their idea of 'Free.'

They put me in the back of the car. My knees pressed against the front seat and there wasn't enough room to shift the position of my feet. The man sat in the back, next to me.

I tried to focus on keeping my breathing steady, but I was feeling slightly carsick. The woman was taking turns too quickly and gunning it out of stop signs and when lights turned from red to green.

She was winding away from the university district and out toward the countryside. We drove for a while with no talking, only the whine and rattle of the little car's engine and the darkness in my mind.

Now we were out of town and in the forested, rugged hills.

"Okay, Jed! Talk to him now!" the woman said,startling me back into the present.

Bearded guy turned to me. He was silent for a moment and his forehead wrinkled with concentration. Then his mouth contorted.

"Grntxlshhl. Hshklcklck. Sshsstpphft!"

I backed away, as best I could, into the couple inches of space I had in the corner of the back seat.

"Jed, you're scaring him!" the woman barked.

"Just a minute! Let me think!" he yelled back.

He blinked quickly a few times, took a deep breath, shut his eyes and was silent for another moment. Then he started again.

"Bra brashtnkikik! Shzingguk. Grak!"

"Oh, just stop, Jed! You fucking idiot! You're obviously doing it wrong and you're scaring him!"

"I..I don't get it!" Bearded guy's eyes were darting back and forth between me and dreadlock woman. "I read every word of that fucking book like ten times! I practiced it with Levi for weeks. In the car on the trip to Seattle we didn't hardly speak anything else."

Oh, Christ, I thought. The book.

Dr. Thurman spent more than a year working on it. Man, did that guy get tedious. I ended up making up a bunch of bullshit just to get the project over with. It would have taken a lifetime for me to have really given Thurman the rules of the language and the basic vocabulary. I mean I don't really know the rules. I never thought of them as rules. They were just ... talking. What did they think I was? A Neanderthal linguist?

The professor didn't want to publish it. When we discussed it, he would look at me kind of sideways. Thurman would stammer through the meetings,

"But ... but professor. My whole life for the past year..."

Carol ultimately held sway. She told the professor that he should view the book "not just as an academic work, but also as an awareness- and fundraising opportunity."

Bearded guy sat there staring at his feet and breathing shallowly with his mouth hanging open as dreadlock woman went on, at length and in detail, telling him how stupid he was.

Her voice rose and fell and as she spoke louder, her words came faster and she pressed harder on the accelerator. The Corolla ripped around tight blind curves on a bumpy, two-lane road through the forest.

"Oh! That book," I said and forced a laugh. "You know, you really shouldn't feel bad. We tried, but you can't really learn the language reading a book. Trust me guys. There's a lot to it."

With that, they were both quiet for a moment.

"Fucking bastards," dreadlock finally said in a voice that was low and quavering.

The car was stuffy and hard to breath in, but I then felt cold.

"They've even exploited your language," she continue and I saw a tear fall from her right eye and run down her cheek.

She quickly brought the car to a stop on a gravel turnout.

Bearded quickly got out of the car, stepped behind it and popped open the hatchback. I turned and saw he was taking out an enormous pair of clippers, larger than the ones my landscaper used to cut dead limbs from the big pine in my backyard.

I tried to scream but my voice caught in my throat as I hyperventilated. "Run!" I thought, but I froze. I imagined the cold as I was lost in the forest at night and the sting of cuts from running through the brush.

Then, dreadlock was standing outside and opening the door next to me and it was too late to run.

She reached out her left hand and started stroking my hair and cooing at me again like she had back at the house, only now tears were streaming down her face.

"Don't worry, Grnnt," she said. "We won't let them exploit you anymore. Now you can be innocent and noble and pure, again."

Beard walked up beside her. I looked between them and saw where he had cut a large hole in a chain-link fence.

Now I recognised where we were. This was the valley where we had lived.

It was the middle of nowhere really. Too rugged to develop, but not as scenic as the state park fifteen miles away or so. Overlooked even by hikers.

So we had lived here forever, hunting deer and rabbit and foraging roots and berries.

Then Professor Hempstead in the geology department did his big survey, using Google Earth images of the entire region. I forget what he was studying. So does just about everyone else who knows the story. Something about rock strata in the hillsides. What he found, of course, was long-range images of the tops of our heads as we sat around the fire and chased down rabbits.

We all nearly shit ourselves when Hempstead and his grad students showed up that day, riding ATVs.

The chief pushed me out in front. What with my lack of hunting skills, he figured I'd be the least costly sacrifice.

The *Homo sapiens* decided I was sent as an 'ambassador.' I never lied about that. Just never bothered to correct them.

Hempstead, humble guy that he is, happily turned me over to the famous and controversial 'Early Man expert' Dr. Oliver Burden and then went back to studying his rock formations.

So now here I was back where it all began, in the valley that was now a 'protected Early Man preserve.'

Dreadlocks and beard led me to the hole in the fence. She hugged me and he patted me on the back. They both backed away, smiling and waving, with big tears pouring down Dread's contorted face.

I smiled and waved back. They took forever to get back in the car. I couldn't decide which way I should run if something set her off again.

Finally the car crunched off of the gravel and buzzed off, trailing a cloud of dust, and I was alone on the edge of the preserve.

I thought if I walked into the preserve, I might be able to locate the tribe. Come nightfall, I would at least have a fire and some bland venison to eat.

But what if I don't find them, I thought, and I felt cold again.

I sat down and thought.

Then from up the valley, I heard a sound.

When I heard it, I knew what to do.

I would not freeze and starve to death. When I realised that, I felt warmer right away.

I am G, I thought. The resourceful 'Early Man' who had survived the whole early part of his life without modern resources.

The sound grew louder.

I stood up and went back to the road, and walked along its edge back in the direction of the university.

As the Volkswagen approached, I stuck out my right hand, thumb pointing up the road, and smiled back over my shoulder.

ABOMINATION

Matthew Sylvester

The doors to the lift ground open, dust in the tracks making a hair-raising noise. People who were already hunched over various desks and consoles hunched even more at the sound.

"This way please, ladies and gentlemen." The speaker was a fastidious little man in a spotless lab coat, hands covered by datagloves. "As you can see, and no doubt hear, the bombardment has reached even the confines of our lab. I am, however, assured by Bunker command that nothing the Enlightened have can reach us here. Not even a kinetic nuke."

He extended his arm, sweeping it out in a clear attempt to keep the party of officers moving.

"That's all well and good, Surgeon-General, but we're all veterans here. The only thing we"re worried about right now is whether the weapon will be ready."

The Surgeon-General stopped and faced the soldier. There was an impressive array of ribbons and campaign markers on his uniform, and a certain weariness that spoke of sleepless nights filled with memories of a past the General would like to forget.

I know that feeling all too well. I might not have been on the front lines, but I am still fighting as hard as they are, and making the same sacrifices as they. My life might not be in danger, but my soul, my soul is a different matter.

He forced a smile onto his face, the feeling completely alien. He couldn"t remember the last time he had genuinely smiled, and laughter seemed to be a dim and distant memory, almost mythical in nature.

"The weapon will be ready. Of course, the final decision will be left to the Military and the Papal Command, but I think that you will be pleased with the results. Follow me please."

He turned and walked away, not bothering to check as to whether they were following. He knew that curiosity and the need for a weapon that would mitigate the losses they were suffering in the war against the Enlightened would set their feet in motion.

***

General Mattheson watched as the Surgeon-General led them down corridor after corridor, sweeping past hermetically sealed rooms full of Bunkees in spotless lab uniforms. Signs on the walls were populated with writing that looked as if it was foreign, "WeaTechRKT", "RobPath" and "CybEnh" were just three of the signs he saw.

Please, Lord, let this weapon be worth all the effort, and resources, and aid us in our struggle against the those that would destroy us. The prayer was one he used daily, usually as he read through the latest casualty figures and watched as the Enlightened forces slowly pushed those of the Righteous back.

He bit back a snarl as he thought of the two sons he had already lost in the war, and of the two sons and a daughter that were currently topside, fighting in the shattered remains of once-beautiful cities that filled the nuclear and chemical wastelands.

Finally, they came to the end of the corridor, a door much heavier than any others he had seen preventing further process. Two guards wearing full combat gear stood with their weapons at port, and above them hung another sign, "NeaDNAthal".

What the fuck does that mean?

***

The room that they were led into was spotless, but this time there were just as many guards as there were Bunkees. All of the guards wore full combat gear, their body armour the latest and heaviest design in use.

Mattheson noticed a certain tension in everyone present. Normally guards stand as still as rocks, but these ones were constantly flexing their fingers, shrugging their shoulders and shifting on their feet, just like when a man is gearing himself for immediate action. The Bunkee technicians scuttled about like white ants, shooting nervous glances towards yet another door that was signposted as "Holding Cells".

What the hell is going on?

His curiosity was more than piqued. For everyone to be physically afraid of the new weapon, it had to be something far more unusual or effecting than a new bomb or weapon. To make them this scared, it had to be something truly unique, terrible, or effective. *I bloody hope it's all three, the bastard Enlightened are wiping us from the face of the planet. Just the thought of* the Enlightened was enough to make his stomach churn and his mouth dry. He had thought that he led the best soldiers there were, but the faith of the Enlightened was something that literally needed to be seen to be believed. They were more than happy to sacrifice themselves, building living bridges in the bio wire so that their comrades could gain a few extra yards, charging across a minefield in order to clear it for the regiments behind them.

Although his people believed that they were the Righteous, martyrdom was something that was still alien to them. Although in the dim and distant past many people had been martyred in the name of the Lord, it was incomprehensible that people would have such scant regard for their own lives. The body and soul were gifts from the Lord and gifts from the Lord were to be treasured, to be looked after. Such had been their belief at the start of the war. When faced with insurmountable odds, the Righteous would surrender, believing that they were saving not only their own lives, but also lives of the enemy. It was only when the Enlightened revealed that they would take no combatants prisoners, that the Commanders of the Righteous realised they would have to culture a "fight until the end" mentality in their own troops. Now, they fought until they were unable to. When they run out of ammunition they used their rifles as clubs, when they broke they used their knives, when they broke they fought literally tooth and nail. However, sacrificing their lives the way the Enlightened did was anathema to them, and so they continued to be forced back.

"Before we enter, I must warn you that what you are going to see has not been seen for millennia. Prepare yourself for something that *will* shock you to the core." The Surgeon-General quickly typed a passcode into the pad next to the door and stood aside as it hissed open.

Good Lord!

From the outside the door was deceptively normal-looking, but as it slowly opened, Mattheson could see that it was actually nearly two feet thick.

That must weigh tonnes. What the hell have they done here?

As the door opened, a cacophony of noise from the room beyond sprang forth as if it had been trying to escape the confines of the room all that time. Without a word, the Surgeon General stepped through.

Bastard's enjoying this.

Mattheson was always suspicious of scientists and weapons technicians. Even though they created weapons and defence systems that enabled his troops to perform to the best of their capabilities, they did so without a true understanding as to the effects that their developments had on their fellow human beings. They never truly saw, felt, heard, smelt or tasted the effects. Nor were they on the receiving end of the devices their opposite numbers within the ranks of the Enlightened developed.

Taking a deep breath to settle the cloud of flutterbys that threatened to fly up his throat and out of his mouth at any moment, he motioned to his entourage and stepped through the yawning doorway.

Inside the lighting was muted, blue light contrasting strongly with the harsh white glare of the room behind them. To either side of the room, bunk units formed a corridor of sorts, with solid-looking cell doors preventing anyone from seeing what was making the noise, flaps at eye height ready to be opened by the curious or those delivering meals to the occupants.

"General Mattheson, if you would care to be the first to see what we have ...created."

He looked over and saw that the Surgeon-General was stood by a door, fingers poised to open the hatch.

The flutterbys had turned to rocks, and his stomach churned, but curiosity and a fear of being seen to be afraid set his legs in motion.

By The Lord!

Eyes stared back at him, their sudden closeness causing him to jerk back and a strange hooting noise to come from the creature? *Man?* Inside.

He gingerly looked back through the hatch and saw what he first took to be a hairy man in a one-piece combat suit. The man, no, not a man, a thing, stared back at him.

Something tickled the back of Mattheson's mind as he took in the low brow, jutting jaw and small eyes of the cell's inhabitant. It stretched and he realised just how broad it was, just how powerful and deep its chest was, and just how strong it was as it flexed its arms, muscles standing out.

"What in God's name is that!" He spun towards the Surgeon-General, sending the little man stumbling backward, it was almost as if he thought I was going to hit him!

"It's the perfect soldier. Strong, obedient, intelligent yet unsophisticated and it suffers no mental injury from killing a human."

"They are from a long lost strain of human, pre-diaspora. Their genes are present in all of us, more so in those unfortunate enough to have ginger hair." The Surgeon-General paused, almost as if he was waiting for a laugh. When none were forthcoming he continued.

"We have broken every code of Genetic Conduct, gone against the teachings of our church, and created life when only The Lord can create life. We have created a weapon that will drive the Enlightened back, and put the fear of God into them."

Mattheson rocked back on his heels, opening his mouth to speak and closing it when he found himself unable to speak. The scientist was right, every law ever created with regard to genetics had been broken, every teaching from the Church of the Righteous ignored. This was blasphemy, heresy, immoral and, he sighed, necessary.

"I take it they have been tested in combat?"

"Indeed, we pitted them against enemy prisoners and members of the Penal Battalions. Even when outnumbered three-to-one they prevailed. It seems that they might actually enjoy fighting."

"If you give us the resources we need, we can accelerate the programme and have a regiment birthed in one month, combat-ready six weeks after that."

Mattheson looked at his entourage, all of whom had looked through the hatch and stood, pale-mouthed and slack-jawed. "Bishop, you speak for the Righteous Faith. What say you?"

The Bishop smoothed his burgundy red uniform, starting then stopping to speak several times before saying, "It is an abomination, but without this abomination we shall be wiped from existence by the Enlightened. You have our blessing."

Mattheson released a breath he did not realise he had been holding, "You better crack on Surgeon-General."

***

"Enemy heavy infantry, approaching, estimate platoon sized, engage at will."

The commbead clicked as she and her comrades acknowledged the order. Taking a better grip on her rifle she made sure it was snug and tight into her shoulder. Sensors in her glove interfaced with the targeting system and an aiming dot appeared on her visor.

Satan knows what these fucking creatures are, but after years of campaigning, I have never been part of a retreat. Satan willing I won't be today either.

She knew that was probably wishful thinking as only the day before the entire Western Front had been overwhelmed, panicked units streaming away from their positions in the face of this new threat.

A rifle cracked as one of her squad mates took a pot-shot at the approaching enemy. All of a sudden they surged forward, charging towards the improvised defences, hurling grenades and firing their guns from the hip as they did so.

She spotted a target, her sight automatically showing where she should fire in order to hit a moving target. One squeeze and three hyper-velocity rounds cut their way through the air before punching into the target's body armour. It barely paused as it leapt into the air, covering at least two meters in one seemingly effortless bound.

She adjusted her aim and fired again the rounds hitting dead centre but the target barely slowed.

What the fuck!

Even if the armour had stopped the rounds, the impact should have knocked the target off its feet, the internal dampers of her rifle preventing her from being blasted back.

Oh Lord Satan!

She slapped her commpad.

"It's them! The Abominations!"

She had barely finished speaking before the first of the Righteous Soldiers leapt the barricade, screaming a war cry that raised hairs all over her body.

Another trooper fired, blowing its rifle to flinders. Before they could fire again, the Abomination grabbed their head, and with a mighty wrench, yanked their head off.

Bile spewed from her mouth, splattering over her chest as she repeatedly pulled the trigger, emptying her magazine into the Abomination, the first bullets shredding the armour, weakening it and paving the way for the following bullets to blow fist-sized cavities in its torso.

Finally, and with a low, gurgling moan, the Abomination collapsed to the ground. She pulled the trigger once more and heard a click as the firing mechanism found no more rounds. Hastily she ejected the magazine, fumbling to find another when she heard a soft chuff of air next to her, the stench of halitosis attacking her nostrils.

She turned, her rifle dropping from her nerveless fingers as she looked into the face of an abomination, mere inches from her own. Blood caked its lips and the soft down that covered its face. It smiled slowly, revealing bloodied, jagged teeth, bits of flesh stuck between the gaps.

Pain exploded in her face as it snapped its head forward, slamming the front of its helmet down onto the bridge of her nose, shattering her visor. Before she knew it she was on the ground. Pain came again as it head butted her again and she watched as it drew back once more. The last thing she saw was the head descending again.

***

Mattheson watched as the Supreme Bishop of the Faithful paced in front of those gathered in the briefing room.

"For the first time in decades we are finally driving the Enlightened back, gentlemen."

"The NeaDNAthal units have been an unqualified success. Their deployment in areas of heavy resistance has proven to be crucial."

Mattheson could not resist a smile as he looked around at the men and women surrounding him and saw the life returning to their eyes. And yet, they can all tell there is a but coming.

"However, we have had some disturbing reports. Mattheson, if you please."

He stood, his mouth suddenly dry as the words he had prepared failed to emerge from the desert his tongue had become.

"Ahem." he cleared his throat as he looked at the expectant crowd in front of him. "Right. Yes. Well, there's no way to say this gently. At present we are now winning this war. Our NeaDNAthal units are, as the Supreme Bishop says, and I"m paraphrasing here, kicking the living shit out of the enemy."

He paused as laughter and raucous shouts came from the crowd. None were ranked less than Colonel and all of them were seasoned veterans but the joy they were experiencing at the sudden turnabout in their fortunes could not be contained.

"But. And this is a fucking big but if you"ll excuse my language, there have been reports of units failing to obey orders."

I've got their attention now. Poor sods.

"In some cases, they have exhibited a wilful tendency to capture the wrong objectives. This is despite the Behavioural Modification Collars."

There was a collective gasp at this. One of the caveats that had been put in place prior to full development was that Behavioural Modification Collars be used as a form of reward and punishment. They were supposed to be foolproof.

"That's not the worst of it. There has been one report of a trooper asking 'Why?'"

Silence reigned for a second as that last statement made its way to their brains. That silence ended as indignant shouts, shocked exclamations and even laughter rang out.

"Calm please. At present it has been decided that these incidents are too isolated to be a cause for any great worry."

The lie sat on his tongue like a fresh turd and he had to resist the urge to spit.

"The troopers in question were executed. Any other breaches of discipline should be recorded, reported and the perpetrators executed. Carry on."

***

Onethreefiveslashnine laughed. It felt good to squeeze the life from the human. They screamed and squealed like a female being taken for the first time, their fear filling the nostrils with a heady perfume. He dropped the dead trooper and stood to see how his brothers fared.

The hatred he felt for them went beyond being forced to fight for them and against them. Something, some *memory* at the back of his brain *itched.*

His brothers surged past him, ripping the Enlightened troopers apart. He laughed in sheer delight as he watched a pair of them pull the arms from one of the humans, clubbing him to the ground with the limbs before beating him to death.

"Stop wasting time! Move forward you dumb fucks" he cringed at the words, knowing what was to come next. Pain filled his body, his entire *being* as his human controller keyed their collars.

Gritting his teeth, refusing to cry out he turned and faced the human. Looking at him, he marvelled that they had survived for so long. He knew that they were obviously more intelligent, that they had been able to craft tools more efficiently, but he also knew that they had made a mistake when they birthed him and his brothers. They had granted far too much intelligence.

"Get moving you fucking monkey!"

The human thumbed the controller again and pain blossomed. His teeth felt as if ants were trying to dig their way out of them and the marrow of his bones as if it was molten lead. Still he resisted, relishing the look of dumb surprise on the human's hairless face.

Slowly, fighting the need to scream in an attempt to release the pain, he reached out, gently cupping the sides of the controller's face.

"Why? Why hurt us? What afraid of?"

The language he had been taught lacked the finesse of his people's true language which involved posture, gesture, tone and inflection.

The human opened his mouth, whether to answer the question or curse him again he neither knew nor cared. Instead he quickly twisted his hands and thrust his thumbs into the controller's eyes, pushing, he sunk them to the second knuckle, hooked and then gouged them back out drawing not only the eyes but also brains out. He let the screaming man drop to the floor, relishing the sound of his screams.

Turning he faced his brothers.

"Spread the word: from now we fight for ourselves."

***

M attheson rubbed at his eyes, wishing that they did not feel so gritty, and that he was not so tired he could barely see straight. Sighing, he looked at the woman opposite him.

Not bad looking if you like the hard-nosed-bitch type. Great tits.

Tits, he struggled to remember the last time he had actually seen a pair outside of the communal showers. It had been so long since he saw his wife that just trying to recall her features was an effort he found too hard to bother with.

"Look, you can throw all the blame you like our way. We fucking know that we were wrong to create the NeaDNAthals. However, if you hadn"t started this war in the first place, and allowed us to just get on with things, we wouldn"t have done it."

"Now..."

The bitch stopped talking as he slammed his palm down onto the table, his calloused hand making a snap that caused everyone around the table to start.

Fuck, that hurt more than I thought it would.

"I'm not casting blame, woman! Both sides are as guilty as the other, and blaming each other for wrongs done will not get us out of the shit-hole we have created. Now, unless you have something other than religious rhetoric, political dogma or any other such nonsense, I suggest that we discuss how the Hell we deal with this threat."

He leaned forward and looked down the table towards the two glowering priests sitting opposite each other.

"And I firmly suggest that you two stop pulling bloody faces."

He jabbed his finger at each of them as he spoke.

"Forget the differences in ideology and remember that you are *both* responsible for the souls of your flocks. If these talks fail, their souls will be lost.

"With that in mind, I declare the first peace talks between the forces of the Righteous and the Enlightened formally open. Bishops, you will begin."

He sat back in his chair, pretending to not notice the daggers that his counterpart was shooting him. *It's my bunker, my command centre and my fucking meeting, deal with it.* He found it both funny and sad that even when both sides had a common enemy, that she was still more interested in scoring points over him, than looking at how they could work together and counter the threat.

***

Muffled screams came from the burning tank. The missile had penetrated the rear of the turret, fired from within the rubble and targeting the weakest side of the armour. Flames shot from the vision slits and a great cloud of burning smoke puffed into the air as the commander's hatch opened.

What emerged was barely recognisable as human. Low moans escaped from a charred mouth, the eyes burst in the extreme heat, skin burned off and body fat running down over teeth exposed by lips that had been cooked off.

Hands that were little more than claws tried to get a purchase as survival instinct refused to let the commander give up, with one last moan he froze in place, the superheated smoke and gases from below finally killing him.

With the tank dead, the infantry it had been supporting were suddenly vulnerable. Panicked orders were shouted and men and women dashed for cover, trying to spot their ambushers, listening for the next shot.

"Go."

One simple word. A mere breath when compared to a full sentence. A word that was death to the huddled troops. A word that he relished giving.

NeaDNAthals popped up from hidden positions, some in the very middle of the human soldier's positions. Whilst those on the outside shot the soldiers nearest them, those in the middle were the best close combat troops the humans would face.

Armed with what most would call primitive weapons, the close combat specialists ripped into the humans. Knifes slashed and stabbed, spears were thrust clean through body armour, maces crushed bones and smashed visors and swords cut and chopped through limbs.

In less than ten seconds, an entire platoon of the newly formed Army of the Faithful lay in the rubble, dead or dying. No prisoners was a mantra that all sides understood and followed. The Army of the Faithful could not let the Abominations continue to survive, and the NeaDNAthals wanted nothing more than to kill as many humans as they possibly could.

"Withdraw."

What passed for silence in a war-zone suddenly descended as the sounds of hacking, stabbing, shooting and dying stopped, the NeaDNAthals moving swiftly away from the scene of the massacre.

Quickly they made their way to the next rendezvous point, jumping into pre-prepared positions next to those already there. The wait was short. The dust on the rubble started to shift, gently at first, but then more and more vigorously, the sound of tanks growing louder and louder, the vibrations from their power plants working its way into the bodies of the waiting NeaDNAthals until they thought their teeth would chatter themselves to pieces.

"Wait."

Joy filled him: even working together, the humans were struggling to destroy his people. The capture of the breeding centres meant that his people were able not only replace their losses, but to grow the population far beyond anything the humans had ever conceived.

Even now, as he and his brothers fought and died in the ruined cities and barren planets the humans had created in their war of folly, others of his people prepared to leave. War, although glorious, was sustainable. Survival of the species, survival of any species, should always take precedent. Whilst he and his brothers fought the humans to a standstill, space-worthy merchant ships, cruise liners and private yachts were being repurposed and stocked, made ready to take his people away from human-space.

The first of the tanks rumbled out of a side road further up the street they were on, turning to face towards them. Infantry fanned out to either side, dashing to points of cover, and pepper-potting their way up.

More armoured vehicles and infantry followed, until at least one hundred infantry, a scratch company, were making their way forward. He laughed silently as, even though they wore body armour, he could see their fear. It was as plain as their ugly noses. They scuttled, like drunken beetles, moving from cover to cover, knowing that the enemy was near, but unable to detect them.

His people had discovered a number of innate skills, skills which the Elders had claimed came from a past that not even the humans truly remembered. A time when they lived on only one planet according to the records they had captured. Fighting and hunting were two examples, with concealment being another. Combined, these skills made them consummate soldiers, exactly what they were bred to be. However, they were far more than what they were bred to be.

The Elders had read the medical reports, in which the scientist's pride of success was clearly mixed with the fear of what they had created. The NeaDNAthals had surpassed all of the targets originally set, but rather than redesign the strain, the scientists had just raised the bar, pushing further and further into a science that had been banned for centuries.

Now, their people were paying for their arrogance. He took aim at a non-com directing a heavy weapons team. He knew no further orders needed to be given. He was the Hunt Elder: when he shot they shot. When he moved, they moved. It was the way of his people. Be One, in order to be one. Stand together in unity.

He took a slow breath, breathed out and held it. A gentle pull on the trigger was all it took to send a burst of rounds through his target's visor, blowing the back of his head clean off mid-order. As soon as he did so, the rest of the Hunt opened fire. Missiles and rocket-propelled grenades raced through the air towards the armour, whilst high-velocity rounds, grenades and gouts of napalm cut the infantry down.

Surrounded on three sides, with the armoured support either disabled or destroyed, the infantry panicked. Fluster fire sprayed in all directions, with all semblance of fire-discipline flying out of the window. Contrasting orders by the human commanders sent some squads into a counter-attack, whilst others were told to withdraw, the NeaDNAthals taking lethal advantage of the confusion.

'Sweep."

Slowly but surely, his people moved through the ambush site, finishing off the wounded, setting traps beneath the bodies, and then returned to their original positions to wait for the reinforcements their victims were sure to have called for.

***

People often wonder why retreating armies suffer such heavy casualties. The simple reason was that when an army is retreating, its focus is on the direction it is moving, not the direction from which the enemy is coming, usually behind.

Defensive formations are also nigh impossible to form, which is why rear guards are used. They dig in to hastily prepared defences and fight for as long as they can before they are either massacred, or allowed to pull back to the next defensive line.

Retreats turn once-proud soldiers into haggard scarecrows that walk with their shoulders slumped, twitching at the slightest threat – real or perceived – and often losing equipment on the way, further reducing their combat effectiveness.

Knowing this was of no help to Mattheson as he roared past column after column of soldiers shambling along the highways and through the fields. Time-after-time they had launched counter-attacks in a desperate attempt to hold the NeaDNAthals back, and time-after-time they had seen those attacks not just defeated, but destroyed, vital men and materiel lost.

He looked down at his pristine uniform, the HQ braid serving to make him stand out even more than the fact that his uniform was clean and his face shaven. The men standing aside to let his command vehicle past resembled shabby, haggard shadows of their former selves. Looking closer he could see men and women wearing a mix of Righteous and Enlightened equipment, forced to scavenge from the dead in order to keep fighting.

A sudden screeching filled his ears and a shadow raced overhead. Explosions thundered behind him, barely giving him a chance to duck his head and cross his hands in the brace position before his car was struck. There was chest-crushing impact, a sudden absence of air, sharp pain and then nothing.

When he came too, it took him a while to realise that the vehicle was upside down. Blood covered what was now the roof and he knew without having to look that his driver was dead. A quickly as he could, he unbuckled himself and then opened the escape hatch in the floor.

Oh Lord!

A combination of smoke, heat and the stench of burnt flesh forced him back into the vehicle. He scrabbled around and finally found a respirator. Taking a deep breath he put the mask on, then released his breath in one big push, expelling any bad air that might have been trapped.

Reaching up he pulled himself out of the wrecked command vehicle, gasping at the sight before him. Where before there had been a column of men and women, plasmapalm burned, turning the earth and highway beneath it, to glass with the heat.

Those soldiers that had not been within the blast radius were still recognisable as having been humans at some point, but they were still charred husks of flesh.

Even those that had been more than fifty feet away from the bombs had been killed by the heat; burning to death and suffocating as the air around them was sucked into the firestorm.

He turned, bile rising as he tried to scrub the sight from his memory, looking for anyone that might have survived. On the other side of the broad highway he spotted soldiers returning from the fields where they had scattered for cover. Staggering towards them, his legs feeling as weak as a newborn foal's, he located a commtrooper.

Snatching the voice unit from the trooper, he keyed in a code, "This Mattheson, the 25th Combined Operational Corps is, of now, combat ineffective. Approach five to the capital is open, repeat, open. Strongly suggest we consider asking for terms of peace."

Tossing the voice unit back, he started walking, praying that he could find a serviceable vehicle and get back to command central.

***

I *can't believe the bitch is still trying to score points.*
Mattheson was relieved he had been required to handover his sidearm prior to commencement of the meeting, the way that his opposite number refused to see sense was causing him to start to lose all sense of self-control.

He could sense that others in the room were becoming just as irritated, which was why he also wished he had the comforting weight of his pistol at his hip. *Not that a pistol would be much help, they'd kill us before we had a chance to get more than one shot off.*

"Semantics aside, who's right and who's wrong aside, I think that both the Righteous and the Enlightened are in agreement that further combative actions against the NeaDNAthals are futile at best and are detrimental to the ongoing existence."

"Similarly, we are in agreement that not only is it impossible for the Righteous and the Enlightened to co-exist, it is impossible for Humans and NeaDNAthals to co-exist. Does anyone wish to dispute these two statements?"

He raised an eyebrow, staring at his counterpart, daring her to contradict points that had been discussed at length for the last two hours.

"Good."

He smiled, relishing the way her fists clenched, her jaw muscles standing out as she forced herself to remain silent.

"Then let us discuss a Concord of Peace between the Righteous and Enlightened, and a Treaty of Exodus for the NeaDNAthals."

Stick that in your pipe and smoke it.

***

The whiskey burned its way down his throat, leaving a lovely numbness on his tongue and just a hint of honey and cinnamon. He chased it down with fresh spring water, preferring that to mixing, *Good Lord that tastes good.*

Mattheson turned the volume up on the tridee, taking another sip and relishing the pictures that were being broadcast system wide. It was broken into a triptych consisting of the reporter, ground-based shots and shots taken from one of the off-word spaceports.

The ground-based one showed ship after ship launching, great clouds of fire, dust and exhaust fumes rushing along the ground as the ships literally punched their way through the sky. The camera panned to show lines of NeaDNAthals making their way into other ships, to wait for their turn to leave.

The camera in the space port also showed ships, but these were completely different to those that the NeaDNAthals were using. These could never truly be mistaken for anything but combat-ready ships. Even if they were decommissioned and had all of their weapons and sensor arrays stripped, they would still look like predators that were merely biding their time.

Mattheson grinned, relieved that the Enlightened had been forced to leave under the terms of the agreement, their shattered forces limping away to lick their wounds. He knew, deep down, that this was a pyrrhic victory, that they would be back once they had had time to recover. Next time, surprise would no longer be on their side. Next time they would be facing an enemy that was battle-hardened, with a population still ready and willing to defend themselves, their loved ones and their faith.

He flicked his eyes to the ground-based camera, watching the slow procession of NeaDNAthals as they entered their ships. This too was a Pyrrhic victory: a new race was taking to the stars, heading to planets that had been earmarked for colonisation by both the Righteous and the Enlightened once proper terraforming had been completed. These worlds were too difficult for humans to live on, with harsh climates and apex predators that would cause more trouble than it was worth, but had been accepted by the NeaDNAthal elders with what he could have sworn was well-disguised glee.

Another sip, another smile.

Yes, they'll both be back, but for now, we're at peace.

THE NEANDERTHAL SOLUTION

Anne Henderson

The red-headed people sat around the circle of fire singing about the snow that would come as soon as the wind from the moon side began to blow through the rough vegetation of the plateau. Later, as the temperature dropped, they would walk in their strong slow gait to their shelters and wait for the sun to rise again so they could see the mountain in the distance.

The not-as-white people would come from the mountain before the snows arrived. They moved quickly like the animals of the forest when there was no snow, much more rapidly than the red-headed people. The songs from long ago told of the killing of the red headed people many suns ago by people who moved quickly. The not-as-white men caused babies in the women. The births sometimes died, but all were buried with the elders in the burial cave decorated with pictures of animals that could be used as food for the dead spirits. The ones that lived were not light skinned with red hair. Their hair and big eyes were dark. They were called the strange ones. The not-as-white people came to get the strange boys when the snows stopped and took them away to a land on the other side of the mountain.

Dawid left the circle of fire. He moved swiftly and quietly through the brush and headed to the dark side of the mountain called Anboto. He had left supplies in a small shelter made of bones on the side of the mountain. He knew that the not-as-white people would not look for him near their pathway; they would head straight for the circle of fire. Dawid was a strange one. His mother had hidden him from the not-as-white people since birth and he grew up to be the singer, the teller of tales for the white ones. He sat in horror in his little shelter as the not-as-white people came over and down the mountain and destroyed his little community of red-haired people. He watched his mother die.

Dawid put his head in his hands and whimpered like a young animal. After many days, he felt a hand touch his back. It was a young girl of the not-as-white people.

"Food," she said quietly, one of the few words that remained in common between the two groups.

Dawid began to cook the grains he had in his bag. Hot stones from the fire were removed with a skin glove and thrown into water in a leather pouch. Once the water was hot, he threw the grains in and they waited watching each other carefully. Mari was crippled. Her group had left her to die in a small cave.

The progeny of Dawid and Mari became the Basque peoples. They made their own language, a crude mixture of the languages of people who would later become known as the Neanderthals and that of a similar people (and perhaps the same species, *Homo sapiens*). The years passed and a little community formed in the Pyrenees, all directly related to Dawid and Mari. The strong people raised goats and learn to cook the goats with the wild grains of the plain around the mountain. They ate and knew the green plants and used those with medicinal qualities. They also protected their people from the roaming remaining Neanderthals as well as the encroaching not-as-white H. sapiens peoples. Dawid and Mari became the gods of the people. Mari's cave is now a shrine.

After hundreds and thousands of years the remaining small populations of the Neanderthals were diluted by the other peoples of the world, and now all Indo-Europeans have Neanderthal DNA. The singing red-headed people were and are still viewed by many, including some religious sects, as monkeys, a species with little connection to the H. sapiens people. But they were us.

***

In a massive, but ugly, church in the Midwest USA, a minister of the Lord is defining evolution for the vast congregation using an over juiced loudspeaker,

"We have people standing by to take your donations for Jesus. Yes, we take credit cards, and for each $100 dollar donation, you will receive free, absolutely free, my latest book on evolution, called *The Bible and Evolution*. Think about your savings for a new car - your money squirrelled away for a vacation. These are temporary pleasures. Your money invested in Jesus will bring you a real miracle, an everlasting purchase. Just use your money for Jesus. Operators will be standing by for 17 minutes to take your calls for donations to this important endeavour of telling Christians about biblical science."

The minister cleared his throat and looked straight into the TV camera.

"Over the years people have wanted proof that God created us … Hallelujah, you know the answer, but let's talk about this. Science can only exist in terms of the Christian mind. Even great scholars know this to be true. It required God for us to have a mind that can understand what is happening in the universe. "

He stopped and took off his jacket and wiped the sweat from his face. He then continued more forcefully, banging his fist against the podium in impatience.

"The operators are still standing by waiting for your pledge. Send them $100 today. What you need is a miracle and Jesus will give you a miracle. How do we know what happened in the past? We weren't there, but thank God we have the Bible to tell us events in the past. Human arguments may be powerful, but it is the Bible that gives people the truth. The bible teaches us science.

"Jesus said: "But from the beginning of the creation, God 'made them male and female.'"

"When did this happen? The evolution people say it all occurred billions of years ago. Puh lease, if you believe Christ is Lord and are dedicated to following the words of Jesus, then this becomes an enormous problem. Do you think Jesus lied? No indeed, Jesus does not lie. That means that evolution as discussed in all of those expensive textbooks is a big fat lie.

"God made the laws of nature. Evolution is thought to be millions of years of probabilities. There are people who believe … yes believe …. that God created people using evolution. They are avoiding the truth.

"And who were the Neanderthals you will ask and what do they have to do with the so-called evolution theories? Some believe they were monkeys, one of many animals in the Garden of Eden. I give you proof in my book that they were early human nomads, one of the groups that left Babel. The difference in skulls between ancient people and modern man is probably just the result of differences in inbred family traits. The differences don't appear to have happened until the Neanderthals were of an advanced age. Perhaps they were the group of people that lived hundreds of years as described in Genesis and the really older people, like Abraham, had slightly misshaped skulls. The Neanderthals were just a tribe created as the result of a union between Adam and Eve."

***

An e-mail campaign was started by the Associated Churches of America Group, an offspring of Serious Conservatives for Christ, all of whom believed the Neanderthals to be great big ugly monkeys. The religious war was on.

The e-mails started to flow.

From Willy PhD:

"I am attaching a scan of an unconfirmed report of early religious warring. Now you will know—every time you see someone with red-hair, a long torso and short legs you will realise that the Neanderthals did not lose, they just got integrated into us.

Willy

Attachment...NEWS FROM THE WEB - Neanderthals Lost the Religious War

By Felice Cohen

Date: July 20, 20xx

Evidence has been gathered from recent archaeological digs which suggests that religious wars are not a feature of advanced civilisations. The Neanderthals that dwelled in the last outpost near the Pyrenees lost their final battle to the emerging species of Homo sapiens. *They were the last of the peoples that believed in the gods that caused the sun to rise and set. The* Homo sapiens *group, on the other hand, believed in the sacred fire. The religious wars destroyed the Neanderthal culture forever. All remaining males and a portion of the females were rushed into battle in their struggle for survival. (Click on the little Neanderthal man for further information)*

And in the E-mails all over the USA on the next day -

People of the Faith,

May god be with us (and I mean our god) and our campaign to teach the ignorant about how mankind came to be on this earth. The university professor and even some of our religious brethren actually believe that we were once animal- like creatures like Neanderthals. We should forgive their stupidity. They are looking at monkeys fighting it out and calling this a religious war to confuse our children and all children of god.

God did not look like a monkey nor did Adam and Eve. Evolutionary theories are a plot of the Devil. The scripture tells us this. God created the world in 6 days, not billions of years. Anyway, the laws of thermodynamics refute evolution.

Have a blessed day
Your friend in Jesus
REMEMBER TO PASS THIS MESSAGE ON TO AT LEAST 20 PEOPLE, If you don't pass it on, we cannot guarantee that your next six weeks will be happy.

***

It was a public statement made by a scientist that he was searching for a mother as a surrogate to produce a cloned Neanderthal baby that sent the news agencies into full gear. It certainly enraged those who strictly believed in the Bible's interpretation of the beginning of mankind.

"There is a *99.7%* correlation of DNA base pairs between moderns and the ancient Neanderthals and something like 3 to 4% of the DNA of modern man was derived from Neanderthals. The original Neanderthal population even shared some basic language capacities with *Homo sapiens*. So a portion of the Neanderthal's DNA remains in all people except those that came from Africa. Assuming that the chromosomes of Neanderthal people were relatively close to those of more modern peoples, there should have been no problem with interbreeding between the two groups, and inbreeding did occur, probably from members of the original group in the Pyrenees, but also from mating those due to slave trade. Strangely, there is no direct inheritance in the female line, only the male. The closest fit to Neanderthal could be the Basque peoples which have the highest population of Rh negative and type O blood in the world, as well as a large percentage of peoples with red hair and green eyes.

" I am seeking a surrogate to give birth to a cloned Neanderthal baby. We should prepare now for scientific breakthrough that should occur in the next few years." The scientist closed his notes, looked up and smiled.

Newspapers from the NY Times to the National Enquirer ran the story almost as soon as the appropriate DNA analyses were complete. There were imagined pictures on the front pages, everything from the monkey-like dark hairy caveman with a huge browline and large nose to more modern depictions of a rather dishevelled hairy person in a business suit carrying a briefcase.

The headlines were screeching, "YOUR NEW NEXT DOOR

NEIGHBOUR? NOMINATE A MOTHER!" and from the Daily News, "THIS COULD BE A HAIRY SITUATION."

The evangelist continued the diatribe.

"God made man in his image, not man made man in the image of a monkey. This will not tell us anything about evolution since there is no such thing as evolution. There is nothing in the Bible about evolving. We were put here by God and it is a sin to mess with what God did. The Bible says so."

A special session of congress was held to discuss government funding of DNA research, particularly the sequence and cloning laboratories. This was a contentious discussion since the latest polls showed that over fifty percent of congress does not believe in evolution.

"Scientists are agents of the devil," the senator exploded for all of TV land, "We cannot in good conscience fund this anti-religious crap. God's word is the only truth. There are hundreds of scientists with all kinds of scientific prizes who believe that intelligent design is the only way that makes sense. There are too many holes in the theory of evolution. "

The senator had red hair and a short torso.

"These scientists are the same ones as those running around in snowmobiles in Alaska trying to shut out pipelines down. They just say they are digging up frozen dinosaurs. They just like playing out there in the snow using our money."

Pickets formed outside university laboratories:

DON'T PLAY GOD WITH MY TAXES
THERE ARE ENOUGH MONKEYS INSIDE THIS BUILDING.
WE DON'T NEED TO MAKE MORE
TAKE YOUR DNA AND SHOVE IT

A lot of the people looked like the same guys that picket abortion clinics. Every state legislature had a different view, but many voted science labs in general out of existence with little forethought. The result was the closing down of the manufacture of antibiotics or development of artificial limbs. If one laboratory went down, they all went down. The general populace was so brainwashed that a vote of the populace was useless. The decision for scientists to continue to be funded for evolutionary or any studies ultimately went to the Supreme Court.

The real question was whether the government should allow research that was contrary to religious beliefs in the country. The controversy was particularly aimed at situations where state schools were involved, but the intent to close laboratories also extended to private laboratories and foundations. Some intern had dug up evidence that most government funding goes to private, not public education. The Court was pushed back to the same old argument and debates would go on for years.

In the interim, European laboratories began the Neanderthal project. The Neanderthal genome was sequenced and plans were made to clone a Neanderthal person. Then someone had the brilliant idea to take two individuals with distinct Neanderthal features, both physical and genetic, have them mate, and test the DNA of the offspring for similarities to the Neanderthal genetic pattern. The initial offspring were short, stocky, light skinned and Rh negative. The experiment has been going on for some generations now (using in vitro fertilisation), each generation showing a higher and higher percentage of Neanderthal DNA.

It was back to the Supreme Court when one of the individuals applied for US citizenship.

"We don't want Neanderthals in our country," announced the conservative leader of the senate, "Never had 'em, never will. They can go back where they came from, wherever that was. And no, they cannot marry in my state or in this country as far as I am concerned. We cannot have monkey-like people and their children running amuck in our country."

The decision is still out. The Neanderthals have formed their own community while they wait for the results of the Supreme Court Ruling. I cannot tell you where it is.

A NEANDERTHAL IN BOHEMIA

Christer Van

In the year 1888 I took up residence in the city of Paris, establishing my practice to meet the needs of a very special client. While I have no need of other custom, my methods require the knowledge that can only be gained from contact with the public, although such matters need not involve me on a personal level. There are, throughout the city of Paris, several large rooms retained to further my investigations, occupied by those whose call upon my services have established a degree of loyalty that most employers could never enjoy.

The term armchair detective is one that I have heard—suggesting that only the power of critical thought is needed to find the hidden secrets that unlock the mysteries of the world. Such ideas are patent nonsense, for only through observation, induction and deduction can the truth be found. I am merely fortunate that I do not usually need to leave my chambers to observe. The city has eyes and ears, and many of those are in my employ. Researchers, advertisers, telephonists, nightwatchmen, postmen and more, they need only employ the tricks I teach to do my work for me, and they need only report their observations for me to learn.

The following narrative, however, came from a different source.

There is, somewhere in the 18th Arrondissement an old curiosity shop, and it is here, in a dimly lit room surrounded by the stacks of old worn books that gather dust over the antique space beneath, that I received a visitor. Alerted by the tinkling of the shop bell I felt, rather than heard the soft tread on the stair. It was enough for me to determine that this was a tall man, but of slender build—wiry rather than heavy—and that he was used to making a cautious entrance. Here then was a professional gentleman, carrying out his business, and that business involved a great deal of stealth and attention. A light measured knock on the door was followed by its opening before permission was granted—a confident man, then, and the catch of metal against the door frame told me he held a stick—doubtless the lack of care meant that he held his hat in his hand, although the absence of a pause told me he had not removed his coat.

I am not a blind man, but I find it useful to secrete myself behind a sturdy bookshelf out of immediate view—either through the windows, or to anyone entering through the door.

"Mr Sherlock Holmes, I believe." It seemed rude not to let the man know I had his measure. "Do take the seat provided. How can I be of assistance?"

I heard Holmes cross the small space in which an armchair had been prepared for visitors. It groaned slightly as he sat, and he wasted no time reaching into his pockets and withdrawing a cigarette.

"I shall not take up much of your time, sir. I simply wish to pass on a client."

"There is nothing simple about such a passing. Your personal attention in the matter offers three possibilities. Either you are curious to meet me and require an excuse, or else you are in Paris on a matter that demands too much of your attention to properly consider your case."

"Both are accurate, but I suspect the third possibility is the more relevant."

"It is a local case then?" I asked, already certain of the answer. "Someone recognised you or discovered your whereabouts and took the opportunity to present themselves or their case."

"Indeed," said Holmes. "I see that you use similar methods to my own, and that your premises are deliberately disadvantageous to those methods. I cannot determine anything other than that which I already know."

"Just leave the note for me on the side table," I said. "Unless you have other information you consider pertinent."

"Out of curiosity, how did you deduce that I had a note?"

"Can you not guess?"

"I do not guess, sir. I observe, I measure, I test. I was observed, or else I signalled my intention to reach into my pocket."

"Both. You were observed by agents acting on my behalf, because the movements of the great Sherlock Holmes have value, and may have bearing on investigations of my own. Had I not been aware of that fact, your mention of a case rather than a client would have alerted me."

"We are but fencing, sir. I leave the note here for you, and I am confident no information that I provide will illuminate you further. I also leave my card, and ask that you update me once the matter is concluded."

With that, the detective lit his cigarette, rose from the armchair, and departed. I, not having risen from my own chair, turned to the bookshelf beside me. The two chairs had been arranged in the fashion of a Catholic confessional, but instead of a grill the space between myself and my visitor had been taken up with a false panel, made to resemble an armful of tightly packed books. Sliding it aside, I reached through and retrieved the note.

From my agents I had already ascertained that the man who thrust the note into Holmes' hands had done so as the detective left the Paris Central Station. He had, based upon his clothes, been an itinerant war veteran who—unless he had acquired the clothes from someone else—had served in the Austro-Prussian War. The note confirmed this observation, having been written in German. It had been hastily written using a blank page torn from a small book, although the length of the note suggests he wrote it whilst travelling on the same train as Holmes, whom my sources told me had been in Vienna. The paper itself had been blank, although the dimensions and water-staining suggested it was something the man always carried on his person, while the implement used to write it—a red grease pencil—was not a common possession. The note itself contained a heartfelt missive from a concerned father seeking help for a lost son. Apparently the boy had been determined to enlist in the Landwehr, despite being a cripple. The father had approached the recruiters and been turned away with denials, and claimed to have been evicted from his lodgings for being 'unpatriotic'. He immediately sold what little he had to pay for passage to London to seek out Sherlock Holmes to ask if he would return with him to Prague in order to investigate the boy's disappearance.

Now here was a thing. A war veteran whose patriotic son wants to follow in his footsteps does not sound like a dissenter, so the eviction was for another reason. The idea of a father so convinced of wrongdoing that he crossed half of Europe to get help would certainly appeal to the detective's ego, but from my knowledge of Holmes his interest is only in the most particular of cases. This was just a missing person. Like Holmes, such matters do not usually command my attention, although I would happily pass it on to those who would track down the boy on my behalf, confirm his whereabouts, and draft a letter for me to sign informing the father of his son's predicament.

I dismissed arrogance as Holmes' motive for passing the matter on, concluding instead that this was a test of my methods, and that my response would provide him with more information than my offices had. Taking the case out of curiosity, I set the wheels into motion, and soon I was on my way to the city of Prague.

***

With the shadow of a major conflict hanging over continental Europe, uncertain alliances were being forged with Royal blood of the major nations. Flimsy treaties were binding hostile states together as the old alliances and confederations gave way to the new.

Newly separated from the mighty German Empire by its defeat during the Austro-Prussian War, the Austro-Hungarian Empire was still the third great continental power, and the possibility of future conflicts had forced the Reichsrat into dangerous territory.

The security of the Empire was under threat from all sides—the war had seen to that, triggering military escalations between its growing arsenal and those of the other great powers. As well as Prussian, there were British and Russian interests provoking the actions of well-funded anarchists and assassins desperate to undermine the Empire. Already the suicide of Crown Prince Rudolf at Mayerling had left Emperor Franz Joseph without a direct heir, throwing the Habsburg succession into turmoil.

As the hereditary King of Bohemia, Wilhelm von Ormstein was at the centre of a power-struggle with his cousins, desperate to find political leverage to reinforce the legitimacy of his bloodline. Already he had become the figurehead for a Czech and Bohemian nationalist revival while his secret police, the Fekete Osztály, allegedly named after the famous Fekete Sereg, the Black Legion of Matthias Corvinus in the fifteenth century, was certainly not a band of mercenaries like its forbears, but a highly organised force that combined the ethics of the Petrograd Okhrana with the methods of the ancient Fida'yin of medieval Persia. They had already infiltrated much of the Landwehr and the loose web of autonomous regional institutions that held the lands of the Empire and the Crown of Saint Stephen together. The marked differences between Austria and Hungary made it difficult to have influence over both, and so the King had been keen to back any strategy that might bolster his ambitions.

The Fekete Osztály had easily uncovered the whereabouts of one such opportunity. There was a Jewish scientist, Professor Albert Loewenstein, said to be descended from the famous Rabbi Loew of Prague, the notorious mystic rumoured to have created an artificial man from clay. His career marred by such nonsense, the professor had abandoned the major universities, preferring to stay among his own people, relying instead upon correspondence with his peers—men like Corazón, Knox and Moreau—chemists and vivisectionists who had themselves been tainted by the controversies of their experiments.

It had been Major Dvořák, the Chief of the Fekete Osztály and Wilhelm's personal security adviser, who had alerted the King to Loewenstein's interests. There had been rumours that the scientist had been frequenting various sites in Germany, Moravia and Croatia, interfering with the work of zealous palaeontologists who—either from anti-Semitism or professional jealousy—reported his activities in an attempt to deter him from his own excavations. Further investigation had uncovered the strangest of experiments, which Wilhelm had agreed to fund in return for certain assurances.

Booted heels clicked as the Major drew to attention before his King. Dressed from head to toe in a smart black uniform whose cut closely resembled the piped blue livery of the Landwehr, but with a single exception. Instead of a peaked cap, Dvořák wore a close-fitting Uhlan cap—better known since the Crimean war as a balaclava—which covered the whole of his face with the exception of his eyes. Anonymity was an essential part of the Fekete Osztály ethos, and only the identifier —X-1—which replaced the more traditional rank insignia at his collar, betrayed his identity.

"Your Majesty!" he barked, coming to attention three feet short of Wilhelm's desk.

The King of Bohemia was a tall dark-haired man with strong cheekbones and the slightest hint of a duelling scar on his right cheek. His straight, prominent chin and thick, hanging lip belied the cruelty of his eyes.

"All is good, I hope, Dvořák," he said. "What matter brings you to me today?"

"The genizah is ready for inspection at your convenience, Your Majesty."

In the Hebrew language a genizah was a temporary repository for worn-out books, which was traditionally situated in a synagogue or cemetery—the Jews forbade the throwing away of books containing the name of God, and required them to be properly buried—but in this case the term referred to the hiding place of Rabbi Loew's Golem, and to the old secrets that Loewenstein, at the King's behest, was resurrecting.

"Already? That is excellent news, Major. Have an unmarked carriage prepared. My convenience is now."

***

According to Dvořák's files the boy, Gerhardt, had been a patriotic simpleton whose deformed arm and clubbed foot rendered him of little use for service in the Landwehr. The Major had been present on the day he had attempted to sign up, and had seen the fire in his eyes and the eagerness in his belly. Choosing to spare him the life of a pauper, Dvořák had made the arrangements which saw his assignment to Loewenstein's experiment. This had not been an act of kindness—the boy was otherwise useless, but his simple ways had made him easy to persuade, and the promise of a cure for his afflictions in return for a life of service to the Emperor had been readily accepted. There was some trouble when the father came looking, but the matter had been dealt with swiftly, and simply.

Placed into the professor's care, Gerhardt had been billeted in a small room, unfurnished but for a single bed and a washbasin. This was luxury to a boy who had grown up on the streets, and his gratitude had been expressed through volunteering for menial work in the scientist's service. Sweeping floors, fetching and carrying while Professor Loewenstein worked on the cure. When he wasn't working, Gerhardt was subjected to a variety of tests and examinations which he had been assured were of vital importance, determining the physical and mental limits of his health so that the correct dosage might be administered when the cure was ready. This meant little to boy, whose only thoughts were of being fit, healthy and able to serve his country when the time came. He had been spared the truth—that he was as likely to die as to be cured, and that the cure might effect such an extreme transformation that nothing of the original Gerhardt would exist.

Summoned to the professor's *chedar*—his study—Gerhardt waited as the white-haired old man stood, his back turned, testing the cloudy contents of an Erlenmeyer flask that cooled on the instrument-filled workbench before him.

"Boy," he called him over, "see here."

"Yes, sir," Gerhardt complied, standing beside his master as the scientist poured the contents of the flask into a drinking glass.

"Once you have imbibed this condensate there will be no turning back. The process will have begun. It will quickly enter your bloodstream and prepare you for what is to come. I have taken what precautions I can, but there will be pain beyond description as your body adjusts, and the shock of the treatment could kill you as much as cure. Do you understand me?"

"Yes, sir. I have been as good as dead for all my life. The pain in my joints is with me every day, and the shame I feel when people look away from me is more than I can bear. I want this, sir."

"You are a brave boy. I just wish you could better understand what lies ahead. Whatever happens you will both further the interests of science and bring mankind closer to hokhmah. Now, drink," he offered the cup, "and when you are done you should rest until we are called."

***

Josefov, the former ghetto still referred to by the citizens of Prague as der Judenstadt, was well known for its educated émigrés. The Jewish population had waxed and waned over the centuries, alternately welcomed, scapegoated and exiled according to the politics of the day, but in the present climate Prague had become a refuge for those facing persecution in the other continental states. With almost a quarter of the city's population being of Jewish origin, clashes between a handful of Zionists and the growing number of Czech and Bohemian nationalists had seen relationships strained, and now the threat of political repercussions hung over the Quarter once more.

Being popular with the nationalists, King Wilhelm could not risk his reputation by receiving Jewish visitors at his home, nor could he risk being seen within the boundaries of the Judenstadt itself. The current situation, however, called for desperate measures, and as darkness shrouded the city an unmarked brougham bore him towards Loewenstein's laboratory.

Despite the unmarked brougham and a change into civilian clothing, the Landwehr and agents of the Fekete Osztály had been despatched, out of uniform, to secure the King's route. Adopting the mask of the fictitious Count von Kramm—an incognito Wilhelm often assumed during his more pleasurable assignations—he was borne deep into the heart of the Jewish Quarter, where the carriage came to an abrupt halt outside the Old Jewish Cemetery. Here they disembarked, entering the graveyard through the old walled entrance.

The irony of the location was not lost on Wilhelm. The anti-Semite Goedsche had written of the Prague Cemetery, describing it as the place where Jewish elders met in secret, conspiring to take over the world. It was patent nonsense of course. Yes, there were secret places here, but the only planning being done was in the name of Austro-Hungary.

Dvořák, retaining his balaclava but otherwise dressed as a civilian, conducted Wilhelm through layer upon layer of tightly packed tombstones until, at last, they came to a domed mausoleum—the genizah after which the experiment had been named. Here they were greeted by another of the Fekete Osztály, who ushered them inside the barren space that lay beyond. The chamber was empty but for a flaming faggot set into the wall and two small piles of old books and letters. In the centre a circular stone cover had been set aside to reveal a shaft and ladder which would lead them underground. Following Dvořák, the King descended into the secret necropolis that lay beneath the cemetery.

Moving along the narrow passageway, the King's small entourage picked its way past corpse-filled shelves and ancient tomb-markers. After several hundred metres they emerged into a large circular space lit by a chain of evenly spaced bullseye lanterns, making the ancient auditorium feel more like a modern lecture theatre. In the centre of the chamber was a laboratory workspace that included an upright tilt table with sturdy leather straps designed to secure the head, wrists and ankles. Beside this was a long table on which a diverse selection of beakers and scientific instruments was laid out. This included a row of stoppered phials, each of which contained various coloured liquids.

A young man, plainly dressed, welcomed the party, escorting them to the surrounding circle of ancient stone benches where, besides the King and his companions, a number of the Empire's leading scientists were already gathered.

"Your Majesty," said the young man, "with your permission we shall convene the presentation. Professor Loewenstein will deliver his report before we commence."

"And where is the professor?" Wilhelm asked.

"He will be with us momentarily," replied the young man, before turning his attention to the layout of the long table, making some final preparations while his guests waited.

When he eventually appeared, Loewenstein was accompanied by a young bald-headed, slack-jawed boy, who shuffled slowly into the room, drawing attention to his poor health and disabilities. Cautiously, the boy joined the professor in the centre of the room as the older man addressed his small audience.

"Your Majesty, gentlemen, let me introduce you to our subject, Gerhardt. He is a willing volunteer whose disabilities have prevented him from serving the Reichsrat, but whose body has been vigorously examined to ensure, as well as we can manage, the best results."

Turning to his assistant, there was a brief exchange of words before the younger man passed a slender white object to the professor.

"This relic," said Loewenstein, "is a femur. It was recovered from a limestone quarry at Neandershöhle near Düsseldorf in 1850. Mistaken for the bones of an ancient bear, these fragments have since been confirmed as those of an ancient human. Not like you or I, but perhaps one of Lyell's missing links. Within a few years the scientific community was afire, debating the origins of these bones—from those of Mongolian Cossack to an Ape. We are settled upon the consensus that the bones belong to an ancestor species, *Homo Neanderthalensis*.

"But whatever the creature's physiology, we can be sure of the qualities that it may have. Stronger, more bestial and most probably microcephalic. I am not, however, a palaeontologist, and I do not, therefore, seek to put forward such arguments. Instead I mean to unlock the answer to these debates by another route—a process, if you will—one which has the untapped potential for creating a new and capable force from amongst the alien, the weak and the infirm."

"*Homo Neanderthalensis* would appear to be quite different to modern man, and I believe that a more primitive consciousness might produce a more compliant people, easier to teach, to command, and to exploit. These may only be theoretical assumptions on my part, but based upon work I have previously conducted with other colleagues."

"These"—he indicated the rack of liquid-filled phials—"contain the product of my research. For six months I have been working on the difficult and dangerous task that you have set me. Using cells extracted from the bone marrow of our primitive cousin, I have successfully isolated the chemical characteristics which define the species, distilling them into an unique serum."

Calling his young assistant over, Loewenstein guided Gerhardt to the tilt table, where they secured the boy firmly with the leather straps. Satisfied that the boy could not do himself any harm, the scientist returned his attention to his audience.

"Due to the pain of the transformation I am about to induce, Gerhardt's skin has already been administered with a desensitizing solution of morphine and iodine. You will also note that his body hair has been removed to enable you to observe the transformation with greater clarity."

"Unfortunately, the boy must remain conscious throughout the transformation. This process has its risks, and it is possible that he may be driven mad by what we are about to do."

"What are you about to do, Professor?" Asked the King, "And what do you mean by 'transformation'?"

"Note the facial features and the shape of the boy's cranium, Your Majesty," Loewenstein replied. "They are unique to *Homo sapiens*. On administering my serum, the hard bone tissues will break and the softer body tissues will warp. The physical body shall be changed beyond recognition, imbuing Gerhardt here with the physical properties of *Homo Neanderthalensis*."

"Professor," the boy called out, interrupting the old man, "will all of my bones break?"

"Hush, boy," the scientist whispered, "we are committed now; and yes, they will break, and stretch, and reform. Otto."

At the professor's nod, the young assistant placed a harness over the body's head, fixing a strap into his mouth to stop the tongue from choking him, and to prevent him from biting into his own flesh. Ignoring the boy's widening eyes and muffled screams, Loewenstein returned to his work. Pulling a small trolley from beneath his work table, the professor moved the rack of phials and placed them beside a series of steel-tipped hypodermic syringes.

"Now, observe. I shall inject each condensate in order. This will ensure the appropriate nutrients have been infused before the final serum—the catalyst—is introduced."

"Forgive me, Your Majesty," said Major Dvořák, attempting to rise. "I must check that everything is secure."

"Nonsense," the King took his shoulder and pressed him back onto his bench. "Your men have the place secure. This is the good part, No?"

Reluctantly, the Major acquiesced. When he had risen, the eyes of his men had fallen upon him. They were certainly alert, and this was not the time to distract them. Back in the centre of the auditorium the professor had been loading the syringes with the contents of the phials. One by one he plunged them into young Gerhardt's veins, infusing the boy with their unique chemical cocktails whose effects were almost immediate as each serum coursed through his blood, rapidly being absorbed into the organs, the muscles, the bones, the brain and the soft tissues in between.

One by one the audience rose in shock and wonder as the physical transformation began. The sounds of cracking and stretching preceded the slow trickle of blood and clear fluids from the boy's ears and nose and the stifled ululation of his blood-curdling screams.

Whispers passed among the King and his companions. It was working—the boy was changing before their very eyes, swelling up, his limbs thickening, his stature shifting, his pores sprouting a mixture of greasy perspiration and fine lengths of hair, as if he were turning into a bear or a wolf. Some could not tear their gazes from the scene before them, while others buried their faces in their hands. King Wilhelm chose the former, transfixed by the scene that played out before his eyes.

"Behold!" Cried Loewenstein in triumph, "Neanderthal Man is among us!"

***

The room was silent. The beast—such as it appeared to be—was silent, its head slumped against the leather strap that held it in place, as it had been since the boy lost consciousness. It was covered in a light skein of downy fur from head to toe, and its muscular body sagged into the restraints. The barrel chest—which rose and fell with each deep breath—and the ape-like cranium were not so different from those of a modern man, but different enough to be remarkable. King Wilhelm was the first to his feet, his hands applauding vigorously. One by one the other witnesses stood and started to clap.

Loewenstein beamed. He had not been certain of success, but it had worked!

"This, gentlemen, is an achievement I could only dream of. Note that the transformation has produced a healthy, toned specimen. The legs are even, the arms fully functional, and where we previously saw a malnourished boy, you see before you a very healthy specimen. Now, I hesitate to mention the consequences of our success. It may take a year or two, but by replicating the process we can transform the sick, the weak, the stupid and the disabled. Imagine a wounded soldier, unfit for combat, taking up a hospital bed, doomed to a slow and agonizing death. Now imagine administering a serum that transforms him from one form to another. Rejuvenation, gentlemen. The complete cellular transformation of the body. I believe that with my serum it is possible to imbue men with other qualities—not just of *Homo Neanderthalensis*, but also with animal characteristics. Teeth, claws, sense, there may be no limit to what we can achieve."

"This is most excellent," said King Wilhelm, leaning in to share his thoughts with his security advisor. "From what this Jew says, perhaps we might be able to transform the ignorant African into the superior Saxon!"

"I've heard enough," said the Major, drawing his side-arm and thrusting it into King Wilhelm's ribs. His accent had shifted from flawless Czech to something with a hint of French. "This is one scheme I cannot allow to reach its conclusion."

"What are you doing?" King Wilhelm demanded, his voice shaken. As he glanced towards the gunman, he saw the man reach for the Uhlan cap, which he pulled away to reveal a face unlike any he had seen before—almost any, for it bore a striking resemblance to the brute that young Gerhardt had become. The bald head, deeply scarred, bore the heavy brow and prominent jaw of the Neanderthal. It certainly wasn't the face Major Dvořák. "Who—what—are you?"

"My card," I said, bowing slightly as I offered up my carte de visite. It had been a simple enough disguise, and the stupidity of the military balaclava had made it the simplest infiltration I think I have ever achieved. The King, feeling the pressure of the gun barrel, graciously accepted the card, giving it a cursory examination. On the front was the black and white portrait taken when I was a much younger—and much less self-conscious—man. On the opposite side it introduced me:

"M. Sauvage
Trouveur de secrets cachés
82 Boulevard de Clichy. Paris"

"Finder of hidden secrets? You are a French detective?" The King was clearly distressed at my duplicity. The anger in his eyes was dangerous, so I increased the pressure on his ribs to deter him from any unnecessary bravery. I may be a nihilist by choice, but I had no desire to become an assassin.

"All you need to know is that I am a concerned citizen, Your Majesty." Stepping away from the King, I turned my gun towards the centre of the auditorium. It barked as I fired two shots, which crashed into the professor's workbench, shattering two beakers whose contents were guaranteed to react. The bench erupted into bright red flame, licking Professor Loewenstein's sleeve as he ran for cover. Beating at his arm he fled from the chamber, while I used the brief distraction to quickly clamber over the stone benches towards the centre of the room, turning once to let off another shot over the King's head.

With their monarch out of immediate danger, two of the audience—plain-clothes officers of the Fekete Osztály—drew side-arms of their own and began to fire at me. Given the ridiculous protocols of the organisation, they had probably never seen Dvořák's face, and I couldn't be certain if they were poor shots or missing me on purpose. A third officer, meanwhile, ran over to the King, shielding him from further danger and escorting him from the chamber. The various scientists and other dignitaries similarly withdrew as I took shelter behind the tilt-table and its semi-conscious occupant.

"Don't shoot the beasts!" Ordered Wilhelm. "Withdraw! Place a cordon around this place and flush him out later; and find out what happened to the real Major Dvořák!"

***

The auditorium emptied quickly as the King's party disappeared into the Prague necropolis. Surprised at how quickly they had vacated, and how few men had stayed to shoot at me, I turned my attention toward the boy, Gerhardt. Releasing his straps, I lowered the youth carefully to the ground.

"Gerhardt, isn't it? I'm M. Sauvage. I'm sorry I couldn't get to you before this happened. I am here on behalf of your father."

Neanderthal eyes flickered open and Neanderthal eyes stared back. Gerhardt took a deep breath and instinctively knew that mine were of the same kind. He wouldn't understand what was happening to him. His mind would feel stronger than he had ever been, but his thoughts would be... different. Given that I have only ever thought like a Neanderthal, I am perhaps not the best person to judge.

"It's your brain, Gerhardt. It works differently. Let me ask you a question. Why did you volunteer?"

"I am... was...loyal to the Empire. My father and my father's father were Magyars, but I see things differently now. I am no longer Magyar."

"No, you are not. Could you kill another man?"

"A man?" A frown crossed Gerhardt's troubled brow. "Why would I want to do that?"

"An enemy of the Reichsrat, perhaps? Could you shoot him?"

"No. I abhor violence. I wouldn't want to kill."

"Excellent," I said. It seemed that the way he thought now mirrored my own. This was a relief, but it also meant the experiment was a complete success. "Our people have always been pacifists, and those fools wanted to make a soldier of you. Had I not intervened they would quickly have realised their failure. You need to come with me—what you see will help you to understand."

The boy blinked, and wordlessly rose as I helped him to his feet. Pausing to retrieve the femur, we left the burning chamber together, making our way out towards Loewenstein's *chedar*. By the time we arrived the room had been abandoned. Papers had been hastily disturbed and the scientific equipment was untouched. Setting the remains of the room alight, we made our exit, following the winding passageways of the necropolis in total darkness. As we walked, I knew that Gerhardt's eyes would be adjusting themselves to the shadows. We have better night vision than *Homo sapiens*, and even without a light source we could see the path ahead. He probably watched me discard the professor's lauded femur bone among a similar pile stacked up in one of the funereal niches. Rather than finding the nearest exit, I suggested that we take random turns until we found a distant way out far from the guns and eyes of King Wilhelm's secret police.

***

For all of its resources, the Fekete Osztály had little chance of finding the boy, or I. My methods are thorough, and my precautions are considerable. We may not have destroyed Loewenstein's work, but at least he—and his fellow vivisectionists—were on my watch list. He would be gone for a while, hidden away from prying eyes, deep within Josefov. I felt sorry for those around him, who might think of him only as an achiever, the son of a Rabbi and a pillar of the community, rather than as the antithesis of his people. At least I knew better, and they will be better off without him. There are ways of destroying a reputation, and that would be a priority for me long before finding him became a priority for the Fekete. They would find Major Dvořák easily enough, locked inside a basement room deep beneath Prague's Old Royal Palace. With luck his job will be secure—better the devil you know—although the King had been quick to order Fekete agents to Paris without consultation, which could mean his most influential days are over. Their investigations will draw a blank—they will discover that my given address is none other than the location of the Moulin Rouge Theatre, whose community is a tight-lipped bunch as hard to infiltrate as any secret police force. Harder, if my own experience is anything to go by.

Which leaves the boy. I should be sorry that he was forced to undergo such a painful transformation, but I am not. The new Gerhardt is far from simple. A quick learner in fact. There may be trouble ahead with his father—I have postponed reintroducing them until the boy is sure it is what we wants. I had been alone in the world, but now—for a while at least—I have a protégé.

THE DISTANT APE

Andrew Freudenberg

Marko yawned and forced his eyes open. The combination of the *Tereshkova*'s constant rumble and the expansive command chairs was extremely soporific.

"Welcome back to the world of the living."

Anya grinned and unbuckled her seat harness. She floated over to him and kissed him on the cheek.

"I was dreaming about the village again."

"Well that's nothing new."

"This one was different. In the dream we weren't just an experiment. We were real. It felt…"

"Good?"

"No. That's not it. It felt natural. I'd forgotten that feeling."

"I know Marko. I was there too. Remember?"

Marko grunted and looked past her into the blackness beyond the cabin window. Mars was visible in the distance, a dim red baseball. Stars glinted like a blanket of sparks behind it. He rubbed his eyes. It was two months since launch and the novelty of space had worn thin. This was different though. Now he was looking at his future home.

"Sorry. I need some caffeine."

Anya stroked his cheek with the palm of her hand.

"Would you like me to get you some?"

"That would be great. Thanks. Sorry."

She gave him a reassuring smile and disappeared through the exit. Once she was gone he sighed and tried to push the shadows from his mind. Memories of their old lives bought the worst out in him. He tried not to dwell on it. He was angry enough already. Anyway, it was time to make his report.

"Computer ready transmission."

"Transmission mode online."

"Spacecraft *Tereshkova* reporting. All systems are optimal. End report."

"Transmission mode offline."

Anya reappeared with a canister of hot coffee.

"Chatty as usual?"

"They might still respond."

"I doubt it. I think they're starting to think you don't like them."

Marko glanced at her and saw from the sparkle in her eyes that she was playing games with him. He allowed himself a small smile. Fate hadn't often been kind to him but in this case it had outdone itself. She was both a great beauty and a borderline genius. He loved her distinctive facial features. Her prominent brow ridge and protruding nose were pure Neanderthal. Wide shoulders and a long neck topped a body that was strong in a way no human female could ever be. He acknowledged that his disgust for *Homo sapiens* may have bolstered his desire for her, but his feelings were unquestionably romantic. They were the last of their kind, born for each other. How could there be any doubt that they were meant to be together?

"Less than a week to go now Marko. Is it time yet?"

Her words woke him from his reverie and he sat upright, suddenly wide-awake.

"I think so. Are you still one hundred percent with me? I know I've asked you a dozen times but I don't want you to have any doubt."

"For the thirteenth time … I have no doubts. It has to be done."

"I was planning to do it in a couple of days but I don't suppose it really matters."

"I'd just like it to be over with. Then we can move on."

"Then I'll do it now. Then there's no time like the present. Keep an ear out for control. If they call, tell them I'm on a comfort break."

She grabbed his arm and pulled him to her as he stood up. She stared into his eyes.

"I love you, you know."

"I love you too. I'm sorry it has to be like this."

"It is what it is. We didn't choose this life."

"I know. I just wish…"

"Well don't. Do what you have to."

Marko kissed her forehead. He unfolded her arms from his waist and took her hands in his. He squeezed her fingers and kissed her again.

"I'll be back soon."

The *Tereshkova* was essentially a long tube split into two levels. The top was divided into living quarters and the various technologies required for the journey to Mars. Most of the bottom layer contained what they would need to establish the colony. Robots waited to build them a domed Eden;

mechanised farmers stood primed to unpack their precious cargo of plants and animals at a moment's notice. It was also where the 'coffins' were.

As he descended he could feel the ambient temperature dropping. His breath became visible under the dim orange lights. A small artificial gravity well gave him some weight but his feet still drifted as he used the handrails to push himself down. At the bottom stair he rubbed his hands together.

"Let's do this."

The four human members of the crew were encased in their own personal biotech sarcophagus. Each glass sided container lay sandwiched between steel blocks that contained life support hardware. A thick control column dominated the centre of the room. Marko walked around looking through the misted windows at his sleeping crewmates. He felt no remorse for what he had to do.

System management was protected by a thirteen-digit password. Supposedly the designers had felt that the software needed no manual intervention. Access would only be granted by Control under extreme circumstances. These were the kind of details that Marko disliked and so he had found the code and decrypted it. He had a remarkable aptitude for hacking. This was a skill set that he always played down in the presence of his handlers. The touch-screen granted him administrative privilege. He pulled up the page for Abram Azarov and highlighted 'oxygen mix'. A vertical slider filled the display.

"This is for my brothers and sisters."

He hadn't seen them for ten years. Not since it all ended. Reading between the lines it was obvious that they were dead. He hadn't been able to find even a fragment of careless data that suggested that they survived beyond that day. It was still sharp in his memory. It had been a classic Siberian autumn, grey and cold with a biting Northerly wind. The smell of rotting leaves was all around. His brothers and he had been tracking a wild boar for at least an hour. They had laughed and joked with each other, all boasting that they would be the one to make the kill. The hunt had taken them as far as the mysterious wall that marked the edges of their world.

"I think we lost it" Gavrill had spat.

"I think it lost us," Marko had laughed. "Never mind, we're not hungry. Perhaps we'll run across something on the way back."

"I hate when they get away."

Marko slapped Gavrill on the back.

"You hate it but they are happy for another day."

'Good for them. Race you back."

"You're on."

The forest that they lived in stretched for six or seven miles in one direction and was three miles wide. In places scrub ran around the edges separating the trees from the boundary. Their encampment sat on the Southern edge along the tree line.

As they ran they heard the sound of the helicopters overhead. It was totally alien to them, an abomination to their ears. Although sometimes they imagined that they heard strange noises on the breeze it was never anything they could identify. It was attributed to spirits whispering nonsense in an attempt to confuse them. They were children of nature, or so they believed, and these machines smashed through their fragile concept of reality.

"Marko, what is that?"

"I have no idea."

They stopped in their tracks and stared up at the shapes in the sky as they passed overhead. A cold chill ran down Marko's back. He had suspected for some time that something was wrong with the life they led. It was nothing he could ever quite explain, either to himself or his tribe. It was instinct and nothing more. Standing in the passing shadow of these metal creatures was like being vindicated and damned at the same time.

"They're heading for the camp."

They ran again. The camp was a mile away. By the time they arrived, lungs and hearts straining, it was too late. A dozen faceless demons were dragging their screaming women away. With roars of fury the hunters charged towards them, flint axes raised high. Three shots rang out and three men fell. He never saw his brothers again. Of his sisters only Anya remained.

On board the *Tereshkova* a warning siren was ringing. It was tolling for Abram Azarov as he suffocated. Marko watched as Azarov faded away by numbers on the screen in front of him. The green display turned red in alarm. Once there was no more activity he called up the details for Irina Toporov. A sub menu revealed controls for the cardiac stimulator. He engaged it and watched as Toporov's heart rate soared.

"This is for my mother."

After the Village they had taken them to a grey hospital prison. At first he had suffered from crippling attacks of claustrophobia. He had yearned to see the stars again. Being without them was almost as shocking as any aspect of the whole experience. The featureless rooms and dry motionless air had challenged his sanity.

The humans had come to him and introduced themselves. They had a lot of explaining to do.

"We are like you but we are not the same."

"Why do you speak our tongue?" he had asked.

"We do not. You speak ours. You have much to learn about the world, Marko."

Then they tried to explain who the Neanderthals were.

"You were an experiment."

Marko had looked at them blankly. He had never heard the word before. The scientists quickly realised that they had their work cut out for them. They set about filling his head with information. It was a month before it dawned on him what his life actually meant. He didn't speak for a week.

For reasons known only to them his captors granted a visitor's permit to his mother. He had never quite figured out why. He was certain it hadn't been intended as an act of kindness. After being removed without warning from the program when Marko was fifteen she had campaigned to return. Officialdom had slammed the door in her face and warned her to keep quiet or suffer the consequences. Eventually the frustration had broken her and she had retreated into the shadows. It came then as a great shock when she was summoned without explanation. It had taken her two days by bus to get there and she was ragged and pale by the time she arrived. After she had reassured him that she was not a ghost she attempted to apologise.

"I never wanted to leave you Marko. They took me one day while I gathered berries. They said that I was no longer required. I tried to fight them but they knocked me out."

"You came from this world before... before the Village?"

"Yes, I grew up here. I was poor. I signed up as a subject for medical research and ended up here. They made me sign lots of papers. They made me promise never to tell any of you and never to tell anyone on the outside either. I'd be in prison now if I had done.'"

"Prison? Like me?"

"Oh Marko. It's not the same. Who knows where your life will lead."

"My life is so strange mother. At first I thought these people must be Gods." He laughed aloud. "How wrong I was."

"I am one of these people you know Marko. You are partly human too."

"Where are my brothers and sisters?"

"I don't know. Marko, you were my only biological child. They wouldn't tell me about the others. I thought of you all as my children but they came from different mothers."

She looked at him desperately. Tears had been streaming down her cheeks for as long as she had been speaking. A wall of plexi-glass separated her from him and she put one hand up against it. He did the same, his face a morass of conflicting emotions.

"I love you and I will always love you my son. I will probably never see you again but always remember me. You are in my heart."

The encounter had left him with a bitter anger towards his captors. He had thought that he had come to terms with the deception but now this had destabilised him again.

In her cool chamber Irina Toporov stopped twitching and he closed the control window. Anya's disembodied voice sounded in the room.

"Control has started raising hell. They're screaming about the diagnostics and demanding to know what's going on."

"Tell them you'll get back to them. Then switch them off."

"Will do. How are you doing?"

Of course she knew already. The ship's computer would have made sure of that. He told her anyway.

"Abram and Irina are gone."

There was silence for a moment.

"Good. Right then. I'll talk to you later."

The controls for Sergei Manovitch appeared on the screen. Marko frowned. He had felt impersonal about the previous two executions but he actively disliked this man. He was a brash moron who had made no secret of his dislike for the two Neanderthals. 'Abominations' was his favourite insult. Marko tried to deny the small flush of pleasure he got as he looked at Manovitch's details. His mission was justified. In fact it was justice itself. The purity of it shouldn't be sullied by personal agendas.

Long-term sleep involved having ones plasma mixed with a variety of nanotech additives. These ranged from radiation scrubbers to kidney monitors. The mix could be set manually and Marko set about flooding the man's system with microscopic devices. The ship's onboard factory could churn out an endless quantity.

"This is for my people."

When they had introduced Marko to computers he had taken to them immediately. In general his capacity for learning was exceptional but these machines fascinated him. Something about their empty 'minds' and adherence to logic had set off a light bulb in his head. It came to pass that an important friend of the space program heard about him and talked to some even more important friends of his. The end result was Marko found himself transferred to an extremely remote base somewhere up North. He had become a 'person of interest' to the Mars mission planners.

There he was surprised to be reunited with Anya. He felt a little less lonely and found the strength to cover up his inner turmoil. Both of the Neanderthals had performed spectacularly throughout a barrage of tests and it started to emerge that there may be a place for them onboard. To his face they told him that it was his superior strength and admirable brainpower that had earned him a seat. In truth he felt that it had more to do with being expendable. Staying awake and not remaining under a powerful radiation shield had risks. There was also much talk of pressures on an astronaut's sanity during the long journey. Either way his life had taken another astonishing turn.

The base had a small garden. Every night Marko would circumvent security to go and stare up at the heavens. As he lay on the grass he would contemplate his journey from prehistoric man to space traveller. Soon he would be journeying towards the lights that he had been staring at all his life. Despite all the changes that he had been through this still held an incredible magic for him.

Afterwards his mood would plummet. It depressed him that only he and Anya were left to see these wonders. While he mourned his immediate family he also grieved for the never born. There was no doubt in his mind that *Homo sapiens* were responsible. He couldn't accept that his people had merely dissolved into the human gene pool. He looked at the world through the lens of the Internet and saw chaos; man killing man, consuming and destroying without any thought for the future. It wasn't hard for him to imagine them slaughtering his people for being 'different'. Even if interbreeding had produced progeny those born with Neanderthal features wouldn't have been allowed to survive. He began to picture himself as a lone warrior, the last of his kind. It was a fanciful notion but it was always at the back of his mind. On the surface he showed only calm and told the humans whatever they wanted to hear.

Manovitch's monitor gave a final shriek and fell silent. Marko walked over to the only remaining container with a contented green light blinking on the top. He tapped a flush panel on the curved top and it swung open. Inside were two large red handles. Marko grabbed one with each hand and pulled. The green light turned red.

"Emergency eject."

"Confirm."

A cacophony of pops and hisses emerged from the machine before the side panel slid down and the bed swung out. On it lay the Captain. Mikael wasn't a bad man. He was a product of the system but he wasn't unkind.

Marko looked down as he struggled to open his eyes. He was pale and clammy.

"What?" he managed.

"Mikhail? Captain. I have woken you up to apologise in person for what you and the rest of the crew have had to suffer."

"What?" he repeated, attempting to lift up his head. He was still too full of drugs to manage it. "Apologise for what?""

"You have all had to pay the ultimate price for something that is not your fault."

"The others?" A whisper.

"They are all dead Mikhail. I'm so sorry but your species has left me no choice. Anya and I need to be alone."

"But we were all…"

"Mikael, no files are unseen by me. I'm clever like that. I know you were authorized to kill us either if ordered or you felt we posed a threat. We are not human. We cannot be protected by your laws."

"I thought you liked being a part of the crew. I thought you were proud of your position."

"How could I be proud when you hid me from the public? How could I be proud when you told them I was a product of 'genetic manipulation'? I am not an invention of the Russian people. I am Neanderthal. That's what I'm proud of, not your games."

"You could go back. I'll tell them what a hero you are."

Marko put his hands around Mikael's neck and slowly squeezed. Mikael could barely find the strength to lift his arms let alone to resist.

"More lies," said Marko. "We cannot hear anymore. We do not want to hear anymore."

The Captain started to cough and gasp for breath. His eyes bulged and then there was a loud snap. His corpse fell still.

Anya greeted Marko with an extended hug when he came back up.

"They're still shouting at us. I think they want to talk."

"Oh, they can wait. We'll give them a call when we get settled in."

He reached down and patted her belly.

"Perhaps once the baby is born."

ARC

Derek Muk

Jan kept staring at the block of ice. "That thing gives me the creeps."

Albert Taylor studied the cave man encased in the ice, a look of fascination on his face. He felt like a kid in a candy store. The cave man was of average height and stocky, and had dark, shaggy hair, wearing nothing but a piece of animal fur around his genitals and buttocks. Frozen in its hand was a lethal looking club that looked like it could do some serious damage like crush someone's skull.

"If you keep thinking like that you're not going to learn anything," Taylor replied. "Don't be so negative. You still want to be an anthropologist, don't you?"

"Of course."

"Well, one of the key qualities of an anthropologist is open-mindedness, the ability to accept different viewpoints and ideas, and also to be inquisitive and curious about the world. They're ravenous for knowledge and love learning. Most of them would be jumping up and down at a find like this."

She nodded. "You're right. I should be grateful I'm in this program considering how hard it was to get in. But what do I know? I'm just a lowly teaching assistant slash grad student."

He turned to her and smiled. "You're not *lowly* to me. C'mon, just be positive, Jan, and everything will just fall into place. You'll see. Good vibes go a long way, trust me." He turned back to the cave man. "Besides, look at this guy! He's living history! How often does a fully intact artifact like this pop up?"

"Don't forget that mammoth you and Professor Reynolds found," Jan interjected.

"Yeah, but that wasn't nearly as intact as this. Plus, this man has been preserved in ice."

Her eyes widened. "Meaning he could be resurrected?"

"I'm not saying anything just yet but I'm not discounting that theory, either. Remember, I'm an anthropologist and I have-?"

"An open mind," she finished for him, grinning. She was a young, slender woman with shoulder length red hair.

He smiled. "You got an A for today's lesson." Taylor studied the cave man some more. He was a tall, lanky man in his early fifties with long dark sideburns and narrow, slanted eyes. "Several years ago a colleague of mine at Harvard returned from the Arctic, where this fellow primitive man was discovered, with seeds he had unearthed there. Interestingly, he played around with them and they grew to be a type of vegetable that's never been seen before. He figured the seeds were millions of years old."

"Wow. Is that how old this guy is?"

Taylor nodded. "Give or take hundreds, if not thousand of years." He adjusted the controls of the tank that held the block of ice.

"What are you going to do with him?" she asked curiously.

"Well, there will be the perfunctory scientific tests and analysis, and of course there's the new exhibit on prehistoric peoples. In my opening speech I'm going to mention old Arc here," he said proudly.

"Arc?"

"That's the name I gave him." When she looked at him quizzically, he continued: "It's short for Arctic."

***

Over the next few days preparations continued for the gala opening of the exhibit on Saturday. Taylor, Jan, and museum employees placed the final finishing touches the day before. When the big day finally arrived Taylor stood behind a podium in front of a large audience in the campus museum's auditorium.

He smiled at the crowd. "Ladies and gentlemen, thanks very much for coming. You lucky folks will be the first to see and experience the Prehistoric Peoples exhibit. And believe me, you're in for a real treat. A lot of exhibits have focused on dinosaurs and Stone Age animals but very few concentrated exclusively on early humans. Who were these people? What were they like? What did they eat? Wear? How did they behave and think? What were their customs and traditions? What happened to them? This exhibit addresses all those questions. Later, I'll talk about my latest discovery, aptly named Arc. So now, without further ado, let me show you folks some slides." He looked at Jan, sitting in the middle aisle behind a laptop. "Jan, could you turn off the lights and begin the show? Thanks."

***

The security guard made his usual rounds in the anthropology building, checking to make sure all the doors were locked and all the lights were off. When he reached Professor Taylor's laboratory he saw that the door was ajar and the lights were still on inside. He went inside but didn't find anyone except a primitive looking man being held inside a tank-like container. The guard didn't see that the ice was melting, nor did he see the water leaking from the tank. He simply did his duty: turning off the lights and locking the door.

***

On Tuesday, Taylor returned to his lab to find the cave man gone. The tank's door was ajar and the interior was wet and smelled of mildew. He checked the tank's control panel and noticed that someone had defrosted the block of ice. *But who? And why?* He was certain that when he left here last week all the controls were normal. Frowning, he examined the laboratory's door and lock and saw scrape marks on the keyhole and the door handle. He called security. Moments later, the same guard came.

"No one broke in?" Taylor asked.

"No, sir. However, the door was open a little."

"I'm positive I locked the door when I left."

"Are you the only one that has a key?"

"Yes."

"Perhaps someone else has one, too, sir."

But who?

***

"Who would want to steal a cave man?" Jan asked. Taylor wished she wasn't so naïve but she was a student, after all. "Treasure collectors, hunters, jealous professors and scientists who wished they could've discovered something like Arc, black market dealers, the list goes on." He frowned, seething inside. "Whoever did this I'm gonna bury them."

"Now, now, Professor, calm down. You don't want to do anything rash. You've got your career, your tenureship, your lengthy body of academic journals and work, all your degrees, your wife and children."

"I'm not married and I don't have kids."

"Oh, sorry," Jan said, embarrassed. "If you need to talk to someone, you can talk to me."

He didn't look at her. "Thanks. . .I should've gone to the lab over the weekend and checked on Arc but I was swamped with the new exhibit, opening weekend and all. You know. You saw how busy I was, people were following me everywhere asking questions like they were my groupies or something."

She chuckled. "Yes, I saw that. Hey, you're an important man, an expert in the field."

He sighed. "Yeah, yeah, yeah."

"So the police already talked to you?"

"Yes."

Jan's brow furrowed in thought. "Where would you take a million year old prehistoric cave man? Or where would he escape to?"

An imaginary light bulb popped above Taylor's head. "You think Arc left the lab on his own?"

"You implied that anything's possible."

He crossed his legs, thinking a moment. "Hmmm. Well, if I was a cave man I'd go to a cave or an underground chamber, or tunnel, away from people. Seeing the mass of people on the streets would probably startle him." He grabbed his corduroy blazer. "C'mon, let's go."

***

He navigated himself through the unfamiliar terrain, this new, confusing landscape that he suddenly found himself in. Waves of nausea, dizziness, headaches, and body aches rippled through his body. On top of all that there was disorientation, puzzlement, and hunger. The latter was really a problem now. He hadn't eaten in a long time. It was time to hunt and he gripped his long club tightly. He staggered his way across the campus, the lawn's soft grass under his bare feet, steering away from groups of strange looking beings. They looked like him and yet looked different, too.

He took refuge in a small creek that was under the shelter of some trees. Walking along the creek he eventually reached a wooded area on the edge of the university. He embraced the silence, the solitude. Where were his fellow clan members? He did not see them. His hike through the forest brought him to a young couple who were necking and making out under a tree, oblivious that he was observing them. He watched in fascination as the woman kept sticking her tongue into the man's eager mouth, noticing the way the guy fondled her buttocks. Amazingly, their lips never separated. He wanted to keep looking but his ravenousness prompted him to action and he stepped forward, crushing a small twig with his foot.

The couple stopped kissing, turning in his direction. The woman gasped.

"Get the hell out of here!" the young man said.

He approached the couple slowly.

"Are you deaf?" the man said. "Go away or I'll kick your ass!"

"Let's go, Ronnie," the woman said, clutching his hand tight.

"Let me take care of this, babe," Ronnie replied, pushing her behind him. Ronnie stood his ground as he got closer.

But before Ronnie could even blink Arc swung that long, lethal club at him viciously, smashing young Ronnie's skull. The peaceful tranquillity of the forest was shattered by the sound of bone being crushed. The woman screamed. Ronnie collapsed on the dirt like a sack of potatoes, blood pouring from his head. His eyelids fluttered quickly and his body started convulsing. The woman tried to intervene but Arc pounded his club on his face until it was unrecognisable. The woman continued screaming. Arc simply grabbed her by the arm so hard that it popped out of its socket. She cried in agony. To silence her he knocked her on the back of the head and she went limp immediately. Then he threw her across his big shoulder like a ragged doll and disappeared into the forest.

***

Taylor and Jan searched around Tilden Park, the Berkeley Hills, and some wooded areas on campus but didn't find Arc. It was sunset as they trudged down a grassy hill towards the university. Taylor closed his phone.

"What did the police say?" she asked.

"They've sent out search crews but no luck yet. It's going to be dark soon."

"So he'll be returning to his cave?"

"Most likely."

"Wait, this is crazy! So we're assuming he was revived and is lurking around out there. A million year old man, and boom, he's alive."

"Stranger things have happened. Remember those seeds I told you about."

Jan nodded. "I'm trying to keep an open mind about things but this idea just seems wild. You're sure you don't have any enemies that could've stolen Arc for their own twisted fantasies?"

"I wracked my brain but couldn't think of anyone. Are you hungry? All this running around has my stomach growling."

She chuckled. "Thought you'd never ask. Let's go to Fat Apples. My treat this time."

***

A few days later, Taylor was sitting in his office scanning the news headlines during his lunch break. An article about the discovery of a dismembered, half-eaten corpse caught his eye. The female victim was a student of the university but not one of his. A second body, that of a young man, had also been found. No witnesses, no leads yet. What piqued Taylor's interest was the fact that the police had found bare human footprints and animal fur near each body. He immediately thought of Arc for he was barefoot and thought about the animal fur he wore. Now call it coincidence or what have you but he couldn't stop thinking about the possible connection. It was a crazy theory but he decided to go with his instincts about this. If Arc was responsible for these grisly murders he had to be stopped.

A knock on his door brought him back to the present. He went to it and opened it. Standing there was a stocky twenty something woman with dyed purple hair and numerous tattoos.

"Hi, Professor Taylor."

"Hello, Kim. Still have questions about the paper?"

She beamed at him. "You got it."

"Come in."

She sat down in a chair before his desk, taking out a notebook from her backpack. "Hey, I swung by the museum yesterday. The new exhibit rocks! I love the realistic, life-like figures of the early humans. My little brother and sister went with me and they really liked the interactive features, playing with each one, pressing every button, listening to all the audio."

Taylor smiled. "It wouldn't be a real exhibit without that. Glad they enjoyed it."

"Ooh, tell me about this cave man you dug up in the Arctic!" Kim said enthusiastically.

"Well. . ." he replied, stalling for words. "Well. . ."

***

He built a small fire in the cave, sitting next to it. The flickering orange flames created eerie shadows on the walls. Among other things, there was numerous graffiti. He studied the spray paint in fascination. None of it made any sense. He liked the colors, though. Trash was scattered everywhere. He sifted through empty potato chip bags, candy bar and gum wrappers, cigarette boxes, empty beer cans, and plastic bags. All of it puzzling to him. He sniffed them, licked them, twisted them, bent them, ripped them apart, rubbed them against his skin. He was in awe, trying to absorb and learn about this new world as much as he could. Perhaps he would understand things over time.

He heard a rustling sound outside the cave and spun around quickly, staring at the entrance. Nothing. Seconds later, something shuffled around in the cave. He grabbed his club, trying to find the origin of the noise. He pounded the club in a dark corner of the place, snatching a dead mouse up by its tail. He buried the animal in the dirt, covering the mound with a rock. Then he left the cave.

He walked through the forest. Moments later, he approached a two-lane road. Parked on the side of the road was a car with three people in it. Arc watched as two men pulled a young woman out of the back seat and dragged her, kicking and screaming, into the woods. One of them gagged her. Arc followed the three as they walked down the dirt trail. His facial expression grew hostile as he saw them going towards the cave. Following the trio silently, he observed as the men yanked the woman into the cavern. He saw one of the men, a tall, heavyset man with wispy dark hair and a goatee take the woman's jacket off as the other one held her. Before the goateed man could touch her slacks Arc entered the cave, his club clutched in his hand at the ready.

The men turned towards him, surprised. The woman looked astonished, too, but more out of relief than anything.

"Who the fuck are you?" the goateed man said.

When Arc remained silent, the other gentleman, a guy with a close cropped afro and a tear drop scar on his left cheek, said in a Caribbean accent, "You heard da man. Get the fuck out of here!"

Arc stared at the men challengingly.

"Ahh, so you wanna stare fight now, huh?" Goatee asked. Arc didn't respond. "Who is this joker? Look at the way he's dressed, like some savage."

"I'll take care of him," the man with the tear drop scar said. He approached Arc. "Go! You hear me? G-"

Before he could finish the word the club had already swung as fast as a baseball bat, striking him squarely in the face. They all heard something crack, specifically bone. Teardrop's eyes were as big as saucers, his jaw dropped wide open. He didn't even know what hit him. The next blow smashed him again in the face, and so did the next one and the next one, until rivers of blood flowed down his head. He crumpled to the ground.

His buddy, Goatee, couldn't believe what had just happened. He just stared at his fallen friend, at Arc, and back to his friend again. He was hoping to get some quick pussy and leave without any problems. Boy, was he so wrong! He held the woman in front of him like a shield.

"Step aside!" Goatee ordered.

Arc merely gazed at him and the woman. She was crying, trying to free herself from Goatee's grip.

When Arc didn't budge he moved forward, pushing the woman ahead. Suddenly, he shoved her hard towards Arc and tried to make a run for the cave entrance. Before he could reach it Arc jumped him and they landed on the dirt. They wrestled on the ground. The woman bolted out of the cave. Goatee was big and strong and it looked like he could easily beat Arc but he couldn't fight him off. Goatee reached into his pocket and took out a knife, hoping to end this fast. He should've prayed, it might've helped.

Arc knocked the knife out of his hand and grabbed his club. Before Goatee could get up Arc hammered the top of his skull with a crushing blow. And again, and again, and again, and again, until his bloody head rolled loosely on his neck.

***

The lecture had ended and afterwards there was a question and answer period. Taylor remained on the stage. He recognized quite a number of his students in the audience, including Jan. The rest were museum patrons.

A nerdy looking man in his early twenties with big glasses raised his hand.

"Yes, Roland."

"Is it true that early humans were omnivores?"

"Yes, that's correct," Taylor replied. "They ate berries, nuts, as well as meat."

"What about human meat?"

"I have read articles supporting that theory. If food was scarce or unobtainable cannibalism was an option."

Someone in the audience snickered.

An elderly woman sitting in the front row raised her hand.

Taylor nodded at her. "Yes, ma'am."

"Could they talk?"

"The brain capacity of the Neanderthal was similar to that of modern humans and a limited range of speech was possible. Earlier humans also showed indications of intelligence by way of the tools and clothing they made, by their customs and traditions, by the fact that they buried their dead. These same peoples were capable of some speech but it was probably not as advanced as that of the Neanderthal."

"Were they violent?" the elderly woman asked.

"Well, it was a volatile time they were living in and they had to survive. The world was constantly evolving. They had to defend themselves from predatory animals, not to mention each other at times. They had to defend their homes."

Kim raised her hand and he nodded at her. "Can you talk about the recent murders on campus? Rumour has it that a primitive, savage person committed them."

Taylor cleared his throat. "Uhhh, I do not have any information on the subject." He looked at his watch. "Well, thanks very much for attending, folks."

***

"Did you see this?" Jan asked, bursting into the empty lecture hall, waving a newspaper in her hand.

Class had just ended and Taylor gathered his papers and folders and put them in his briefcase. "What is it?"

She ran down the stairs of the amphitheatre-type room to where he stood on the stage, showing him the paper. On the front page was a headline that read: *Remains of two more bodies could be the work of "savage throwback."*

He scanned the article. "'Bare human footprints and traces of animal furs were found at the crime scene,'" he read aloud. "'Police also uncovered a campfire in the cave and grilled meat hanging over the fire. Police said the meat was human and had come from the two victims.'" He skipped down to another sentence and read: "'Primitive cave drawings depicting humans hunting animals were on the wall.'"

Jan frowned. "What are we dealing with here, Professor?"

Taylor thought for a moment and then said, "C'mon!"

***

After Taylor explained to the homicide detective in charge of the investigation what his theory was the detective looked at him impassively. Taylor thought he might explode into laughter or something but he didn't.

"Look, Detective Kwan, I know it sounds crazy but please trust me on this one," Taylor continued. "I've studied primordial humans for a long time and know how they think, how they act. Please let me assist you with this investigation. I don't think you're looking in the right places for this man."

"Where should we be looking?"

"In caves, in tunnels, underground dwellings, away from crowded urban areas."

Detective Kwan considered this for a moment, tenting his fingers together calmly. "There's someone I'd like you to talk to. Come with me please," he said, leading Taylor and Jan to an interrogation room down the hall.

Sitting alone at a table was a young woman with bruises on her face. She looked sad and tired.

After Detective Kwan closed the door he said to the woman, "Alice, this is Professor Taylor and his assistant, Jan. Can you describe to them the individual you saw in the cave?"

The detective, Taylor, and Jan sat around the table.

Alice dried her eyes with some tissue, looking at them hesitantly. "Well, he wasn't wearing anything except for a piece of animal hide around the lower part of his body. . .he looked, looked kinda . . . kinda like one of those indigenous Indians down in the Amazon rainforest but not exactly like that . . . he, he, uhhh . . . he was more like a . . ."

She trailed off, not being able to find the exact word.

"Cave man," Taylor finished for her.

Alice nodded slowly, drying her eyes. "Yeah, cave man like from the dinosaur era . . . and he had this long club . . . he bludgeoned those guys to death with it. I'm grateful to this man because he saved me."

Taylor nodded. "Did he say anything during this incident?"

Alice shook her head.

"Is there anything else that stuck out in your mind about this man?"

She looked away, licking her bruised lips. "Can't think of anything more ...I'm just thankful that he saved me. When you find him I want to thank him personally."

***

Taylor and Jan went to the cave crime scene with Detective Kwan. The Professor studied the primitive drawings on the wall. It showed humans hunting the woolly mammoth.

Jan covered her nose and mouth. "Oh, God, what's that smell?"

Taylor squatted down in front of the extinguished campfire, seeing bits and pieces of blackened meat in the pile.

"Hey, check this out," Jan said.

He walked over to where she was and saw footprints in the dirt. They appeared to be about the size of an average human foot.

"Where are you, Arc?" Taylor asked quietly.

***

Taylor strolled through the university museum, looking at the various artifacts on display. Even though he had seen them a lot he tried to view them with a fresh, objective eye as if he were a first time visitor. He stopped before one of the centrepiece dioramas of the exhibit, a large reconstructed cave with a family of early humans. The life-sized, life-like figures were skillfully crafted and created and appeared very realistic. The period detail had also been captured pretty well, Taylor thought, looking at the drawings on the cave wall as well as the clothing, the tools, and down to the condition of the family's teeth, fingernails, and toenails.

The males squatted over the bloody carcass of an animal, preparing to butcher it with some knives made of stone. The females were sitting on the ground, stretching out animal hides that would be made into clothing.

Taylor moved on to another diorama. This one had cave men figures holding spears, hunting a mammoth in the snow. He went further on, stopping in front of a complete skeleton of a Cro-Magnon man. Next to it was the skull of a *homo erectus* human.

Suddenly, someone tapped Taylor on the shoulder and he spun around.

Jan stood there, smiling. "Can I join you?"

"Don't do that again! You scared me. Sure, tag along. You know, I'm really amazed by our exhibit."

Seconds later, a man wearing a Cal sweatshirt approached them with a book and a pen in his hand. "Professor, could you autograph this book?"

He eyed the cave man book he wrote, grinning proudly. "Nice to know there are still copies floating around out there, Brian," he said, signing the book.

"Yeah, thanks to eBay," Brian replied.

Taylor laughed. He and Jan walked on. To their left some children were pressing buttons at an interactive booth where they could listen to Stone Age humans 'talk' and explain to them what a typical day in their life was like.

"Wow, you're famous," Jan remarked. "I'm honored to be in the presence of a celebrity."

"Oh, hush. Don't tell me you're jealous. Oh, by the way, remember the cops dusted my lab and the door? Well, turns out the only fingerprints they found were mine and some other ones they couldn't identify. I think whoever broke in used gloves."

Her brow furrowed. "Hmmm. Who could it be?"

***

He had to move on. His home, the cave, had been boarded up and sealed with yellow police tape. He had pounded the wooden board angrily but it wouldn't budge. So he stormed off, hiking through the woods for miles. The sunlight felt nice and warm on his face. He stopped for a moment, marveling at a large bird flying in the air. Further on, he saw a squirrel and tried to catch it but it raced up a tree.

Soon he approached the end of the forest. Strange, shiny machines cruised up and down the road before him. He looked at them curiously and when he got too close to one a loud noise emanated from it.

"Get outta the way, dipshit!" someone said from one of the machines.

He gazed at them with hostility, making a low, growling sound, raising his club. When another shiny machine came by the loud noise was repeated.

"Look out, you idiot!" a woman said.

He swung his club at the machine but missed. Another machine approached and he tried to hit it but missed again. He growled angrily, running across the road before other machines came. When he reached the other side he walked down a road with large dwellings on both side of it. Some as high as a tree. Humans standing outside these dwellings stared at him as he went by.

"Cover yourself up, mister!" an elderly man said. "There are children around."

He saw little humans throwing a round object to one another. One huddled behind his mother's skirt. Another said: "Hey, look it's a cave man!"

"Vince, get away from him!" a tall human said.

Arc kept walking, ignoring their stares. He kept going down a tree lined street that took him all the way to a busy thoroughfare with even bigger machines that were louder and faster. Humans backed away from him as he walked by. He reacted the same way, avoiding big groups of humans. He saw a sign outside an entrance, eyeing it with an innocent curiosity. What did it say? He ran down the stairs of this place. When he got to the bottom other humans were waiting on a platform as a long, large machine approached. The machine carried lots of humans, zooming off fast. Arc watched as it went away, looking at its bright lights.

He jumped down onto the tracks, walking along them towards the dark tunnel.

"Hey, you're gonna get killed, blood," a human said to him. "A train's coming."

Arc looked at him and kept going. A cool draft blew out of the tunnel, blowing his long, unkempt hair back. It felt good. The tracks were cold beneath his bare feet. Soon he was in the tunnel, his eyes adjusting to the darkness momentarily.

The nausea and body aches persisted but he kept moving forward. It would be okay. He would learn to adapt to this new world. But where was his clan? And the animals he once knew were all gone.

He hid in the cool comfort of the tunnel, away from the bizarre humans and their unusual ways.

***

Taylor and Jan followed Detective Kwan down into the BART station. "We have eyewitnesses reporting that they sighted this man in the train tunnel," Kwan said. "One person claimed that the suspect tried to stop the train, standing in front of it. We followed him into the tunnel but haven't been able to locate him."

"Did he hurt anyone?" Taylor asked.

"No."

They reached the platform and saw a train departing. Mobs of people had gotten off of it and were in their face now, trying to see what was going on at the opposite track. The police had cordoned off that track and directed the rubbernecks to exit the station.

Kwan led the Professor and Jan to the edge of the platform. "I'm going to have to ask you two to wait here," he said. "It's too dangerous."

"Oh, c'mon, Detective, we've gone this far," Taylor said. "I know what we're dealing with here. I've lectured, studied, wrote books on the subject, quizzed many students on this topic. You're gonna need me in there to communicate with him."

Kwan looked straight in his eyes. "Okay."

Taylor turned to Jan. "Stay here. I–"

"No way!" she protested. "I'm not going to miss seeing possibly the greatest anthropological discovery of the century. And one that came back to life!"

"All right. Stay behind me."

The trio went into the dark tunnel with some uniformed officers who had their guns drawn. Taylor felt a cool draft blow against his face. It felt refreshing. Millions of thoughts raced through his mind, the top one being the excitement he was trying to contain. He couldn't believe he might actually encounter a live prehistoric human. The prospect was both daunting and exhilarating. For someone that had slaved behind years of academic work, teaching, doing research, writing in journals, this was a dream come true. He felt like a kid again, as corny and clichéd as that sounded. Some of his fellow colleagues at Berkeley and at other universities were probably jealous of his find, though he didn't know who offhand. Whoever it was they *may* have a key to his lab and they *may* have. . .no, no, no, he didn't want to go down that path, especially since he didn't have any substantial proof to back it. *Yet it still bugs me,* he thought. His mind turned to the fame and glory he'd get from this, the money, endorsements, financial backing for more projects and excavations, book and movie options, numerous talk show interviews, he'd be in the limelight for years. Not that he cared for it. Indeed, Taylor was definitely not a self-centred ego maniac, though some of his friends probably thought otherwise. No, he'd be in control and would handle things responsibly. Or would he? *Would fame change me?*

Another cool draft blew against his face, bringing him back to the present. His eyes had adjusted to the darkness of the tunnel.

"So where did you find this man?" Kwan whispered.

"In the Arctic. I led an archeological expedition there."

"What's it like out there?"

"Well, there's still a lot we don't know about the area, like what's out there, who or what lived there in the past, what could be buried there. A lot of research is being conducted, however."

The group continued walking down the tunnel, not seeing anybody. They heard a train pulling into the station in the other tunnel, in the opposite direction. About ten minutes later, Jan whispered to Taylor and Kwan, "There's someone dead ahead, to our left."

Taylor squinted his eyes in the darkness and was able to make out the shape of a person. Their physical features were as black as ink, however. "Good eyes, Jan," he whispered.

An eerie silence filled the tunnel. The person just stared at the approaching group.

"This is the Berkeley Police Department," Kwan said. "Step forward with your hands on your head."

The dark figure didn't move from his position near the wall.

"This is the police," Kwan repeated. "Step forward with your hands on your head."

An uneasy stillness hung in the air. That's when Kwan flicked on a powerful flashlight and pointed it ahead. The person put their arms before him, shielding himself from the light. Taylor saw Arc. In Arc's right hand was the long, deadly club. There was dried blood on it.

"Drop the weapon!" Kwan ordered.

"Let me work my magic," Taylor said.

"Go for it."

Taylor approached Arc slowly and cautiously. The cave man stared at him with dark, penetrating eyes, his club raised. Taylor looked at the club, keeping a safe distance between the two of them, and kept his hands up in the air. Taylor maintained a calm, harmless demeanor and Arc acknowledged this by lowering his club. Moments later, Taylor took a step forward and Arc did the same thing. Taylor mimicked throwing a weapon down on the ground, slowly and carefully, like he was teaching a child. Arc studied him but did not part ways with his precious club. Taylor repeated the gesture. After what seemed like an eternity, however, the cave man finally released the club and it landed on the ground with a thud, echoing throughout the tunnel.

Taylor pointed towards the opposite direction, to the station. He mimicked walking towards the station. Arc watched him and after a moment followed, like a dog following his master.

When a uniformed officer bent down to retrieve the club Arc turned around quickly, glaring at the officer and baring his sharp teeth. The officer tried to grab the weapon but Arc beat him to it, wielding the club proudly once more.

When the officer aimed his gun at Arc, Taylor screamed, "No!"

Arc swung his club at the officer's face, cracking his skull open. He then tried to hit the other officers and that's when they opened fire, bringing him down in a thunder of bullets that echoed loudly throughout the tunnel.

Taylor watched in horror, his eyes wide open. Jan covered her ears with her hands.

Smoke blew in their faces. Taylor ran over to Arc's bullet-riddled body, kneeling down. Arc coughed up blood and appeared to want to say something, raising his head a little. Taylor leaned in close to listen but no words escaped the cave man's mouth. Only a sad, hopeful look remained on his face as he grabbed Taylor's hand. The last thing he did was squeeze the Professor's hand gently before he took his final breath. Then it was all over.

"Sorry," Kwan muttered behind Taylor's back.

THE MODERN WOMAN

Christine Morgan

"Dr. Mervin?" I steered my crinoline and bustle a weaving path through the other noonday diners. "Dr. Clarence Mervin?"

The shabby little café was well off the beaten track of usual university haunts or museum gathering spots. Finding this man here instead, given the reception he'd recently received in those august scholarly quarters, was therefore no great surprise.

He glanced up, shoulders making a furtive twitch as if in anticipation of a blow, either of the verbal or physical varieties. The fact of it being a feminine voice thus addressing him did nothing to assuage this, nor did the sight of me, that voice's owner.

"Yes?" he asked in a tone so hesitant it bordered on the quavering.

I am not, for the record, of imposing stature or build. I've been described in terms like 'angular' and 'severe.' Or, to put it another way, in terms of an hourglass, I'm more a grandfather clock. Tall, straight, and wooden. Even the tightest-laced whalebone corset can only do so much with so little.

That said, it saves me a fortune at the dressmaker's. I have no need for frills and fancies. A simple tweed skirt and cape-jacket over a prim blouse, high-button shoes, and a cap with only a token bit of feather did the trick as far as I was concerned. I wore the hair – an unremarkable shade of brown – drawn back, caught at the nape in a netted snood.

Given the temperate nature of the day, I was not even carrying a parasol or umbrella with which I might have suddenly beset him a barrage about the head and ears. I had only my clutch-bag, held at the waist in walking-gloved hands.

I suppose that the very elements contributing to my lack of threatening physical appearance may have lent themselves well enough to the threat of a verbal tirade. On first acquaintance – indeed, often on second, third, or fiftieth acquaintance – I seemed to convey something of a stern headmistress or humourless governess note. The thin lips, pressed together in what was often taken for a disapproving scowl … the sharp eyes behind the spectacles … the posture … I tended to give the impression of being on the verge of cutting loose with a tongue of ice and acid, wielded with rapier-like efficiency.

This was not, as it happens, unwarranted when the situation called.

Since this situation, however, did not call, I mustered the thin lips into a smile. "I am Dr. Genevieve Delaney of the Delaney Institute for Feminine Wellness and Well-Being. I was privileged to attend your presentation, 'The Revival of Primitive Man' at the recent Scientific Discoveries Symposium. Might I join you?"

Had he been doing more than merely picking at the toast-crust, I daresay he might have suffered an asphyxiational mishap. I'm not sure which element of my speech was the primary cause, or if it was a combination thereof, but the results left him boggling at me, gulping, mouth working like that of a landed trout.

He started to stand, struck the table's underside with his thighs, clattered the crockery, dropped his napkin and nearly upended his chair.

I took this as permission to join him, seating myself opposite. I set my clutch on the table and folded my hands atop it.

Clarence Mervin sank back down. He blinked.

He, too, was far from imposing. The physiognomy was boyish, of a round-cheeked variety, the skin that fair sort made for going the most florid shades of red. The hair was sparse, sandy, and in need of barbering. The eyes were owlish, wide and of a watery blue disposition.

Judging by the way his clothes hung on the frame, he'd once been well-padded if not trending toward stout. For all that, when I'd first spotted him, it was to find him brooding over a meagre repast of tea with toast, plucking at the crusts in a manner that could only be described as 'desultory.'

Speaking of his clothes, not only were they ill-fitting, but several seasons out of style even amongst the staid, stuffy, and even stagnant social circle to which he nominally belonged. This defect in tailoring, combined with the aforementioned meagre repast, convinced me of what I had hitherto only – but with good reason – suspected. The man was, as they say, barely keeping body and soul together. Broke. In the dire straits chin-deep and rising.

I therefore offered to buy him lunch.

Part of it was, I must admit, to observe the anguish of his inner struggle. Men, you know. As if it wasn't bad enough, the very idea that some strange woman should march up unannounced and introduce herself, that she should then also be the one to foot the bill? A female doctor, no less?

But, pride doesn't put much food on the table, and after a moment's agonising, Dr. Mervin accepted. The next bit of time was taken up with the rituals of signalling the waitress, ordering the edibles, having the teapot replenished and glasses brought of iced lemon-water, and the arrival of a basket of only barely stale rolls with jam.

"You ... you attended my presentation?" he ventured.

"I did," I said. "It was most fascinating."

The owlish eyes peered at me with searching suspicion. He then swiftly scanned the café, perhaps expecting to see a host of sniggering professors and curators looking on to see how well the prank was going over.

"We'll get someone to approach him," these conspirators might have plotted to one another. "Someone earnest, very sincere. A woman, perhaps? Yes, a woman, that would be an excellent touch. Really let him make an ass of himself!"

They had, of course, soundly denounced him. All but laughed him from the podium, or driven him from it with a barrage of rotten vegetables – which were, for precisely these sorts of reasons and occasions, banned from the Symposium floor.

It was a disgrace! they'd cried. A discredit to higher education, to the university, to his peers! An insult to the entire fields of paleontology, archaeology, anthropology, evolutionary studies and the humanitarian sciences!

Not that they'd quite been howling for his blood, but, honestly, they may as well have been. Instead of having his work rewarded with prestige, tenure, a comfortable funding grant, and his name immortalised in the hallowed halls alongside those of the giants, he'd been ousted. Accused of attempting to perpetrate a hoax. Given the bum's rush.

I didn't doubt they would have tarred and feathered him, if they'd had the supplies handy. Right when he'd been expecting triumph and acclaim, to boot. That had to make it an all the more bitter pill to swallow.

"...most fascinating?" he echoed when the owlish gaze returned to me.

"And a shame you weren't allowed to finish," I said. "I very much wanted to hear the rest, not to mention have the opportunity for follow-up questions."

"Ah," he said. He fiddled with his cuffs. He slathered jam on a roll and devoured it in three bites.

By the time our meals arrived, I'd managed to convince him of my bona fides and that I was not part of some scheme to mock, expose or ridicule him. The way he fell to, all but wolfing his food, lent credence to my notion that he'd been on a diet restricted by frugal necessity.

"What does he eat?" I asked. "Your Primitive Man? I would guess that our modern fare, heavily salted and sugared as it is, has made for a rather drastic change."

"Absolutely," said Mervin, wiping his chin with a napkin. "He won't touch tinned or processed meats. Got to be fresh. He prefers beef or pork to fish and fowl, though in a pinch he'll suffer the latter. What he likes most is calf's liver, if you can believe that."

"It makes a certain amount of sense, given a hunter-gatherer lifestyle."

Mervin nodded. "Same for greens and vegetables. Fresh, fresh, fresh. Won't touch the tinned of that, either. Except when it comes to fruit. Funny you mentioned sugar; he will guzzle as much in the way of canned peaches or apple-sauce as I can lay my hands on. Salt, too. Never seen the like! I've wondered if I oughtn't get a salt lick to hang on the wall!"

"I shudder to think of your grocer's bill," I said.

He groaned. "I'd never understood my parents complaining about my brothers and I eating them out of house and home until this."

"What about candy, pastries, other sweets?"

At that, he shook his head. "Less so. At first, yes. Stuffed himself. Gorged, even. The same for cheese and butterfat; he ate an entire brick of lard once!"

My nose, I must admit, wrinkled. I began to regret opening the conversation in this direction before we'd finished our own lunch.

Now that he'd gotten going, however, Mervin kept right on.

"Fortunately," he said, then caught himself with a scoff. "Fortunately? I say that now, but at the time it was another matter. Regardless. Fortunately, it made him sicker than I've ever seen. Thought he was going to die of it. Both ends and --"

I held up a hand and tipped my head toward the neighbouring tables. "Doctor."

"Oh. Yes. Sorry. Suffice, he hasn't touched the stuff since."

"Alcohol?"

A grimace wracked his features. "Those spirits which turn the most civilised of men into beasts? That's how I got tossed out of the cottage I'd been renting. The brute half tore the place to pieces, and when my landlady came by to complain, he..."

A crimson flush flooded his face. He coughed, and cleared his throat. I think he'd forgotten for a moment he was conversing with a member of the so-called fair and gentle sex.

My eyebrows climbed. "Did he knock her over the head with a club and drag her off by the hair?"

"Dashed if he mightn't have tried, if I hadn't been there!"

"How ever did you dissuade him?"

"A shock prod."

"You use a shock prod on him?"

"Not anymore," he hastened to assure me. "Only at the start. In the early stages, don't you know, as a training tool, an aid to learning."

"An aid to learning," I repeated.

"It's no different from a schoolmaster with a birch switch."

"Or a horse-drover with a goad."

"No harm was done!"

"What about modern pharmaceuticals?" I asked. "Drugs? Laudanum, say, or a tincture of opiates?"

Mervin hesitated. The flush, which had faded, resurged. I held the thin line of my lips against an impulse to smirk at his discomfiture. Would he tell me?

Stammering, mumbling, and stumbling over his words, he did try. He told me that most patent medicines had little to no, or adverse, effect. And that opiates, well, that opiates did not send the specimen on a destructive rampage as the alcohol had done, but ... well, had inspired other ... cravings ...not unlike those in the manner of which the landlady had nearly been accosted...so it had become necessary to...well...

It occurred to me that this mortified fellow had not once so much as even hired a girl for himself, let alone for something like this. I had to press the lips more firmly against the smirk that so very much wanted to surface.

Little would he have any reason to suspect that I'd already interviewed both the landlady and the girl in question. But he'd understand, in due time.

Meanwhile, and perhaps eager to move on to other matters, he mentioned that there'd been hardly any further need at all for the shock goad, once they'd gotten communication sorted.

"So you've taught him to speak?"

He shrugged, jabbing an asparagus spear. "His mandibular and laryngeal structure aren't suited for complex utterances. He understands well enough, provided a clarity and slowness of enunciation, but full speech? No. Some simple words. The rest is gestures ... we've devised a fairly sophisticated sign language."

"Interesting," I said.

"I'd been going to demonstrate at the Symposium, but, as you saw, they didn't give me the opportunity." He jabbed another asparagus and bit it in half with a savage snap of the teeth. "I barely got through the accounting of the expedition and discovery, let alone the revival or anything further."

I nodded, well recalling the uproar.

Having by then warmed to his subject, Mervin went on more expansively. I was familiar with the articles he'd had published – in somewhat sub-optimal scientific journals, it must be admitted – detailing his earlier work at the *Vallée des Arbres Pétrifiés*, near the Franco-German border. But I chose not to inform him of that at this time, and let him continue unabated.

The region had long been of scientific interest, of course, initially to geologists and vulcanologists. The petrified forest there was unlike others of its kind, the stony trees curiously porous and even hollowed. The prevailing theories maintained that a volcanic eruption, earthquake or meteoric impact had released a pocket of superthermal subterranean gases. This produced such a blast of intense heat that the moisture within the trunks and branches had been flash-boiled away, even as the harder wood became calcified and ceramicised, instantly baked like pottery in a kiln.

When signs of neolithic settlements were uncovered in the vast warren of limestone caverns beneath the petrified forest, archaeologists and anthropologists also flocked to the valley. Cave paintings, ancient midden piles, flint-knapped tools and evidence of ritualized burials tantalized those excited by the 1856 discoveries in what was now more properly known as Neanderthal.

Those such as Doctor Clarence Mervin. He'd begun his research in the caverns, then shifted to a site further down the valley. There, on what had once been a riverbank, were the buried remains of a prehistoric hunting camp, as well as the remains of prehistoric hunters.

His theory, expressed in his papers and a condensed version of which he related now to me as we finished our lunch, was that the event responsible for the petrification of the forest had not just boiled away the tree-sap and resins, but vaporised them into a dense airborne cloud. This cloud, according to Mervin, sank back to earth, settling over the hunting camp on the riverbank in a manner similar to the pyroclastic flow of ash and mud that had famously engulfed the ancient city of Pompeii.

"Under normal conditions," he said, having by then ordered a ham slice and scoop of egg-salad on lettuce to supplement the gluttonous meal he'd already dispatched, "the process by which resin or tree-sap solidifies into what we know as amber requires millions of years. However, the presence of gaseous molecules, mineral dust and other substances – combined with a marked drop in local temperatures, as borne out by the botanical and sedimentary records of the time --"

"Indeed," I said. "It cooled and condensed far more rapidly, with the result that the hunters at the camp became encased in amber ... or, this amber-like hardened resin ... much as insects have been."

"Precisely. And, as in Pompeii, it happened so quickly, so thoroughly, that they were caught in place, locked in that final, fatal moment. All of them except one, that is. Were you able to see the slide-projection photographs before they jeered me from the podium?"

"I was. The one specimen preserved perfectly intact. With, as you soon observed, gas bubbles and air pockets trapped in the resin with him. Inducing ... what was it that the test samples suggested?" I knew, of course, but many men preen and enjoy being able to show off their learnedness, and this one was no different.

"A chemical anesthesia capable of inducing a state of torporific catalepsy." As expected, he did preen. "It's been linked to cases of premature burial, as I'm sure you've heard."

"Oh, yes," I said. Safety coffins had been all the rage when I was a child; family lore had it that a great-uncle had been buried alive.

Even now, in these days of enlightenment, modern medicine and embalming, people fear that fate. Poe's famous but sensationalistic popular tales had only added to the lingering dread. And no wonder ... the prospect of falling into a cataleptic trance, only to waken in the grave ... that could send a shiver up the steeliest spine.

The thought of Poe led me also to recall another of his stories, the one in which a hapless sailor brought some ape or another back from foreign shores. It had escaped, and, whilst attempting to imitate the habits of its master, committed murders. I thought of mentioning this to Mervin, but decided he would see no humour in the comparison.

He went on to relate how he had, upon determining this one particular specimen to be intact and perfectly preserved, speculated at the amazing scientific possibilities should it prove to actually be alive, or revivable. Through a careful series of experiments, he'd devised a way to remove the resinous prison without causing damage, and invigorate the long-dormant tissues in the process.

"The answer, obviously, was electricity," he said, in a tone that gave me reason to second-guess the decision of pandering to his ego and offering him the opportunity to preen. "We get the very word from *ēlektron*, the Greek word for amber, by virtue of how when rubbed with fur, it acquires a charge."

"I'm quite familiar with the principles and applications of electricity, thank you, Doctor," I said. Mildly enough, but the rebuke brought him up short. Chagrin flickered briefly in his eyes. When he continued, it was with a rather less patronising manner.

The upshot of it all was that he'd succeeded. Against all odds and reason, he'd done it. He'd revived a living example of Primitive Man.

It should have been the find of the century, sure to leave the world awestruck. He'd be more famous than Darwin, who may have devised evolutionary theory, but here was proof in the actual, breathing flesh!

Think of what could be learned! A window to mankind's own past! If such a creature could be tamed, socialised, communicated with --!

Fine and well, as far as it went, but as Mervin had since become very aware, all those lofty plans and dreams fell apart when one was denounced as a fraud.

Farewell, fame and fortune. Farewell, hopes and dreams.

A fraud, they'd said. A hoax. Taking some miserable, deformed wretch ... what did he suffer from? A bone disease? Or was his grotesque appearance faked as well? Gum-rubber prosthetics and glued-on hair? Was it madness? Retardation? All an act? A sham?

The nerve! The gall! For Clarence Mervin to think he could make fools of them in such a manner? They were esteemed professors, scientists, the learned men and great minds of science! They were nobody's laughing-stock to be tricked with anything as blatantly ludicrous as this!

I, having been on the receiving end of no small amount of disdain for my profession myself – a woman? a doctor? the very idea! – was not altogether without empathy for his plight. He'd put everything he had into this. His savings, his reputation, his career, everything. What did he have to show for it? A smashed-up cottage, an angry landlady, a mountain of bills and debts, a house-guest of voracious and costly appetites ...

No, I was not altogether without empathy for him. But, by the same token, it did mean he'd be more inclined to accept my offer.

"And now ..." He raised his hands and let them drop, one to either side of his emptied plate. A hopeless bark of a laugh escaped him. "I might as well buy a striped suit, join the circus, and take him on the road as a sideshow attraction!"

"I think I can offer you a far more preferable alternative, Doctor Mervin."

He looked at me, not without skepticism. "How so?"

"My purpose in seeking you out today was not solely my own," I said. "I represent a small group of influential personages – wealthy, respected, influential personages – with a considerable interest in certain aspects of the physical sciences and humanities. An educational society, of sorts."

The man perked up visibly, though a shadow of the skepticism remained. I suppose he was wondering again if this were all some prank sprung on him by his erstwhile peers.

"Do go on, Doctor Delaney," he said. "This … educational society you mention …?"

"… is conducting one of their meetings tomorrow evening," I said, sliding him one of the Chesterton's gilt-embossed cards across the table. I'd already written the time on the back. "I do know it's woefully short notice, and for that I cannot apologise enough, but I ran across some difficulties locating you --"

"Yes, well, never mind that." He flapped my apology away with a hasty wave and snatched up the card. His owlish eyes widened further as he recognised the noted judge's address, smack amidst the city's very best neighbourhood. "A meeting? Tomorrow, you say?"

"They would be most gratified if you and your – does he have a name, by the way?"

"The nearest I've been able to pronounce it is Jayok," Mervin said, sounding for a moment like he'd caught a bone in his throat. "We've agreed, for convenience's sake, to call him Jacob."

I inclined my head in gracious acknowledgment. "If you and Jacob, then, might be available to --"

"Absolutely!"

"Because it *is* such short notice, naturally, a substantial financial compensation would also be in order. The society would insist. An educated professional deserves something for his – or her – time. Provided, of course, the prospect doesn't insult you."

"No insult at all!" he assured me, with enthusiasm so ill-concealed he could barely keep from bouncing in his seat. "I mean yes, obviously, I'd be delighted for the opportunity to present my discovery, but it would be rude to decline a well-intentioned token of appreciation."

"I'm glad we see eye to eye on this, Doctor." I smiled.

He looked at the card again, running a fingertip over the lettering that read Chesterton House. "Are you a friend of the Chesterton family, Doctor Delaney?"

"Mrs. Chesterton and many of the ladies of her acquaintance are faithful, unfailingly generous patrons of my own work."

"Ah. Patients? At the … what was it again? Institute of …?"

"Feminine Wellness and Well-Being," I told him. "For the treatment of maladies such as hysteria, and other female afflictions."

His expression changed to one with which I'm very familiar. I see it all the time on the faces of the husbands who set out to inquire about just what these treatments entail and why they should cost so much. Within seconds of my beginning to explain, they inevitably decide they emphatically do *not* want to know the particulars. Desperate to escape before I can say anything more, they cannot write the cheques fast enough. Ignorance, they tell themselves, is not just bliss. In some matters, it's a bargain at any price. Even the esteemed Judge Chesterton had harumphed and gone purple.

Clarence Mervin clearly had no further curiosity on the matter. He pocketed the card, beaming like a boy at Christmas. "So … tomorrow evening?"

"Yes. Shall I bring a motorcoach by your cottage? Perhaps at, say, six-thirty?"

"A motorcoach?"

I honestly thought the man might swoon. He collected himself as I settled the luncheon tab. We walked out together, exchanged farewells and pleasantries, and then he went on his way with a spring in his step.

As for me, I caught a cross-town trolley, dispatched a wireless to inform Mrs. Chesterton that everything had been arranged, and returned to the Institute at a brisk pace. Ensconced in my office again, I brought down the large leather-bound journal filled with news clippings, sketches, photos, mimeographs of academic papers, and page after page of my own notes.

Primitive Man.

Those stuffy old fools had laughed Mervin out of the Symposium. Mocked him, discredited him, barred him from the university. They could hardly have been more offended had someone presented them with half a monkey stitched to half a flounder and claimed it was a mermaid.

I slept well, passed the following day tending to rounds and appointments, and dressed for the meeting in slate-blue with black trim. No jewelry, minimal cosmetics, the sole nod toward finery being a lace snood to hold the hair rather than the usual netted ones.

The motorcoach arrived promptly on time, and rolled up outside the front garden gate of Doctor Mervin's rented cottage with five minutes to spare. I surmised by furtive curtain-movement that Mervin himself had been waiting, anxious, lest it all prove to be a ruse.

He emerged in what must have been his good suit – which no doubt *had* been a good suit, once – and in the company of another figure of far different description. Even at a distance, and concealed as he was in a large over-coat and broad-brimmed hat, there was something about him so strange, so altogether uncanny, that the instincts could not help but respond.

The driver, who'd stepped out to open the back door, shifted from foot to foot as they approached. I saw him toss me one quick glance, as if concerned for my safety, but he had been paid well enough to keep to his own business.

"Doctor Mervin," I said.

"Doctor Delaney."

"And this must be Jacob."

They sat opposite me. The driver closed the door, returned to his upper cabin, and started the engine with a chugging rumble and a back-fire that Jacob did not seem to care for.

I studied him with avid attention. Beneath the coat and hat, he wore baggy wool trousers and a cotton shirt. They did not fit him well. Not in the same way that Mervin's clothes didn't, but in a way that suggested tailoring to Jacob's frame would require an expert. These oversized factory-mades were the best Mervin had been able to afford.

He was barrel-chested and slightly slump-shouldered, broad through the torso, hunched of posture. His thick arms looked disproportionate in length to his stocky body, his legs shorter and somewhat bandied or bowed. He had wide hands, the backs hairy, with wisps of it also sprouting also between the base and first knuckle of each stubby finger. Some uneven success had been managed in the manicuring of the strong, yellowed nails.

"Doc-tor," he said. His voice was a rough bass-baritone, the word glottal, as if uttered through a mouthful of gravel.

His head, though ... his face ... there most of all was where the differences were the most striking. The skull was larger, low-set on a squat neck, the back of it forming a bulge of heavy bone beneath coarse dark-brown hair. Instead of a high and clear forehead, his brow sloped into a prominent and bristly supraorbital ridge overhanging his eyes. His prognathous jaw was immense, like a steam-shovel, the lower pushing forth into a hint of an underbite. Between bristly eyebrows and wiry beard was a flattish nose. His skin was not quite leathery, but sun-weathered and swarthy-complected.

While I studied him, Jacob in turn studied me. His eyes, overhung though they were, gleamed with definite intelligence. They had the color and clarity of strong black coffee, and as much of an effect on the nerves.

And this, the scientific community had scorned as a hoax?

Mervin, who'd brought his presentation case, prattled on with worried questions as to whether there would be a slide-show projector available and how much lecture time should he expect to have and what level of education might his audience have, would he need to simplify it for the benefit of their understanding?

I reassured him – he'd soon find out for himself just what the meeting's actual agenda entailed – and continued studying the Primitive Man as the motor-coach carried us through the city. Only a few months ago, he'd been in an entombed cataleptic state, dug up and transported, and revived. Unknowing that tens of thousands of years had gone by.

In his mind, he'd been hunting with his tribesmates. Making camp on that riverbank, feeling the earth lurch and shake, seeing the sky change hues. Had they marvelled? Had they quailed in terror of angry spirits or gods? Had they tried to flee? Or had there been no time?

Then, oblivion … until waking to a world so alien to him that it might as well have been another world altogether. A world in which Man mastered Nature rather than exist alongside it. A world of cities, rather than wilderness. A world of machines, technology, and invention.

Amazing, really, that he hadn't simply snapped and gone mad. How would any of us have fared, were the situation somehow reversed? Here he was, riding in a motor-coach through a noisy, crowded landscape of monoliths and pollution … but, aside from the occasional clench of a fist or jaw, or narrowing of eye, he was calm.

Had Mervin, I wondered, given any thought to the possible consequences of his actions? The sudden reappearance of Primitive Man in modern society … the effects it would have upon both?

I doubted it. His hurt surprise at the Symposium, and at the barrage of furious letters he'd gotten from scientists and clergymen, were signs of that.

The motor-coach turned in at the gate of Chesterton House, proceeding up the drive. It was a stately place, dripping with wealth and privilege to excess. We disembarked as a footman paid the driver. Moments later, we were shown in.

Doctor Mervin seemed torn between intimidation and envious yearning as he took in the lavish décor. I noticed Jacob's head lift, nostrils flaring, scenting the air.

No butler came forth to greet us. The great house was hushed. I took the lead. "The salon is downstairs," I said. "That is where Mrs. Chesterton does her entertaining, meetings, and social events."

Mervin's nervousness rose with each step we descended. By the time we reached the lower hall, he, too, sniffed at the air.

"What is that?" he asked. "It smells like smoke."

"Opium," I replied, and pushed open the salon's double doors.

Hazy tendrils of it wafted, intoxicating ribbons and fumes. The room, dim-lit by lamps and heavily curtained, was furnished with luxurious cushions, chaises and lounge-chairs.

And here waited Mrs. Chesterton with her guests. Well-to-do society ladies all, the wives of lawyers and bankers, doctors, politicians ... they reclined around the room in languid relaxation.

Mrs. Chesterton herself swayed toward us. "Genevieve," she purred at me. "You are a veritable angel."

Had we been out at some proper function, the judge's wife would have been attired to the very pinnacle of fashion, shaped by crinoline hoops and corset and bustle, confined in stiff satin and brocade. It rocked poor Clarence Mervin back on his heels to behold her ample curves unfettered, voluptuous flesh loose beneath a sheer silken chemise.

The other ladies were in similar dishabille of chemises, cami-knickers, robes and draped sheets. The scene entire was not unlike a painting by one of the old masters, depicting nymphs at some banquet or bacchanal. They regarded us – or, to be fair, they regarded *Jacob* – with half-lidded eyes. Tongues slipped wetly over parted lips.

The Primitive Man, for his part, drew so deep a breath of the smoke-rich air that his chest strained his shirt to the buttons' very limit. What I'd been told by the girl that Mervin had hired, which had been supported by Mervin himself, was confirmed as to the effects of opiates on his system.

"My goodness," said Mrs. Chesterton, removing Jacob's hat and tossing it idly away. "Aren't *you* a magnificent specimen!"

"Doctor Delaney ...?" Mervin looked at me, his owlish gaze more confused than ever. "What is this? What's going on here? You said ... a meeting ... an educational society ... with ... with ..."

I nodded. "... with a considerable interest in certain aspects of the physical sciences and humanities. Quite so. Particularly that which pertains to female sexuality. I believe I mentioned to you that my field involves treatments for hysteria and other such afflictions."

"But ... yes, but ..."

"This *is* our meeting," the wife of the city's police commissioner told him. "This *is* our educational society."

"Oh, yes," said the spinster sister of a captain of industry. "We've had Aboriginals, Plains Savages, Islanders, Orientals --"

Additional voices chimed in.

"Don't forget the albino!"

"And the midgets, oh, the midgets!"

"And Rex," a dowager railroad baron's widow said. "Dear old Rex. He was such a good boy."

"We even had a Shetland pony, once," the commissioner's wife said. "That one was a bit much. Hardly anyone dared to give it a try."

"But *this*!" cooed the mayor's eldest daughter, a recent divorcee. "What a find!"

"I could hardly agree more," said Mrs. Chesterton. She favoured Mervin with a decadent smile. "Doctor, you are to be congratulated. He's perfect. Thank you ever so much." She tucked a folded cheque into his breast pocket, then patted it. "*Ever* so much!"

Mervin just gaped. He once again reminded me of a landed fish. I took him by the elbow and steered him from the room, before the opium fumes could addle him too much. He didn't have my tolerance for them, I was sure.

Jacob, meanwhile, had reached understanding long before his stunned and scandalised discoverer. His reaction as the ladies flocked dreamily toward him was what might have been expected.

At the far end of the downstairs hall was a small drawing room. It was there I led Mervin. I got him to a chair, then poured him a hefty knock of brandy. He downed it at a gulp. His watery blue eyes watering all the more, he blinked up at me.

"Educational society ..." he said in a feeble whimper.

"More of a libertine debauchery society, to be true." I refilled his brandy and poured one for myself.

"They ..." He realised he was still holding his presentation case, and let it fall to the carpet with a brittle kind of laugh. He'd be giving no lectures, showing no slides, not here, not tonight. "They're ..."

I chose my own chair and sat. I sipped. I shrugged. "Roman noblewomen used to enjoy the company of champion gladiators. In the sultan's harem, bored wives and concubines had the services of their eunuchs."

"Well, perhaps, but ..."

"It is much the same for women in this modern day and age, Doctor Mervin. Neglectful husbands, scolding churchmen, physicians who insist that it's all in their minds … craving release is improper, they're told, and unladylike. They're pent-up, frustrated, dissatisfied. So, they seek other options."

"They go to you."

"They come to me."

In the brief silence that followed, we could hear from behind the salon's closed doors the sounds of grunts, moans, squeals and sighs. All seemed to be going rather well.

"There is," I said after a while, "one more matter I'd like to discuss with you. The Institute, *my* Institute, could use someone of your specialised knowledge and expertise."

Face creased with bafflement, he only looked at me.

"Besides my office here in the city," I explained, "the Institute maintains a very nice country estate, with a private boarding school. The staff are of the utmost discretion, and the pupils are … children of exceptional interest and breeding."

Comprehension went on eluding him. I leaned forward in my chair and tried yet again.

"As you are the foremost scholar on the revival of Primitive Man," I said, "perhaps you'd be willing to continue your research." I raised my tumbler of brandy to him, as if making a toast. "In the event that this evening's meeting … this evening's experiment, if you will … should bear fruit."

ENGINEANDERTHALS

Vince Liberato

The worst part about waking up from an extended stasis? The taste. Definitely the taste.

It's like that sour and pungent feeling you get in your mouth after waking up, only magnified exponentially. Like you're passing a near-solid waste through your oral cavity when you exhale. It's stuck inside of you and no amount of cleansing and internal bleaching can extinguish it. And it fills you up too, keeps you from eating. You get that feeling of satisfaction like you ate a large meal, only you haven't eaten in the months or years you have been on ice. Feeling full is okay, until you realise you are only full because of a bloated, fermented build-up of gas in your stomach. A bubble that will eventually burst and leave you completely hollow... empty except for the rotten taste.

When something threatens the primary monopolies of the Horizon Corporation, a problem that needs to be taken care of with extreme speed, silence, and discretion, I am thawed. I can stand being awake while my body temperature is raised from zero to one hundred degrees, when my eyes thaw from a near crystalised state and chunky blocks of slushy, icy blood start tunnelling their way through frozen veins and arteries. The pain is a reminder that there is work that needs to be done and it helps jar me awake from stasis lethargy. But the awful taste...

"Stasis pod bay opening soon. How are you feeling, Mr. Hathers?"

"Great," I lied. Despite what the readouts on my temperature showed me, I still felt like I was freezing and boiling at the same time. The taste was still there as well, gripping my mouth even harder than it had during the last assignment.

"Opening stasis bay doors in ten seconds."

"Thanks, HANK," I said. I don't know why I always spoke back to him. My answers would not matter.

"Five seconds,"

Inside of me, I stretched and extended an organic air bladder located between my lungs. It felt a little like blowing up a small balloon. I shut my eyes.

"Four."

I opened my eyes. Catseye Vision was engaged. Everything was black and white, but nothing obscured by darkness. I exhaled, expunging the air I stored in my bio-bladder. I shuddered involuntarily from the stasis-taste that rushed up.

"Three."

I shut my eyes again to engage my normal vision. I took a deeper breath to fill the bio-bladder. It still was not at full capacity.

"Two."

I opened my eyes and could see in normal human vision again. Instead of releasing the air I had already trapped, I took an even deeper breath. The internally grown body modification extended to full, gently cushioning the organs around it.

"One."

My body was sprayed with a high profiled chemical mixture that washed off the sticky, sulfurous gel that preserved my body while on ice. It melted off instantly, leaving me completely dry. Once, I tried opening my mouth to see if it would help purify my insides. It did not.

"Welcome back Mr. Hathers. Your assignment is waiting for you on your desk." HANK's disembodied voice echoed in my office. HANK, or Horizon Alarm/Navigator/Knowledge database was about as intelligent as any computer program could be. Any smarter, he risked a visit from I-Bola, a hyper-mutated computer virus that preyed exclusively on artificial intelligences. All attempts to contain I-Bola had failed, and traces of it existed everywhere, keeping all computers at HANK's level or lower. That was why HOMEs, Human Organically Modified Enforcers, were created and kept on ice, only thawed in extreme situations. Before I-Bola, this would have been a machine's job, but no machine that could make complex decisions could be built so long as I-Bola could just rip it to pieces as soon as it went online.

The pod door opened and I stepped out. Laying on my desk was a manila folder; my assignment would be written in it, along with any other relevant information. Whatever the job was, it was serious. Only a few tasks have been sent to me in this fashion, an expensive method used in extreme operations. Paper could burn and could not be traced, unlike electronic records, which could be hacked. Only the top executives of Horizon would be aware of my assignment, and most of their identities were paper-guarded secrets as well.

"HANK, what is my temporal age, to the year?" I asked. I opened my bottom drawer and took out a hand mirror.

"Fifty-eight."

In the mirror, my reflection looked back. Steely-grey eyes, shoulder length black hair, and a little bit of dark facial stubble. I hope this look is still in style when I retire. It suits me. "What is my approximate biological age?"

"Twenty-four."

Most of the other HOMEs I had known did not live in stasis like I did. After a successful mission, they would take their checks, cash them, and spend a very large amount of capital in a very short amount of time on drugs, new mods, and the most expensive pleasures money could buy. I was different from them– I wanted to retire biologically young and live out my extended, modded lifespan in extreme comfort. While setting up a stasis pod in my office was expensive, I had spent almost twenty-two of the last twenty-five years preserved, saving all the capital I could.

"What do you think I should have for lunch?" I put the mirror away as I spoke.

"I cannot answer that. Please reword your question."

"Cancel request HANK," I said. My computer, as its name implied, could calculate dates, wake me up from stasis, and autopilot a ship to simple routes, but could not make decisions or choices. Biological science owed its current state to I-Bola. Otherwise, the machines would probably be running everything.

I smelled the crisp yet somehow stale folder. The last time I had a manila folder, its instructions led me to sabotage a satellite wild-life refuge and make it crash on Mars' surface. I did not know why I had to send the last remaining penguins, panda bears, and platypi to a burning extinction but, as one of Horizon's top HOMEs, I did not question the order. I just did what I was told and got paid – very, very well. I opened the folder. On a photograph of a very large Horizon Climate Spire, a small red dot marked clearly a spot on the snow-white superstructure. On the back of the photograph, scrawled in thin ink and a spidery script, was my job:

The Engineanderthals on Europa have taken the Climate Spire and are threatening to blow it up. Regain control of the moon at any cost. Suggested approach: Eject Atmosphere.

I read it over a few times.

"HANK."

"Yes?"

"What is an Engineanderthal?"

"Engineanderthal. A clone whose genetic material is primarily engineered from *Homo Neanderthalensis*, more commonly known as Neanderthal man. Engineanderthals were created by the Horizon Corporation after problems with Europa's proximity to the Jupiter magnetosphere required a non-robotic solution to issues stemming from the planet's radiation belt. Would you like me to continue?"

"Yes," I said. "Explain their body mods. How do they survive?"

"The modifications to Neanderthal DNA are surprisingly minimal. They have central heating diodes lining the skeleton for extra heat, as well as radiation absorbent glands under the eyes, inside the nose, and along the spine. Between the terraforming already having taken place on Europa, the Climate Spire, and the above modifications, Engineanderthals are able to live in comfort on Europa. Their primary source of food are vegetative growths Horizon saturated the planet with, as well as Syntheti-Yetis."

"Syntheti-Yetis? HANK, define."

"Syntheti-Yetis are augmented apes, specifically mountain gorillas, modelled after the mythical Yetis of the Himalayas, who now live on the surface of the planet. They were created to be a source of meat for the Engineanderthals and those of the Horizon Corporation when full colonization of the planet completed. While primarily vegetarians, they are an aggressive species and have been known to catch, eat, and kill, in that order, those that threaten their nests, which are usually located in icy crevices and canyons. Adults range from eight to ten feet tall, and can weigh upwards of a thousand pounds. Would you like to know more?"

"No," I paused, making sure that there was sufficient space between questions. If I spoke too fast, HANK would blend them together. "Are we on Europa now?"

"We just passed through the outer atmosphere and are minutes away from touching down on the moon."

"Excellent," I sat down at my desk and flipped open the office's controls. I was going to have to find a safe place to land, one that would not attract the attention of the Syntheti-Yetis or Engineanderathals. My office, which was also my primary mode of transportation, shuddered as I broke through the spongy layer of sky that Horizon had created. We would be landing a few miles away from the largest Horizon structure on the planet's surface, the Climate Spire. When the shaking stopped, I dropped the folder into the incinerator and watched it burn.

***

There was no telling why the Engineanderthals were rebelling, but I strongly suspected outside interference, perhaps insurgents from Horizon's rivals, like Black Forest or Soviet. I checked the outside conditions of the moon. Normal human beings could not survive long outside, not without bulky environmental suits that would leave them easy targets, but I would be fine with just my snow cloak.

I was unique among HOMEs for how remarkably little I had been modified from the basic human structure. Like the Engineanderthals, I had multiple radiation absorption glands within my body, as well as an internalised heating/cooling regulator. My bio-bladder could sustain me temporarily if the atmosphere turned hazardous, and my Catseye mod gave me perfect night vision. All of these modifications were made to be hidden and to require as little extra energy consumption from me as possible. This was often not the case with other modded humans. On the Mars mission I encountered a group who called themselves "The Bee Team." Each had grafted onto their body an organic laser that replaced one of their hands. They were usually enforcers or soldiers, armed with some other sidearm and deployed more for intimidation than actual combat. Only once did I ever see one use her laser. She fired it a single time and then collapsed. What was once a healthy female body reduced to thin skin stretched over a bony skeleton before it hit the ground. The Bee Team mod was great for a company goon, but it would make for a very short-lived career as a HOME.

The Climate Spire was not an incredibly appropriate name, as there were actually several spires (nineteen total) stretched out over a sphere, which was bisected in the middle, with half of the massive structure buried under the ice of Europa. The spires functioned as a set of mechanical lungs for the planet, taking in atmosphere and exhaling the thin mixture of oxygen, nitrogen, and carbon dioxide that I was breathing now. The spires required constant maintenance and regulation, and due to I-Bola, it had to be monitored by living beings that could make the adjustments to the delicate equipment.

My entrance to the Climate Spire was a small emergency hatch hidden in the side of the sphere, in the spot marked on the picture I had reviewed earlier. The snow cloak I was wearing had masked me from the outer sensors of the Climate Spire, although it had not shielded out the cold effectively, as it was built for espionage first and everything else second. Sprinting across Europa's icy crust left me chilled to the bone, the cold and the bad taste in my mouth (it had not even started to fade) worked in tandem to recreate the misery of my office from a few hours ago. I pulled the grating free and dropped down. I was surprised both in what I saw and what Horizon had failed to mention in their notes.

When I destroyed the Martian satellite sanctuary, there were several mini-climates arranged in small patches across a very industrial looking ship deck. Low strength force fields kept the animals and base environments locked inside of each area that was crisscrossed with metal walkways and conveyer belts. The panda habitat was a patch of bamboo in a warm setting, while the penguins had an icy square. Even the areas where people could walk in and pet the animals were clearly not a part of the sanctuary, just a grassy environmental bubble on a metal slate.

What I saw was an educated approximation of the enviornment that Neanderthal man lived in prior to their extinction. The upper portion of the dome was a free-flowing recreation of the sky, showing an early morning. White clouds lazily crawled above, blocking out a faux sun from which heat emanated. Vast forests stretched in all directions. I closed the hatch, and the visible seams of the access instantly dissolved into a wall that held the illusion of the edge of a steep cliff. I knew the dome was several miles in diameter, but from the inside, it seemed to stretch to an impossible distance. The only indicator that I was in a structure meant to regulate atmosphere were the poorly disguised trees-spires spread about the habitat. Dozens of feet in diameter, each would have an entrance visible from the outside.

Soft snow crunched beneath my feet. There was dirt mixed in with it, along with several downed tree branches pressed into the ground, creating a green and brown carpet in a small clearing in the woods. There were thick tufts of greyish-black hair caught in many of the branches and it smelled of animal waste. I heard an angry mewling from one thick pile of tree branches, and a baby Syntheti-Yeti confirmed that I had dropped down into one of their nests.

A loud roar responded to the baby's cry and the foliage a few yards in front of me started to shake and uproot. I reached into my holster and raised my weapon to the trembling brush. Or tried to, as the baby Syntheti-Yeti burst from its moldy green cocoon and bit down on my raised hand hard enough to completely sever my thumb and three closest fingers. The gun dropped and the baby retreated just as the forest in front of me exploded.

The first thing I thought, before I bounced off of the tree I had been smacked into, was that HANK's data was incorrect. My attacker was at least twelve feet tall and easily fifteen hundred pounds of angry, bulging, modded muscle. I hit the ground and scrambled to my feet. I did not have time to mourn my missing digits. Both they and my gun were behind the parent. It was the owner of the fur I had seen earlier, and smelled worse than the nest it had built. As time tends to slow when one is in danger, a stray thought compared Syntheti-Yetti smell to post-cryo-taste. They were remarkably similar.

The baby scampered behind its parent and hissed. It was roughly four feet tall and a much lighter colored version of the parent, which had resumed its attack by rushing me a second time. I barely rolled out of the way as it took a swing that would have taken off my head. We repeated this again. It attacking and I dodge/attempt to position myself closer to my laser, both of us each time closing the gap to our goal. For a brief moment, part of me wished I had been outfitted with the same mods that those in the Bee Team were. Sure, I would die, but I would not be going alone. Most of me ducked again. A rushing hotness bubbled out from where a small piece of my ear that was now lodged in Syntheti-Yeti fingernail had been. I would not be able to keep this up much longer, enhanced reflexes or not. I was getting slower, it was getting angrier. Luckily, I would not have to. The laser was a few feet in front of me, the adult Snytheti-Yeti a few feet behind. It charged, I dodged, and the gun was within my grasp. I reached for it, and fumbled the gun in a bloody reminder that I lacked all the parts needed to shoot with my right hand. I tried with my left, but was blindsided by the baby Syntheti-Yeit, who tackled me into its waiting parent. I did it again, with my left this time, and was blindsided by the baby Syntheti-Yeti who tackled me into its waiting parent.

It took me in its arms, in an embrace I could not break. Oddly enough, I did not feel any crushing pain. The only two things I could recognize were the grime and grunge of its hard and bristly fur sticking to my exposed skin and open wounds, and the continued aftertaste from cryogenic suspension, which felt as if it were leaking out of me like air from a balloon.

Black dots tinged my vision. It tightened its grip, and my face burned, blinding me. Then, nothing.

***

"How are you feeling, Mr. Hathers?"

"Ugh, HANK?" I said, "Great," I lied. "Your voice is way off."

"That is wonderful! But I am not HANK. And there is nothing off about my voice."

I opened my eyes. I could see blotchy shadows and a light source. I guessed by the way it danced it was a fire.

"Call me Bolotnikov. We have adopted Russian names for the time being. It has been difficult to create a unique culture from the ground up, and there was much of old Russia that we found to be incredibly appealing, not to mention the similarities between Siberia and our race's ideal climate."

"You're an Engineanderthal?" I asked.

"I am. And you are not, although I am guessing that that fact is general knowledge and not news to you."

Colors had not returned, but I could see outlines now. The voice I assumed was Bolotnikov sounded a lot like a grown man trying to imitate a woman – very high pitched and oddly proper.

"What happened?" I concentrated and tried Catseye Vision.

"Well, my comrades and I were out hunting not far from where you broke in and followed the noise. By the way, thank you for pointing out that entry hatch. We were unaware of its existence until today. We are grateful." He paused for a moment, scratching his chin. ""We watched your duel with her from the trees. You see, because she was so occupied with you, she did not notice our arrival, and since you were busy dodging her, I doubted you saw us… But I digress… During that time, we decided whether we should let you live. We have been expecting someone else to come and try to reason with us or assassinate us or something like that. You're not the first, but you did get a lot further than any before. Or than any we allowed. The last guy Horizon sent was butchered in a manner similar to the Yeti mother. Imagine… he walked in our front door and announced our rebellion over. The look on his face…" He chuckled at that."

"What?" I said. Catseye Vision was not working right either. I switched back. My eyes were starting to focus. Bolotnikov was not the only Engineanderthal in the room.

"With a spear to the face," Bolotnikov said gleefully and laughed. "She bled all over you. You were awake for a little of that…… But it was the quickest way to kill her. A few more seconds, I don't think you would have survived."

I blinked and the blurs focused into clear images. Bolotnikov was male, clothed in a fur tunic that was formerly Syntheti-Yeti. He was short, roughly five feet tall, with a barrel chest and tree trunks of rippling muscle for arms and legs. He watched me with eyes that were alert, intelligent, and alternating yellow-orange then green – he definitely had a Catseye mod and was showing me purposefully. The other Engineanderthals behind him were several feet back, huddled together, and all identical; the only difference I could discern came from colors of fur they wore.

"What are you going to do with me?" I asked.

"Well, that is an interesting question... It really is. If you were to ask me what had been done to you, I could answer that rather simply. We treated your injuries... Syntheti-Yeti bites are incredibly nasty. We seared the holes in your hand, applied antibiotics and sedatives, bandaged your notched ear, and then bound you to a post, where you are at present. Had you asked what we are doing with you, in the present tense, of course, I would say we are interrogating you and discussing this very matter at hand. But you asked me what we ultimately are going to do with you... And that is a problem, a problem I do not have an answer to. Do you know why?

"I can guess," I started, but Bolotnikov was clearly enjoying himself and did not let me get another word in. For one with such a cartoonish voice, he took great pleasure in the act of speaking.

"Because we asked your superiors, our creators, to leave us alone. We know we owe them a great debt, for our existence and this environment and all that, and it is a debt we would pay off in full, even with some sort of agreed upon interest rate attached. But we simply cannot allow them to come in on the terms that they had intended. The point when this world becomes fully inhabitable for human beings is the point where we no longer have any relevance. We would be most likely exterminated. Or euthanized. Or disposed of. Whatever term you apply to any beast that needs to be put down. Maybe put in a zoo, which would be all the more tragic."

From behind Bolotnikov, several more Engineanderthals started making small talk. He raised a giant, hairy fist and they lowered their head and immediately silenced.

"I will not ask you what your intentions were, Mr. Hathers. I already know. What we...And by we, I mean our entire species, would like...We are all comrades and need not speak with but one voice... is to send a message to your superiors. We will pay off our debt. We will even work and trade with your company. But we will not allow human beings on Europa. We will negotiate, but we simply cannot have your kind here. The moon is ours and ours alone... Well, we share with Syntheti-Yetis, maybe with other non-sentient, modded species not yet invented, but you get the idea."

"I don't think I do, Mr. Bolotnikov. What you are asking for is simply impossible. What is to keep Horizon from simply sending ships out to reclaim the moon by force?" The Engineanderthals in the back were very fidgeting, apparently uneasy with what I said.

"Another excellent question, Mr. Hathers. But one that I believe you know the answer to. Simply put, we'll blow up the Climate Spire. It goes down deep into the planet, so deep, in fact, that it would damage the moon severely. Possibly enough to blow the whole thing up, but at the very least, enough to make it a complete loss of capital for the company. The moon was expensive, the Climate Spire was expensive, creating a race of Neanderthal men to man the base was expensive, and all of it will go up in a cataclysmic, extinction-level-event explosion if they do not agree to our demands. Our species has been extinct once before, and while it pains me to say this, we will willingly go again if we cannot be left to develop in a method that best suits us."

The Engineanderthals in the back started tittering again. Bolotnikov, in a quick motion, turned and punched the closest in the stomach, doubling him over. The others did nothing to help their comrade, who spat out blood in between gasps for air. They put their hands over their mouths and the chatter ended.

"Like I said, we will willingly go again," Bolotnikov growled in his squeaky voice.

"How did you..." I started, but was cut off.

"How did we go extinct the first time? A cruel ecological joke, played on us by our home planet at the end of the last Ice Age..." Bolotnikov began to pace and rubbed his knuckles as he spoke. "Did you know that after the first Neanderthal skull was discovered and our species first catalogued, that one of the first accepted theories about our species' disappearance was that we were simply out-competed by your kind? After all, how could the brutish, stupid, and slow Neanderthal hope to go against those whose descendants were smarter, nimbler, and more technologically advanced? Of course, this theory was later on debunked and it was accepted that the rapidly changing weather of the death throes of the last Ice Age was the architect of our demise. Imagine if the ecological changes had taken place over centuries instead of decades... or if the ice had not declined, but accelerated! How much different would history be. Perhaps you and I would still be here, but with our positions switched. The moon or planet would have to be different too. Maybe Venus or Mercury... some place where it gets really hot and inhospitable for those built as we are... You would be explaining how your species were the target of a cruel ecological joke...... Did I already say that? I just kind of like how it rolls off the tongue and... Ah, there I go again. Did I answer your question?" He grinned, clearly wanting me to ask about his control of the other Engineanderthals.

"Not really," I said. "I wanted to know how you knew my name."

"Oh," he was clearly disappointed. "We have your file Mr. Hathers. As soon as your ship entered our atmosphere, we identified it and its owner as Gunther Hathers, HOME. Genetic modifications include all the things we know you have... All dreadfully boring stuff really, I won't bore you by listing it."

"I see. No point in trying to awe you with my trick eyes?" I said

"Right. Or challenging any of us to a contest involving holding your breath. None of us have an internal air sac that would allow us to live in an oxygenless environment for a short period of time."

"What else do you know?"

"Well, quite a bit actually, but it would not be prudent of me to list all the things Horizon's electric encyclopedia lists. I will tell you, however, that my vocabulary is purely a result of my own studies."

"Are you the only one that talks that way?" I asked.

"We are all equals here," he said, glancing over his shoulder. The others nodded their heads slightly. Bolotnikov's eyes flashed yellow-orange again. "They can speak as I do, they just have nothing to say to you."

"Is that true?" I asked.

"It is," Bolotnikov said, snapping his fingers. The other Engineanderthals moved forward, keeping a respectful distance from my interrogator and began to untie me. The ropes around my waist were the tightest. While they were being cut loose, I felt something hastily shoved in my back pocket. The shape was instantly recognizable–my blaster. The other Engineanderthals had just secretly armed me.

"Thanks," I said, rubbing my wrists. My fingers ached where they were now sealed stumps.

"No need to thank me yet. There was a vote if you should live," he bared his teeth in a full smile. They were clean, straight, and white. "And it was close. Very close."

"When was it taken?" I asked.

"By the community's leaders, when we took you in. I was the deciding vote." Several questions came to mind about this, but he did not give me a chance to ask. ""But before we let you go, I feel an exercise in judgement and trust is in order. If you pass it, you will get to be a living messenger to Horizon."

"And if I fail?"

"We'll make use of you in other ways, Mr. Hathers. Trust is very important here. You can trust me on that."

***

We walked through the settlement. I could see huts similar to the one I had been kept. Very simple structures, created from wood, dirt, and Syntheti-Yeti. Several fires burned here and there, some with hunks of meat roasting over the open flame. Every time we approached other Engineanderthals, they retreated to their huts as soon as they saw Bolotnikov.

"I suppose you're wondering just how we manage to keep things running on the outside of the planet so smoothly while living in huts like this," Bolotnikov said. He was shouting a little, his high pitched voice was incredibly jovial.

"I wasn't, but now that you mention it, I would like to know," I replied.

"Simple, really. Our instructions, what we were programmed to know from the moment of our creation, was to constantly maintain each of the nineteen spires speckled about this habitat. For some reason or another, our designers left us with the base intelligence that it was assumed a modern day Neanderthal would have. Like you, our brains have grown lopsided, with a much more developed speech center and capacity to solve problems."

"About the spires," I said.

"Yes, of course, of course. The spires require constant vigilance, but since we are several hundred and growing, no more than nineteen Engineanderthals are required for this task at any point in time. We've got in place an adequate distribution of labour. Quite boring, actually, but it works very well. It is very fortuitous that the Climate Spire regulates its own atmosphere as well as that around Europa. It is very pleasant for us inside, and we could survive outside if we had to, but humans simply could not. Even you, with your resistance to cold and radiation, could not stay outside forever, Mr. Hathers."

"I know," I said. I could feel my blaster pressing against me in my pocket. He was too close to me to get a clean shot.

"Also, it keeps us quite safe from outside interference. You would be amazed at the kind of firepower we have access to, compliments of Horizon. They were more afraid of outside interference than internal revolution, and I'm pretty sure were completely caught off guard by our little rebellion."

"They were. I'm only called in to extreme cases."

"I am honoured, Mr. Hathers," Bolotnikov said. I was not sure if he was being serious or not. "Anyway," he continued, "Here we are. This spire actually controls the interior atmosphere of the sphere. From here, you can see everything we can do and will offer for Horizon in an alliance."

We entered the fake-tree. There was cutting edge tech everywhere, from liquid monitors to organic circuitry. All over the surface of Europa, I could see small blips, each representative of the outdoor Syntheti-Yeti population. Bolotnikov could see my eyes wandering and continued talking.

"We have the group of animals living indoors with us. Just on the off chance anyone ever decided to or found a way to destroy our food supply. Think it was once done with species on Earth to control another rebellious group of people - the Fullabo or Ruffalo."

"I think you mean 'Buffalo,'" I interjected. I still did not have my shot.

"I honestly don't care …" Bolotnikov went into Catseye for a second, clearly annoyed at me. A split second later, they were at his normal setting. "But as you can see, we have already set up a few locations that we can mine on the planet's surface and upper mantle. We are also in the process of developing a satellite that could be used to provide food, water, and atmosphere to friendly craft. Its construction could be completed in an Earth year, once a coalition has been established and we have a reason to create such a station."

"I see. You have done great things here," I nodded. From behind Bolotnikov, there was a hint of red in a pitch corner. A button had been hastily, but not completely, covered up by voidlight - projected artificial darkness. Even mostly obscured, I recognised the tiny flare of colour as the cadmium red used to mark Horizon's Climate Spire's atmosphere ejector. I could push that button and be the only thing left alive on the planet in minutes, sustained by my internal air bladder until I got back to my ship. The blaster weighed heavily on my side and I felt a pang of guilt…

"Indeed we have, but it is only an extension of human technology…" Bolotnikov turned his back.

In a swift motion, I had my blaster out and crosshairs over Bolotnikov's heart. Perhaps I would not have to enact a genocide after all.

Oblivious to me, he continued his speech. "I hope that in a few generations, our technology will have evolved to the point to where it is completely distinct from human tech…"

I pulled the trigger.

Click

Nothing happened.

"And not subject to constraints, such as the limitations of modern weapons and their power sources," he turned to face me. In his giant hand, I could see a crushed, now-useless energy cartridge. He dropped it.

"Call me old fashioned," from inside his coverings he produced a long-bladed knife. "But I prefer more personal methods."

There was no way I could take him on. Only one chance now. I lunged forward, towards the concealed atmospheric ejector button.

Workers in Climate Spires are told that atmospheric ejectors are a safety measure for when something toxic invades the air. But it is never used whenever chemical agents hazardous to life are introduced. It is only there when the atmosphere turns acidic and capable of harming the machines in the Climate Spire. When triggered, the atmosphere both inside and outside of the sphere gets ejected into space, killing all that need oxygen to live, but preserving the structure for a new team to man it.

Bolotnikov stabbed at the air, narrowly missing me. I slammed my fist down on the hidden button and engaged my air bladder, bracing myself for the expulsion of the atmosphere around me.

Nothing happened.

For the second time today, time slowed, only enough for me to realise that Bolotnikov's first strike was feinted. He missed me on purpose. The second was intentional. I did not see any movement, there was just the knife's hilt pressed against my chest. I could have sworn I heard a sound like a balloon popping. Pretty sure it was my air bladder. A nauseous gust of air escaped me.

"I'm afraid you failed our test of trust, Mr. Hathers. Twice, actually. I suppose we'll need to find another way to contact Horizon. Perhaps we"ll cure your skin, write our demands on it, and ask the computer in your space ship to take it to someone important. Do you think that would send a clearer message to Horizon?"

"How … " I squeaked. 'How would you?' was what I wanted to ask. Because of HANK's limitations, there was no way such a complex request could be executed. But because of my wound, all I could produce was the first word.

"The gun was tampered with beforehand and the atmosphere ejector you hit was a fake. We destroyed the real one a while back. We learn from our mistakes, Mr. Hathers, even mistakes made thousands of years before our rebirth. Rapid climate change killed us once. Do you think we would allow a button to exist that could return Europa to a wasteland? Or would you want me to explain the process of curing human skin to you?"

I did not respond. Darkness was creeping around me. It was much colder this time. But at least the taste had finally disappeared.

THE UPHILL CLIMATE

Chris Amies

Helen Davit first met Julianne Mestre in the Kaz Bar in the city of Basman, two days before the expedition up Mount Dumaz. Mestre was wearing an orange T-shirt which said A MAD DESIRE TO RUN FOR THE PEAKS.

"That's what I have," said Mestre. "All of them. The eight-thousand metre peaks, and the sevens, and the sixes, and the fives.

"The English with their feet, though," she continued.

Helen Davit looked at her shoes.

"What about our feet?" she asked.

"You do not," Mestre went on, "comprehend the importance of the eight-thousand metre mark. But for us, it is very important that there are fourteen peaks over eight thousand metres."

"And you want to climb the lot," Davit said. "Can we deal with the – hill first?"

The Frenchwoman smiled and brushed near-black strands of hair back from her face.

"Of course," she said.

***

Davit is looking up at the peak of Mount Dumaz, or Mount Doom, as everyone on the expedition has christened it separately. 4,000 metres and change rising out of the rolling hills and forests of the Caucasus. And on the way up, plenty of ice, rock, overhangs, cracks, and the rest of it. It's been climbed before, certainly, but while the rest of the region opened up post-USSR to western travellers, the small landlocked nation of Kazlar has been a lot more secretive until now. There could, Davit reckons, be two reasons for the new openness.

Firstly, the people involved. Sir Henry Challenger is a hard person for even bureaucrats to disagree with. If he said he wanted to tackle Dumaz then tackle it he would.

Julianne Mestre is a media 'face' too, and what with Kazlar wanting to be a European nation, who better than a French star climber to come and get up some big rocks, on film?

The other reason is currently shambling about in a row of orange tents along the little river through the valley. Five large figures, barrel-chested, huge-nosed and beetle-browed. None more than five feet eight tall, but all alarmingly big. Now and again one will come out of a tent, forage about a bit, and go back in. One of them, the individual known as Joseba, shuffles up to Davit and Mestre, looks at them and then walks further along the stream. In a while the women can hear a splashing as the porter washes himself.

Davit shoulders the camera again and takes footage of clouds breaking from the summit. The weather looks set to be a little cloudy but otherwise good.

***

Challenger wanders around the encampment later in the morning. The famous jutting beard has turned grey in recent years and the piercing blue eyes are surrounded by creases, but he is still a formidable figure. Irascible media pundit, climber of everything that could be climbed, and leader of the 2002 Nanga Parbat expedition. He claims descent from Professor George Challenger, the "Lost World" guy but nobody is quite sure if that is a joke or not and no-one wants to challenge him (so to speak) on it.

Helen Davit wasn't on Nanga Parbat, but she has been on a couple of Challenger's more recent trips, video camera strapped to her shoulder as she walked.

"It's a lovely day," Challenger says. "Time to move on up."

The porters go to their packs and shoulder them. Davit watches them move, surefooted and confident, particularly adapted to life at altitude and in the cold. She grabs more footage of them.

The thals don't seem to have a problem with the camera. There's no reason why they should but Davit thinks of remote cultures who supposedly believe that the camera steals your soul. Unless the so called primitives just didn't want their picture taken and thought that claiming superstition was the best way to stop inquisitive westerners from sticking a lens in their face. "It's against my religion" was always a good stopper for some reason, far better than "I don't want to."

***

The thals lumber off among the climbers, up a stony track that leads between thinning vegetation to the first true ridge. There is little sound other than boots crunching on rock. Nobody is speaking. The thals' breath hisses. A bird lets loose a skirl of alarmed notes. Possibly this is the Alpine chough that drifts across the path unconcerned later. Helen Davit notices it and is surprised; she thought they were only found in the Alps and Pyrenees. Clearly they spread Eastwards to this rocky breeding ground between the Black Sea and the Caspian.

Davit, filming from the back, concentrates on Mestre's deceptively narrow shoulders. The Frenchwoman's fists are clenched. Mestre realises this herself and suddenly spreads her hands as she walks. Davit walks past her, still filming, turns the camera on her and Mestre widens her eyes but doesn't smile. Davit walks on and films Rob Hessing and Alex Korylov, climbing buddies from West London, both looking pleased to be away from traffic and out here among the grey rock. Korylov gives a thumbs-up to camera.

She gets a shot of one of the thals, whose tightly-stretched shirt bears the marking 888 JOSEBA. Joseba – or 888 to his masters – looks into the lens. The thals lack much in the way of facial expression but while people at first thought that meant they were either unemotional or stupid, neither seems to be the case. They just don't have mobile faces. To be fair, they are somewhat phlegmatic – lacking much in the way of decisiveness, good workers but poor leaders.

"Kaixo," says Joseba. "Zer moduz?"

"Ondo, eskemik asko," says Davit. This amounts to a long and fulsome conversation for a thal – 'Hello, how are you? Fine, thankyou.' At first Davit had thought the women might be more forthcoming but they aren't.

"They do speak other languages," Mestre pointed out to her last night, as the two of them settled down in their tent.

"That's clever of them," Davit said. "Better than your average Brit, anyway, with their cod and chips on the Costa Brava."

"But," Mestre says, "they've been trained to speak Basque. They were designed in a lab somewhere in the American Midwest, but do they speak English as a first language? No."

"And what do the Basques think of this?" Davit wondered. "I'd be upset. It's like they're suggesting that the Basques are thals really."

"The Basques think it's funny," Mestre says. "They have their own sense of humour. I once had a Basque friend called Edurne. She was a lovely girl but she used to wander off for weeks at a time. Besides, the Basque - Neanderthal thing has been suggested before. It isn't new and it isn't true. I think the makers would rather the thals spoke an obscure language than mangle anyone else's."

"So a minimum of people get offended," Davit said. "Aren't they afraid of being blown up by ETA or something?"

"Why?" Mestre replied. "ETA's been quiet for years and I think they'd be glad of the publicity."

"Ah," Davit said sleepily. "The publicity."

And next she knew it was morning and Mestre was getting ready to face the day.

***

At nightfall they make camp. The summit is in sight and at this altitude the air is thin and cold. A silver near-full moon shines in the sky. Challenger strides about, beaming. This is his element. It's the element too for the thals, who are pushing one another about and giving off alarming roars that turn out to be laughter. One – 709 ARANTXA – comes up to Davit and beckons her into a circle of thals, who demand with gestures that she film them.

Davit feels a lot better about this. Down in the valley she'd felt they were slaves, pack animals designed to carry loads for the expedition and do humanity's donkey-work. Here, they aren't like that at all.

A warm hand lands on her shoulder.

"Are you having fun?" Mestre asks. The Frenchwoman's lovely smile is back.

"Very much," Davit says. "Though I think it will be time to go and eat soon. Bihar arte," she says and leaves the little group.

"Bihar arte," Arantxa calls.

***

The thals eat apart from the rest. The food at the Challenger side of the camp is the regular staple of rice and chickpeas and tomatoes familiar from hundreds of field trips and expeditions. There is no expedition talk while eating – all those decisions have been made before or will be made in the morning when Challenger sees what the weather is like. After supper Mestre wanders off and finds a rock to practice on, climbing without ropes a few metres above the ground. Davit watches with concern but the Frenchwoman moves with a swift sureness. Eventually it is too dark to continue and Mestre comes back. The others have already turned in.

She isn't certain but Davit thinks she sees something moving in the rocks above them. She takes Mestre's arm and points, whispering,

"Do you see anything?" in her ear.

Mestre looks upward. It had been a shadow, something moving across the rocky slopes.

"What was it?" Mestre asks. "Perhaps a goat."

"Too big for a goat," Davit says. "A ... " she forces the words out, "A bear?"

A bear wandering around up here would think the camp was a mobile buffet, tents or no. Davit has had a thing about bears since she was a girl, and not a good thing at that. She usually calls them 'the brown ones', as did her long-ago ancestors, for fear that using its rightful name would summon one. No icy ascent, steep pitch or treacherous crack has ever filled her with so much terror.

"We're too high up for bears," Mestre says.

"Are you sure about that?" Davit asks.

"Quite certain," Mestre says. Davit isn't.

***

In the night she hears something booming outside, something that might at first have been the wind howling through a canyon, but isn't. She is aware of Mestre looking at her, a tousled head raised.

"Do you hear it?" Mestre asks.

"Yes," Davit says. "What is it?"

"No idea," Mestre says. "Not," she says firmly, "a bear. Or a wolf."

The noise carries on. It is clearly far away, carried on the wind as the wind shifts towards them.

There is a crunching and a shifting outside the tent. Someone has got out to have a look.

"I am going to see," Mestre says.

"No," Davit says, a hand outstretched, but the Frenchwoman has already reached the tent mouth and, in her T-shirt and knickers, goes outside. Davit, in pyjamas, follows.

In the moonlit dark they can see the hulking figures of all five thals, standing at the edge of a precipice. The thals are facing away from them and as the sound rises and falls they are moaning.

One of the thals – Davit thinks it is 425 FIRMINTXO – turns and sees them. He makes gestures to usher them away. He is saying something that sounds like "Naya bassa."

Davit doesn't know what this means. The other thals are still moaning away at the booming howl coming from further up the mountain. And all the other expedition members are there. The two younger men look perplexed but Challenger stands there, on a rocky shelf so he can look over the heads of the thals, and in his eyes there is a strange light. Davit follows his gaze up to the rocks of Mount Dumaz but can see only the grey tumbled stone.

"Do you hear it?" Challenger says finally.

"What is it?" Helen Davit asks.

"It is them," Challenger says. "The thals call them the Anaia Basoa. The brothers of the forest."

Davit has a vision of a bear striding out of the mist, descending upon the camp, all teeth and claws. She turns and runs to the rocks behind the camp, falls to her knees and vomits.

The world goes very quiet. The hooting and moaning have stopped. Davit can smell something acrid, a strange nostalgic smell as though tugging at a childhood memory all but lost.

She is still kneeling on the rocks when Julianne Mestre crouches beside her and puts an arm round her.

"Come on," the Frenchwoman says, and draws her upright.

Wide-eyed, Davit looks around the little campsite, but sees nobody.

"Where are they?" Davit asks. "The others."

"They have gone back inside," Mestre says. "We didn't see … whatever it was out there."

"The forest brother," Davit says.

"Yes," Mestre says. "Tomorrow we must climb. Clean yourself up and sleep now."

"We number them," Davit says quietly when they are both in the tent, and couched in their sleeping bags.

"Number?" Mestre asks.

"Yes. 888 Joseba, 709 Arantxa, 321 Igon, and so on. They have serial numbers like machines. Not people. But what was going on out there? Challenger … said the 'brother of the forest.' He knows what it was, and the thals were calling to it."

"I can't answer you," Mestre says. "Maybe we find out tomorrow."

"Does it want us to go back?" Davit asks.

But there is no reply.

She dreams of something huge, hulking, shouldering its way through the trees; a creature that turns a snarling face to her, its eyes lit red. Not a bear, but its equivalent. Something that evolved alongside humans but became vast and solitary, living in the deep woods as humanity settled and made farms and towns and cities, and which finally faded into legend.

***

In the morning she approaches Challenger. The big man is sitting on a rock with two climbing poles by his side, and doing up his boots. He glares at her as she approaches.

"That thing last night," she begins.

"Thing," Challenger says.

"It howled," Davit says. "You knew what the thals called it. You knew what it was."

"I did," Challenger says gruffly. "It is nothing to be concerned about."

"What," Davit says, "I shouldn't worry my pretty head? Is that it? If it concerns our safety we all need to know what it is."

"Please do not take that tone," Challenger rumbles. "I have no wish to condescend to you or anyone else. If you have issues with my leadership of the expedition, raise them. Otherwise may we proceed?"

"Yes," Davit says. "But if that thing out there attacks someone …"

"It won't," Challenger says. "They live in the forests, down below. Sometimes they come up to the high rocks. And they do no harm."

"Are you sure?" Davit says.

"Of course," says Challenger mildly. His voice has lost the bombast and he now sounds genuinely concerned. "Last night it was curious, no more. It is no threat to us. Otherwise the porters would have run for the valley by now. They know what it is."

"I'll ask them, then," says Davit, and stalks off.

***

But she doesn't ask them because the day takes another turn. She returns to the tent to see Julianne Mestre sitting upright, her naked back to the entrance. Then she looks down and realises she is in the presence of two stocky, hairy legs and naked feet with enormous toes.

Mestre's hips are moving up and down as she rides the porter. The thal's huge hands are holding Mestre's upper arms but to Davit it looks like a tender grip.

Davit backs out of the tent.

Some time later the porter eases himself out of the tent, hastily dressed. Davit ducks down and slips in. Mestre, still naked, is lying on her sleeping mat.

"Hi," she says. "They're not so different, you know."

"How was it?" Davit asks.

"Sized in proportion," Mestre says and giggles. "*Chérie*, any of us could die today. I am certain we will not, but even so." Mestre searches about for her clothes.

Up a ridge to the left. The ridge. The one she's been fearing. This one goes all the way up, so to speak. To the summit. The weather looks good to go, a powder-blue sky and fluffy white clouds. Davit can see over the valley to the other, lesser peaks, and in the distance Mount Elbrus, white-shrouded, the highest mountain in Europe.

A line of people on an edge of the world. Roped together, five of them. Muffled in cold weather jackets, orange, blue, cerise. Boots kicking into snow, crampons biting into the treacherous surface. The crunch of climbing poles. Helen with the helmet-cam still running, turns to take in the whole panorama to right of her, where the world falls away into swirling grey rock, and the left, where the distant horizon is blue. Challenger leads. Ahead of them the Tamar Saddle and to its left the ridge that leads to the white peak of Dumaz.

The wind starts up, hissing across the snowfield and blowing flurries of snow downhill, coating the climbers in tiny speckles of ice. The world gets steeper and icier. Helen looks up at the peak again as the climbers move in at the start of the ridge.

The wind is stronger now, screaming across rock. Helen remembers the creature in the night. She wonders if it is there now somewhere, watching.

***

Then as the peak is in sight, snow blowing from it in flurries, there is a sudden noise. Like a gunshot, horrifyingly loud above the sound of the wind, and a rumbling follows it.

Helen Davit looks up and sees a wave of white descending the slope, onrushing. She wonders for a moment if she is still filming and decides that she is as the snow beneath the climbers' feet shifts and slides downslope.

People fly past her and she loses her footing, tugged by the rope. She tumbles over and over, in a world of shouts and the rumbling of falling rock and snow. Something hits her hard.

When she comes to a stop, she lies in snow, wonders what is broken and if the others have survived. Surely the porters - the thals - will have seen. She moves her toes experimentally and feels a surge of relief at the implication of that simple act. Everything is very still and quiet. She lies there for a long time, wondering. She grows steadily colder and knows she should do something about it, but it is easier and less painful to just lie still. She remembers a saying she once heard:

The mountain is always better than you.

Then there is a noise. A voice speaking unfamiliar words.

Large soft hands take hold of her and cradle her head. All she can see is sky. There is that acrid scent again, as before.

A dark-eyed, heavy-browed face comes into focus. The thals, she thinks. They followed.

"Thank you," she says, looking up at a pair of dark eyes beneath heavy brows. "The others?"

Her rescuer crouches over her and makes a strange barking kind of sound. Helen Davit is now able to focus properly. She sees no brown overalls and no name or number. The creature is naked, covered in brown hair, more like an ape than a human, or something between the two. Helen sees flopping breasts among the hair. Her forest brother is a forest sister.

She tries to remember the phrase Challenger used.

"Anaia," she says. "Anaia basoa."

The creature hoots softly and strokes her brow. Davit looks around. They have slid down the side of the ridge, away from the camp. Mestre is already on her feet, and Hessing is cursing. Korylov is curled up, white-faced.

It seems they rolled off a precipice into snow, and they can thank that for being alive. Helen Davit is a mess of aches and pains but doesn't think there is anything really wrong.

With the radios gone in their fall there is only one thing for it; find their way out, the way the forest people got in. Korylov is badly hurt and cannot move. The forest people are there, gently but strongly picking the climbers up and helping them downslope, uttering soft hooting cries from time to time.

***

It seems like an eternity but the sky is only starting to pink with evening when at last they round a rocky corner and there are the Thals, staring at them, beckoning.

The forest people deliver the injured climbers into the Thals' hands and then are gone, as though they had never been there.

***

Challenger sits on a rock, occasionally wincing at the pain of a cracked rib or two.

Korylov is the most badly hurt, a probable broken leg and broken collarbone. The others have scratches, cuts, but nothing too bad.

"Those people," says Challenger, "the people of the forest, have lived here forever. The locals call them the *almas* and their ancestors were those we call Neanderthal."

"Did you bring us here to find them?" Davit asks. "That was the whole point, wasn't it?"

"No," Challenger rumbles. "The purpose was to climb Dumaz and to show that the thals are suited to high-altitude work. To show, let us say, that an uphill climate suits them.

"As it does myself. Note the jaw," says Challenger, pointing to his own face. "And the brow ridges. And the broad chest. I am the descendant of Neanderthals in an unbroken line from the ice fields. I am proud to be their *anaia*. Their brother. And of the *almas* too."

"But you suspected?" Davit says.

"I did," Challenger says. "Now we must leave them in peace."

***

Yes, Davit thinks. But what of our thals? The ones we engineered, made to serve us? What happens when they decide to run for the highest peaks themselves? When they tear off the numbers and live among the rocks like their forest brothers?

Let them do just that, she decides.

Walking back down the trail, she stops for a moment and looks back up, at the rock and the ice and the sky. For a moment she sees something, not so much a figure as the memory of one, moving across the mountain's face. By the time she is able to focus it has gone.

There is only the wheeling shriek of an alpine chough overhead, and the sun sparkling off the eternal snows.

THE LUCKY ONES

Andrew Miller

"Famine?" William said, holding the engagement ring on his outstretched palm. "As in starvation?"

Dr. Karen Frye nodded and turned back to her éclair. She was a tall woman, dark-eyed and radiant in the light that filtered into the hall.

"But I don't understand," William said. "What does famine have to do with us? I feed you enough, don't I? That's your second doughnut."

Karen swallowed. "That's just it. We sit here in luxury, and meanwhile people are starving all over the world. Children, William, in loincloths. How can I marry you when so many people are suffering?"

William frowned. In truth, he had never considered the problem before. He knew about famine, of course, just as he knew about global warming and salmonella; but he had never allowed the knowledge to trouble him. He had only wondered why people didn't just find nicer places to live.

"If you really love me," Karen said, "you'll sell that ring."

"*Sell* it?"

"Pawn it. Give the money to someone more deserving."

"I know what you're doing," William said. "You're using this Finland trip as an excuse. I'll bet there wasn't even a discovery: it's all just a way to get away from me. Me, the man who loves you."

Karen looked at him affectionately. Luggage was stacked against the wall behind her, waiting to be taken down by William's footman, who would place it in the trunk of William's Bentley.

"I'm fond of you, too," she said. "But the world's too awful for love."

***

More than once during the flight to Finland Karen thought she saw the engagement ring twinkling among the stars beyond her window. How many carats had it been? Three? Four? No, she told herself, it doesn't matter. She'd made the right decision.

It was a question of sensitivity. William was the kind of person who could pick up a newspaper and read about massacres and bombings and go right on feeling cheerful. But not Karen. Those weeping faces took possession of her mind and refused to leave. Worse, they gathered recruits: the beggar on her way to work, the flattened squirrels in the road. She was under the constant assault of pitiful forces.

She sighed and turned away from the window. To distract herself, she reached into her briefcase and withdrew a scuffed envelope stamped *Confidential*. She'd read the report a dozen times since its arrival last month, but the words still gave her a sharp thrill of anticipation.

***

"Twenty-six months ago [she read], an ice fisherman discovered what he thought was a small bear frozen in a remote ravine near Ivalo, Finland. News of the discovery soon reached Dr Unnur de Keizer of the University of Iceland's Ice Sciences Division. Dr de Keizer, recognising the true nature of the specimen and having no experience in palaeoarchaeology, consulted myself and Dr Peter Badge of the California Institute of Technology.

"What Dr. Badge and I found when we arrived in Finland was a *Homo neanderthalensis*, fully and perfectly preserved. Howie, as we named him, measured 1.8 meters and weighed 129 kilograms. His body showed no signs of injury. We estimated his age at death to have been approximately 30 years. Carbon dating of his loincloth put its date of manufacture at roughly 29,000 BP.

"With the help of Dr Kimmo Klami of Meilahden Hospital in Helsinki, we attempted to resuscitate Howie by using an array of respiratory and electro-stimulative procedures. He revived almost instantly, and addressed us in a language not unlike Cantonese.

"Since that time Dr Badge and I have studied Howie in a specially-built, top-secret laboratory on the outskirts of Helsinki. We have also overseen his education, particularly in the English language, and we are happy to report that he is making rapid progress.

"It is our recommendation, however, that a cultural anthropologist be brought in to help Howie integrate into human society. We believe that such a specialist will be uniquely qualified to address many of Howie's peculiar psychological traits, including his tendency to engage in what we can only describe as 'flights of fancy.'

— Dr. Richard Spelt, McGill University"

***

Karen was met at Helsinki airport by a government official who drove her to a public restroom on Idrottsgatan Street. Behind a false toilet she discovered a lift that took her down to the secret research facility. After depositing her luggage in her quarters, and after being told that Dr Spelt was currently on medical leave, she went looking for Spelt's younger colleague, Peter Badge.

She found him in an office just down the hall from the canteen.

"Oh, it's you," Badge said, looking up from his desk. He glanced at Karen's hands. "No frostbite, I see."

He waved her into a chair and shut the door. The office was small and unpleasant; a smell of cured meat hung in the air and an ugly Finnish tapestry covered one wall.

Karen sat down. "Frostbite?"

"Lots of people get it up here," Badge said. "The cold is aggressive. That's why I wear mittens."

As if to prove his honesty, he held up a pair of mittened hands.

"Oh," Karen said. "No. No frostbite for me, luckily."

"Awful flight, though, wasn't it?"

"Well, it wasn't the most comfortable--"

"Whenever I fly," Badge said, "I buy the seats on both sides of me. But do you think the university pays for three seats?"

"No?"

"No. Can't blame them, I guess. But still."

"Yes," Karen said slowly. "I was told that Dr Spelt is ill."

"Mmm. Nasty case of frostbite. Ask why he caught it."

"Why?"

"No mittens."

Badge held up his hands a second time.

Karen began to wonder if it had been a mistake to come.

"I'd like to see the specimen now," she said after a pause.

"Mmm?"

"The Neanderthal. Howie."

"Ah." Turning in his chair, Badge pressed a button on his desk. The ugly tapestry rolled aside, revealing a small padded room behind a thick pane of Plexiglas.

The room was simply furnished. There was a sink, a toilet, a table, and a large cot on which a man was sleeping.

Well, Karen thought, not a man, exactly.

He was the approximate size and shape of a man; the lustrous brown hair that fell around his shoulders was the hair of a man; but there was something in his face, something in the strong nose and full mouth that was ancient, exotic . . . and alluring. Karen's heart began to thump.

"Is that him?"

"Unfortunately," Badge said. He pressed another button and a small microphone descended from the ceiling. "Howie? Howie, Dr Frye is here to see you--the anthropologist. Can you wake up and say hello to Dr Frye?"

The Neanderthal stirred, raising a thick hand to rub his eyes. He smiled.

"Hey there," he said.

Karen had expected a deep, inarticulate voice. In the weeks leading up to her departure, she had formed a mental picture that involved animal skins and chest beating. But Howie's voice was high and clear; he seemed to speak out of a space between his mouth and his nose.

"Howie, do you remember what I told you about Dr Frye?" Badge asked.

"Sure," the Neanderthal said. He sat up and stretched, revealing a toned and surprisingly hairless physique. "It's a pleasure to meet you, Dr. Frye."

Karen felt strangely bashful. "I'm happy to meet you too, Howie."

"It's a shame," Howie went on, "that we've come together under such intolerable conditions."

"Intolerable? How so?" Howie gestured. "This place. These people. Have you been introduced to Peter's mittens?"

Karen glanced at Badge, who was watching stonily, his arms crossed over his chest.

"As a matter of fact, I have," she said.

"Then you know what I mean," Howie said. "You have to understand that the human brain is ten percent smaller than the Neanderthal. I don't say that to cause pain: it's simple biology. As a result I have difficulty interacting with certain members of your species. Peter, for instance."

"I see," Karen said. "So you're unhappy here?"

"Aren't you?"

She blinked. "I just got here."

"I'm not talking about the laboratory," he said. "I'm talking about Earth."

"Earth?"

"Don't you find that it's a curiously terrible place, Dr Frye? Don't you find that happiness eludes you at every turn?"

Sweat began to gather on Karen's brow. "Well, that's a difficult question. Everybody has different opinions about--"

"I'm talking about your opinion."

His tone was urgent, but there was a smile on his lips and an intelligent gleam in his eye. Karen considered and rejected the possibility that he was telepathic.

"Yes," she said at last, blushing. "Happiness does elude me."

"I thought so. Or hoped so, at any rate. I didn't want to believe that being stuck in this dimension has robbed humanity of all its sensitivity."

"This dimension?"

Badge stirred, adjusting a mitten. "The caveman, I'm afraid, is insane. Delusions of grandeur, irrational ideas about space and time. He believes that reality exists in two dimensions, but that humans have only discovered one."

"Really?"

Badge nodded. "Would you like to read our notes on the subject?"

Karen looked at Howie, who shrugged.

"Yes," she said. "Yes, that might be a good idea."

***

An hour later Peter Badge sat in the corner of his office, sullenly knitting a scarf. Howie lay stretched out on his cot, engrossed in *Le Côté de Guermantes*. And Karen sat at Badge's desk, a stack of papers spread before her, silently mulling over what she'd just read.

It was a lot. Howie claimed that Neanderthals had never been the dimwitted barbarians depicted by human science. Instead they had been-- they were--a cultured and sophisticated race, much cleverer and wiser than *Homo sapiens*, and much further advanced technologically. They had, for example, invented a method of cryogenic bodily preservation at a time when humans were clubbing their first gazelles.

Howie had been the lead scientist on the cryogenics project, and had agreed to test the first preservation unit. Accordingly he had been frozen in a block of ice in a remote ravine, with the understanding that his colleagues would unthaw him after a fifteen-year interval.

It had been a shock, then, to be awoken thirty thousand years later by *Homo sapiens*--a species he had thought too savage to survive. And it had been even more disturbing to learn that his own people had mysteriously disappeared shortly after he was frozen.

Human science explains this disappearance with a number of competing theories, none of which Howie accepted. He believed instead that his people, in order to escape the increasing aggression of humankind, had departed for the dimension directly adjacent to this one--a dimension known to the Neanderthals as Mirth.

It was his claim that Mirth and Earth form a symbiotic, bi-dimensional unity. All intelligent creatures born in one dimension or the other are expected to divide their time between the two. In Mirth life is an endless bounty of pleasure and delight; in Earth it is nothing but torture and suffering. Only by keeping a foot in both worlds and striking a balance between pleasure and pain can one hope to find happiness.

***

"Well," said Karen presently. She looked down at the surface of the desk, not wanting to meet the eyes of the insane caveman. "Well, this quite a ...this is really..."

"A lot of deluded ravings?" Badge suggested.

"No, not that," Karen said. "Just a surprise, that's all."

Howie looked up from his book. "You don't believe me, Dr Frye?"

"Well, Howie, I'm not really sure what to believe. These are some very strong claims."

"Look at me," he said.

She looked at him.

He stood up and walked to the glass, the same mysterious smile on his lips. He peered into Karen's eyes until she found herself unable to blink.

"Everything I've told them is true," he said. "I'm not lying."

"Howie..." Karen began.

"There's a reason for all this suffering. And you know it."

"But you're claiming --"

"You know it."

Karen closed her mouth. He wasn't lying.

***

At half-past three the following morning Karen heard a knock at the door of her quarters. She sprang out of bed and crouched in the darkness, panther-like.

"Howie?" she whispered. "Is that you?"

"In the flesh, doctor."

She unlocked the door and let the caveman enter. He kissed her immediately.

"For good luck," he explained. "I didn't have any trouble with Badge: tied him to his bed with knitting yarn. You got my note, I take it?"

"Yes, but --"

"Are you packed?"

She hesitated, then pointed mutely to the small black bag at the foot of her bed. Not coincidentally, it matched the pants and coat she was wearing, both of which had been hanging in a Helsinki department store a few hours earlier.

"Good," Howie said. "Follow me."

Karen had never snuck out of a top-secret underground laboratory before. She found that it consisted of a lot of nervous trembling and a fair amount of bruising. Finally, however, she and Howie emerged into the cold Finnish night. A five-minute walk brought them an abandoned field on the edge of the city.

"What exactly are we looking for?" Karen asked.

"You'll see," Howie said. He dropped to a crouch and began walking on his knuckles like an ape, pausing occasionally to plunge a hand into the earth.

Karen allowed herself to wonder what in the name of hell she was doing. Was this rational behaviour--helping a Neanderthal escape from captivity? Should she be worried that she had agreed to Howie's plan without a moment's hesitation, without the slightest qualm about the legal and professional ramifications? Was it odd that she hadn't felt this way about a man since she was fourteen years old?

"Ah ha!" Howie said. "Found one."

He was lying face down in the grass, his arm buried in the dirt.

"Found what?"

"A rabbit hole," he said, and began digging with both arms, widening the hole until it was big enough for a person to squeeze through.

Karen closed her eyes. "Oh God."

"What's wrong?"

"We're going down the rabbit hole, aren't we?"

"Of course."

"That's how we get to Mirth?"

"Yes. Is something wrong?"

Karen rubbed the bridge of her nose. "No. It makes perfect sense."

Howie went first, in order to check for obstructions and angry hares. Karen watched as he lowered himself carefully beneath the grass, his long legs kicking in the air. Finally the last toe disappeared, and then came Howie's voice, oddly distant:

"It's okay, Karen. Come on down."

She sighed philosophically. Suppose the hole just led into a little rabbit house? Suppose Howie really was insane after all, and she was about to bury herself on the advice of a thirty-thousand-year-old lunatic?

It hardly mattered. Her life with William was over. Her professional life would soon be over. Reality and sanity had admitted defeat. She bent her knees, brought her hands together in a diving pose, and pitched forward into the earth.

"All right," Howie said. "Up you go."

Karen felt hands close around her wrists. She allowed Howie to pull her deeper into the hole, and was surprised to feel the poles of the universe reverse as she emerged from the ground, right side up.

She blinked.

"Confusing, isn't it?" Howie said. "You'll get used to it."

They were standing in a small forest, surrounded on all sides by large, palm-like trees. A delicious scent wafted on the balmy air: something between cinnamon and lemon zest. Instead of a sun there was a rosy diffuse glow that suggested hammocks and margaritas. A warm but not-too-warm breeze made music in the branches of the trees.

"Is this . . . Mirth?"

Howie nodded and took off his pants. "Oh, don't worry," he said. "It's customary to go naked here. Otherwise you don't get the full advantage of the breeze."

Karen said that she would remained clothed, and did her best to ignore the more interesting parts of Howie's body as he led her down a narrow path.

Joy was everywhere. Karen felt it seeping up through the ground and into her feet. She heard it on the hypnotic songs of birds, saw it on the faces of the furry animals that scampered through the bright flowers, tasted it on Howie's lips when he turned to kiss her.

"I'm sorry," he said, beaming. "It's just so great to be back. Isn't it great? Have you ever felt so happy?"

"No," Karen said truthfully. She smiled and put her hand on his arm. "Howie, I want to ask you a question."

"Yes?"

She coughed and looked at her fingernails. "Well, is this the kind of thing you do with all women? Am I just your latest — your latest fling?"

He smiled. "Is that what you think?"

"Because if this is just a casual thing," she went on, "or some weird Neanderthal thing, I just want you to understand that --"

Howie turned suddenly and held up his hand for silence. The breeze had stiffened, bringing with it the sound of gently lapping waves. "That's it!" he said, and began dragging Karen down the path.

Moments later they emerged from the forest. In front of them, lounging on a sparkling white beach, were tens of thousands of naked Neanderthals. In the distance stretched a glassy blue sea.

"Brothers!" Howie bellowed. "Sisters!"

One or two heads — no more — turned as Howie rushed across the sand. He stopped at the first Neanderthal he reached, an obese and mottled male, and began to gesture and jabber wildly in his native tongue.

The mottled male didn't respond. He merely glanced at Howie for a moment, then turned back to the sea. The others lay motionless on the beach, their eyes half-closed and unfocused, their bodies great sausages of fat and skin. Soon Howie stopped talking and turned to Karen.

"I was afraid of this," he said.

"Afraid of what?"

A thunderclap muffled his reply, bringing a sudden downpour. With one motion the Neanderthals tilted back their heads and let their mouths fill with rainwater. Howie did the same; Karen hesitantly followed suit. Her thirst was instantly quenched, and in her chest she felt the warm glow that only potent spirits can produce.

For an hour they crisscrossed the beach in search of someone who would respond to Howie's pleas, but met only silence. Gestures went unheeded; diagrams in the sand were ignored. Finally Howie abandoned his attempts and trudged away from the beach, Karen trailing behind.

They climbed a small dune and came to a hill overlooking the sea. In the distance, leading away from the water, was a wide, rolling plain covered by mossy ruins.

"That was Blissopolis," Howie said, sitting down. He pulled up two handfuls of grass, gave one to Karen, and ate the other himself.

"Blissopolis?" she asked, nibbling cautiously. The grass tasted like truffles and pan-seared salmon.

"The largest city on Mirth," Howie said. "Ten million people at its height--the centre of art and literature and culture."

"What happened to it?"

Howie shrugged. "The last time I was here it was as thriving as ever. Over that hill was the Geranium. I spent a week there losing my virginity."

Karen pretended not to hear this last part. "Well, you were frozen for a long time, Howie. They must've built a new city."

"No. There's no new city."

"How do you know?"

He pointed to the beach. "They're stupefied, Karen. Too much pleasure and no pain eventually turns the brain to mush. It's been known to happen to people who stay in Mirth too long."

"Oh." She frowned.

"It's puzzling, though," he went on. "Surely they knew about the precautions."

"Precautions?"

He nodded. "In my time, people occasionally got stuck in Mirth for too long--lost track of their rabbit hole, usually. But there are things you can do, precautions you can take to dull the pleasure and increase the pain. Fasting, for example."

Karen said nothing. She squinted at the remains of Blissopolis, thinking.

"I guess it was too hard," Howie said with a sigh. "They must've figured it was better stay here than go back to Earth and get massacred by humans."

"Mmm."

"Maybe it wouldn't be such a bad life," he went on. "We could go back to Earth once every few years for a break. See your family. Do you have a family, Karen? I hope so. I never dated anybody back in my own time. I was always too busy with my experiments. You're the most--"

Suddenly Karen stood, a look of inspiration on her face.

"What if there was something we could do?" she said.

"Do? Like what?"

"You said that too long in either dimension is bad for you, right? That everyone needs a little pain and a little joy?"

Howie nodded. "Why? What are you thinking?"

Karen smiled and took another bite of grass. "I don't know. But I think I've got an idea."

***

William dreamed that he rode a wildebeest into the depths of hell. For six months he and the animal descended deeper into scorching pits of evil. The heat plucked at his skin and roasted his eyes in their sockets. When he finally reached the bottom he was greeted by Satan, who chained him to a chair and poured hot wax over his body until the skin blistered and sizzled and slid off the bones.

"Mr. Greene?" Satan said in the voice of a young woman. "Mr. Greene, she's ready to see you now, sir."

William awoke with a yelp. The receptionist was standing over him, smiling and tapping his arm. A little globe of sweat was balanced on the tip of her nose.

"I'm sorry to wake you, sir," she said, "but Dr. Frye is ready to see you."

"Oh," William said. "Yes. Right."

He sat up and wiped his face. The plastic walls of the makeshift building seemed to throb in the heat. Outside he could hear voices--foreign, exotic voices. He had never travelled south of the equator before. He had never, in his life, conceived that such heat was possible.

He followed the receptionist down a narrow corridor, past the cubicles where Karen's minions were hard at work. Moments later he was standing in a small office, face to face with the love of his life.

"William!" she said, leaping to her feet. "You made it."

It had been two years since his proposal, and Karen was more a goddess than ever.

"Hello, Karen," he said.

"How was your trip?"

"Oh, fine. Just fine. Well" — he frowned — "a little strange, actually."

She nodded. "The bus from the airport is awful, isn't it?"

"I wouldn't know. The bus was broken, so they brought me in on a wildebeest."

"A wildebeest!"

"Yes."

"Oh, William. Well, that explains why you're late. Howie and I were started to get worried."

William pretended not to hear the name of his rival. "Well, I made it."

"Yes, you did. And I'm very glad you're here. I wanted you to see firsthand what you've made possible. Come with me."

She led him, to his disappointment, outside. The heat was twice as punishing here, in the full violence of the sun; William was blinded by his own sweat. Blurry faces smiled benevolently all around him as he followed Karen through the maze of tents and tables stacked with jugs of water. He thought longingly of home.

At length they came to a wide, barren field. Glistening natives stood in long lines that stretched to the horizon. Not far away, lines of other bodies — paler, fatter — were climbing out of the ground and being led to a cluster of tents. Close by, in spacious cages, were several hundred rabbits.

"Karen," William said, pointing to one of the natives, "why is that man lying on the ground?"

"He's not lying. He's widening his rabbit hole. Haven't you seen the pictures in the papers? You have to burrow to get to Mirth."

"Is that right?"

Karen quickly explained the fundamentals of transdimensional physics. She spoke with the ease and authority of a Nobel Prize-winner, which she was.

"And so these people," William said, indicating the locals milling nearby, "are going to Mirth?"

"Not all of them. Some of them are perfectly happy here, famine or no famine. Howie's theory is that some humans have evolved the ability to be happy and contented even though they're stuck in the rotten half of the universe."

"Ah."

"But most of them choose to go to Mirth," Karen continued. "And for every local who goes through, one Neanderthal comes here."

"I see." William looked across the dusty, hazy landscape. "And how do you trick the Neanderthals into coming?"

"We don't have to trick them; they're excited to come. It's all about balance. We give the locals two years of pleasure and joy, and the Neanderthals two years of hunger and hardship. And then we switch them again."

"On and on?"

"On and on. But not just here. We set up camp wherever there's a high proportion of human suffering. Next we go to Los Angeles."

"I see." William had stopped listening, however. The heat, he felt, would soon kill him. "It's a very nice operation, Karen. Very efficient."

"Thanks. But none of it would be possible without your help. And your money, of course."

He nodded, trying not to vomit. "Glad to be of service."

"But since you're here," Karen said, "wouldn't you like to go to Mirth? You could be there by this evening. Howie could get you a place to stay in New Blissopolis."

"No. Thanks very much, Karen, but no. I'd like to lie down now, if that's okay. And then I'd like to go home."

She smiled and gave a strange little sigh. "You're happy, aren't you, William?"

"Me? I guess so."

"Howie thinks people like you are the lucky ones. He thinks you're the only reason the human species has lasted this long."

William wiped sweat from his eyes. "That's very interesting. Your husband sounds very wise. But I need to ask you an important question."

"Yes?"

"Are any of these buildings air-conditioned?"

RIGHTS

Jon Wesick

Too much liquor! Too much resentment! Juan and Carlos left the bar after spending most of their meagre paychecks on single-malt Scotch. They could have drunk cheaper tequila but both hated the symbol of their native land, a land where they couldn't find decent jobs. No, better to drink like the *gueros* and feel successful if only for a few hours.

It was a long walk back to the migrant camp. Neither looked forward to getting up at 5:00 AM and spending the day bent over a lettuce field but they had wives and children back home who needed the money they sent. They should have kept to the side streets, away from the *gueros'* unwelcome looks. After all, this was Arizona where cities passed laws forbidding landlords to rent to "illegals." They should have stayed off the main road but they had just enough money to buy a six pack at the 7-Eleven. Better to spend their few free hours enjoying themselves, they thought.

***

The clerk gave them the fishy eye but even worse the woman with red hair and a squat body got in line in front of them. If the *gueros* didn't want to share their land with Mexicans, members of their own species, why had they resurrected Neanderthals like her?

"Hey Juan, want to get a piece of ass?" Carlos asked in Spanish after they paid and followed the woman out. "I hear the ugs will fuck anything."

"Yeah," Juan replied, "but who would want to do it with that ghastly bitch. Look at her. She dresses like a truck driver."

"*Yo hablo espanol, pendejo.*" The Neanderthal woman kneed Carlos in the groin, stepped aside as he bent forward, and drove her elbow down into the back of his neck.

Juan wanted to run but couldn't leave his friend unavenged. His loyalty bought him a broken knee delivered by the woman's quick, low kick. From behind the safety of the cash register the clerk watched with amusement.

If a bunch of trespassers beat the shit out of each other, why should he get involved? And if they killed each other, all the better.

**

Deputy Norm Sleater steered his beige Crown Victoria onto 8th Street and drove parallel to the irrigation canal. He always started his patrols out here, not because there was much crime, but because the greenery of the lettuce fields and orange trees allowed for a bit of calm before a day of dealing with drunks and belligerents. Unfortunately, his wife had recently put him on a diet, feeding him oatmeal and skim milk before he left. That was no breakfast for a man! It wasn't even 8:00 and he was already starving. If things were quiet, he planned to head over to Esperanza's and order some *huevos rancheros*, fluffy eggs with tortilla chips fried crisp and glistening. Now that was a breakfast!

"Bravo 3, respond," the dispatcher's voice said over the radio.

"Bravo 3. What's up, Wanda?"

"We got a report of an assault on B Street. Mexican fella's being treated over at the med centre on Fortune."

"I'm on my way. Bravo 3, out."

He drove east toward the foothills and arrived at the medical centre ten minutes later.

"You got a Mexican fella who got beat up?" he asked the receptionist.

"He's in room twelve. Angie!" she called a black nurse in pink scrubs. "Could you take this officer to the beating victim in room twelve?"

"We stabilised his knee but he'll need surgery. We're waiting on transport to Pima General." The nurse led Norm to room twelve, entered, and found it empty. "That's funny. He was here last time I checked. Maybe he went to the toilet."

"Illegals get nervous around cops," Norm said. "I'll check outside. He can't have gotten too far on that bum leg."

The men's room was vacant and there was no sign of him in the parking lot. Searching the migrant camps wouldn't be worth the trouble. Even if Norm found the victim, the chance of him pressing charges was less likely than one of those TV doctors telling you tequila and Mexican food were good for you.

Norm radioed that the complainant had hurt himself falling off a ladder. There would be less paperwork that way.

"We got call that there's a dead body over by the Gundeson Orchards," Wanda said.

"I'm on it." Norm sure hoped it wasn't the Mexican fella. The sheriff would chew him out if his creative incident report got discovered.

He drove to the orchard and stopped by a white pickup truck. Hal Gundeson stood by wearing his white cowboy hat and looking into the gully beside the road.

"One of the workers found her. I been standing here for pretty near a half hour to make sure nobody touches anything," he said as Norm descended into the ditch.

Norm didn't hear him. He was too busy looking at the crime scene. The victim a well-dressed, red-haired girl lay crumpled like a discarded pack of cigarettes. The dried blood on the back of her head indicated blunt-force trauma. There were no footprints. Norm concluded someone must have dumped the body from a car.

"Is it okay if I head on back?" Hal asked. "I can't trust them Mexicans unless I keep an eye on them."

Norm waved him off, circled the body, and squatted. After donning latex gloves, he lifted the girl's head and noticed the thick nose and ridged, bony brow. His life just got a lot more complicated. Unless he solved the case quickly, a dead Neanderthal meant a hate crime investigation and all the interference that came with it.

What was even worse; she was pregnant. Waiting for the coroner, Norm stood by the body while flies swarmed the dried blood. The whine of many tiny wings the only sound. It would be several hours before breakfast.

***

When Norm first started in the sheriff's department, he made of point of attending autopsies to show how tough he was. He soon learned that he could watch the procedure over AZMENET without the smell of formaldehyde and decay. That afternoon he logged onto the computer at the local sheriff's office.

"The victim, an unidentified Neanderthal female, is approximately nine years old." The medical examiner removed a sheet covering the body.

"Could you zoom in on the necklace?" Norm asked through the microphone.

The cameraman focused on a silver pendant of a man and woman standing by a tree.

"Adam and Eve," the ME said. "Symbol of the Mousterian Charismatic Church. The victim appears to be in her first trimester."

Nine years old, Jesus! What the hell do you do with people who can become parents in grade school?

"Can you tell if the father was a Neander or a human?"

"A Neanderthal or a *Homo sapien*," the doctor corrected. "DNA results will take a few days." He spaced the point of his scalpel on the girl's abdomen and began to cut.

Norm turned off the video and listened to the narration. There was nothing surprising. The girl had died from a blow to the head. The ME found no identification in the girl's effects. For some reason, Neander women preferred wallets to purses. The victim had neither. After the autopsy concluded, Norm searched the web and found a branch of the Mousterian Charismatic Church sixty miles away in Brockton. Taking pictures with him, he headed for the car.

***

The church was empty, just pews, an Adam-and-Eve sculpture, and a cartoonish mural of Jesus raising a red-haired Lazarus from the dead. Norm looked in the office and circled to the garden where he found a Neanderthal in a gray shirt with a clerical collar pruning rose bushes.

"There you go my little beauty." The pastor handled the flower with a delicateness that was surprising for someone with such a muscular build.

Norm cleared his throat. The pastor stood. On seeing a policeman his gray eyes hardened to granite.

"What do you want?" His hand clenched the gardening shears. "I already put up the posters about penalties for underage driving."

Norm resisted the urge to reach for his pepper spray.

"Neanderthal girl was murdered, yesterday." He held up a picture of the pendant. "She was wearing the symbol of your church."

"The symbol of our people, Adam and Eve, the Neanderthals brought back by cloning ancient DNA, the ancestors of us all."

"Do you know her?" Norm showed the photo of the girl's face.

"Amy Runswatl. Didn't come here much. Her family runs a garage over in Lukesville."

"Why would anyone want to kill her?"

"Maybe some short-head teenagers were out for a little fun. Maybe some short-head parents were 'protecting the virtue' of their kids. I can think of a hundred other reasons." The pastor glared. "It all boils down to one thing, forcing the People to live like you."

"Thanks for your help." Norm forced a smile and walked to his car.

The nerve of that guy! When Neanderthals were first cloned, Congress and the courts were nearly unanimous in recognising them as fully human, a decision Norm was proud of. Evidently that wasn't enough for that some of them. They wanted special rights. As far as he was concerned, they just needed to get to work and make lives for themselves.

The Runswatl Garage was a clean, orderly establishment with tools put away in spotless cabinets. A boy, who should have been in school, was working on a computer in the waiting room.

"May I speak with your parents, please?"

"Mom! Dad!" the boy yelled through the door to the service bay. "Cops are here!"

A man and a woman both in dark blue overalls came in through the doorway. If anything, the mother had more grease on her hands than the father.

"I'm Deputy Norm Sleater from the Pima County Sheriff's Department." Norm took off his hat and turned to the father. "Is there someplace we can talk in private?"

The couple traded puzzled looks and the man led Norm to a small office with a desk stacked with Chilton's manuals.

"You're Amy Runswatl's father?"

The man nodded.

"I'm sorry, sir, but I believe your daughter was murdered, yesterday." Norm took out the picture. "Is this her?"

Norm never knew how someone would react to the death of the loved one. He'd seen sobbing, rage, and even a steely calm that could lead someone less experienced to believe the parent didn't care. Amy's father collapsed into the chair and stared open-mouthed at an auto parts calendar.

"I thought the trouble was all behind us. She used to stay out late and I worried she was running with the wrong crowd. Irene said we had to let her grow up, that it's the way of nature. When Amy told us she was expecting, I thought she'd settle down and that everything was going to be all right."

"Did she?"

"She was so happy about the wedding."

"Who was the lucky guy?" Norm asked.

"Eddie Treatl, a boy from a good family. They own Checker Ag Supply."

"Sir, I know this is difficult but I need your help to find Amy's killer. Can you tell me about her friends?"?

They talked for over an hour with Norm making notes on his handheld computer. He left the distraught father with his business card and the promise that Amy's death would not go unavenged.

***

It wasn't hard to spot Amy's friends at John McCain Elementary School. The Neander youth were the ones no one else wanted to play with. Norm couldn't blame the other kids. The Neanders were a foot taller and fifty pounds heavier than a Sapien of the same age. Playing with them could get you hurt.

"Red Rover. Red Rover. Let Vicky come over."

A girl with budding breasts ran toward a line of Neanderthals and broke through their linked arms.

"Where's the fire, Smokey Bear?" the boy with whiskers sprouting from his chin asked Norm. "Just asymming you, man." Before Norm could reply, the boy sprang up and chased a little Latino boy. "Hey, you little shit! Where's my homework?"

The Neanders broke up their game and milled around.

"Don't mind Caleb," the girl who'd broken through the line said.

"He's such an ug," said another. "You here about Amy?"

"What do you know about Amy?" Norm asked.

"That she joined the Darwin Club."

"Shut up, Lisa," the first girl said.

"Shut up yourself, Vicky. If Amy wants to go betraying the People, I'm not going to cover for her."

"This Darwin Club," Norm said. "Is it some kind of gang?"

The girls burst into laughter. One laughed so hard she fell down.

"I'd never join the Darwin Club."

"Except maybe with Mr. Walters. He's dreamy."

"Gross!" A boy stood and walked away.

"We've seen how you look at Marcia Summers, Bradley!" Vicky called after him.

Norm wanted to learn more but the bell rang and the kids dispersed. He went to see the principal. The Treatl boy was absent, a seemingly common situation with Neanders. No one at the office had much to say about Amy so Norm went to interview her teachers.

Norm found David Walters in a classroom full of terrariums and posters of the planets. Walters was not teaching at the time. Instead he was putting away some kind of experiment with strings and pulleys. He was a blond, birdlike man with a bulging Adam's apple and piercing blue eyes. When he saw Norm, he straightened.

"Oh, I didn't see you. Is something the matter?"

"You're Amy Runswatl's teacher?" Norm asked.

"She's in one of my classes along with twenty others. Why? Is she in trouble?"

"She's been murdered."

Walters shook his head and leaned on the desk.

"You don't seem that surprised."

"Have you ever been here when school lets out? The big yellow bus picks up the *Homo sapien* kids right there." Walters pointed out the window. "But the Neander girls walk right on by. Why should they take a bus when high-school boys will give them rides in their sports cars? The phrase the football jocks use is, 'tastes like chicken.'" Walters sat down. "They should have never put Neanders in the same school as our kids. They're lovable and clever but they mature much faster. Ever since they came, it's been one discipline problem after another. So no, I'm not surprised. It was only a matter of time."

***

After talking to Amy's other teachers, Norm left the school but he came back at 3:00 in time to see Vicky climb into a red 680 Z. He followed it for a few blocks before hitting the siren to pull the car over. When exiting the police car, Norm grabbed his baton.

"Out of the car!" He slammed the top of the 680 Z's roof.

A pimply teenager in a letter jacket got out.

"Are you related to that girl?" Norm pointed at the underage Neander in the passenger's seat.

"Come on, man. I was just giving her a ride."

"Are you her relative?"

"Look, my father owns the…"

Norm thrust his baton into the boy's gut, doubling him over. Keys fell from the boy's hand and jangled on the pavement.

"If I ever catch you with an underage girl again, I'll take you out to the desert and put a bullet in your head. Do you understand?"

"Yeah," the boy grunted.

"And you," Norm said to Vicky. "Get out of the car." He put her in his Crown Victoria's back seat. "I'm taking you home. Where do you live?"

"314 Maple Street."

Norm turned the big car around and drove north.

"Please." Vicky's eyes opened wide with fear. "You can't take me home. If my mom sees me get out of a police car, she'll kill me."

"What does she say when she sees you with boys seven years older than you?"

"Jimmy lets me out a few blocks from my house."

"I'll make a deal with you," Norm said. "Tell me about Amy and your mom doesn't have to know about this."

"Amy got to be a real bore. Always sucking up to the teachers and making us look bad. She went on and on about Eddie. About how when she moved in with him, she'd never have to work in a garage again. Like Eddie Tree would ever settle for a dweeb like her. Please!"

"So Eddie didn't get her pregnant?" Norm glanced in the rear-view mirror and saw Vicky take a lollipop out of her pink backpack.

"Why would someone like Eddie waste his time with her?"

"Who did?"

"I don't know." She unwrapped the sucker and tossed the cellophane on the floor. "It could have been anybody. It's not like it was an accident, though. She knew about protection."

"Where did she…"

"Can you let me out here? Any closer and my parents might see."

"I don't want to see you with those older boys. Understand?" Norm pulled over. "If I do, I'll have to tell your parents."

***

Having talked with Amy's classmates, Norm felt he had enough background to confront the Treatl boy. He was about to drive to the family home when a call came over the radio.

"Bravo 3, respond."

"Bravo 3. What's up, Wanda?"

"You have a call from the attorney general's office. I'll patch it through."

"Deputy Sleater, this is Steven Frip, Assistant AG for Civil Rights. I probably don't need to tell you that the Runswatl murder is generating a lot of concern in Phoenix."

"I imagine it would, sir."

"I just wanted to let you know that we'll provide whatever help you need."

"Thank you, sir."

"I'm going to be at the girl's funeral, tomorrow. Perhaps we can talk afterwards. We don't want to interfere with your investigation but it would be in everybody's interest to wrap things up quickly."

"I understand, sir. I'll see you, tomorrow."

***

Norm called ahead. You always did that with important families. He had to park on the street in front of the Treatl house because there were three cars in the driveway. The father, William, met him at the door. He was a short man in gray slacks, cowboy boots, and a white dress shirt. Norm followed him into a living room that had a giant TV embedded in the wall. Mrs. Treatl and her son sat on a sofa. The boy wore a loose leather jacket. His mother, the smirk of privilege.

"Would you care for coffee, Deputy?" Without waiting Mrs. Treatl filled a china cup from the carafe. "Dreadful business about that girl. We'll help any way we can."

"Thank you." Norm took the cup and sat down. "Did you know her?"

"Edward was in some of her classes," Mr. Treatl said. "Isn't that right, son?"

The boy nodded.

"So you weren't friends?" Norm asked.

"He hardly knew the girl," Mrs. Treatl said.

"Did she ever come to the house?"

"I don't believe so." Mrs. Treatl sipped her coffee leaving a red lipstick smudge on the cup. "She might have been here for Edward's birthday party last month."

"That's funny," Norm said, "because I heard Edward was the father of her child."

"That's ridiculous!" Mrs. Treatl covered her mouth while she laughed. "I'm sorry, Deputy. You obviously don't know about some Neander girls. They'll sleep with anybody. That usually means some Sapien boy ends up getting them pregnant. Then they blame some innocent Neanderthal so they won't be accused of 'betraying the People' like that ignorant preacher, what's his name, always rails about."

"Pastor Donnatl," Mr. Treatl said. "His message has a lot of appeal to those who blame their lack of success on discrimination instead of laziness. The man just can't face the fact this is the land of opportunity where everyone, Neanders included, can succeed with a little hard work."

"Pastor Donnatl, yes. But we were talking about Miss Runswatl." Mrs. Treatl poured Norm another coffee. "If I were you, I'd look into that school of hers. People say a lot of girls have been engaging in extracurricular activities with that science teacher if you know what I mean."

***

Next morning a sea of red-haired mourners occupied the Mousterian Church. The men's lapels were a little too thin and the women's skirts too short to be stylish but the clothes were clean and ironed. Pastor Donnatl in white surplice and purple ecclesiastical stole delivered the eulogy.

"We gather today to mourn the loss of our beloved Amy Runswatl who was taken from us too soon. Amy was a devoted daughter and a brilliant student, an example many of our young women can emulate but few can match. And though you may miss her, do not grieve. For even now she is walking by Jesus' side.

"To the doubters among you I offer the example of our People. We who were extinct, wiped from the face of the Earth have been resurrected here just like our departed Amy has been resurrected in heaven?"

From the back of the church Norm scanned the crowd and recognised many faces. The Treatl family was conspicuous in its absence.

"Friends, there are some who would take the People's miraculous rebirth for granted," Pastor Donnatl continued. "They would squander their lives on material gain and sensual delights. But Amy's tragic death reminds us that this is an age of signs and portents and that we must not waver in our fight for justice. For only when we reestablish our homeland will Jesus return to judge the wicked and the righteous.

"Friends, do not think Amy died in vain. Think of her as a soldier who gave her life to fulfil the prophecy. May God bless you. Amen."

Organ music played and the congregation lined up to file past the casket. Norm noticed a man in a pin-striped suit and moved closer.

"Deputy." Assistant Attorney General Frip shook Norms hand.

Two things stood out about Frip, the smell of his aftershave and the fact that he didn't sweat. He and Norm stood respectfully until the service ended. Then they moved to the chapel steps where Frip glad-handed the exiting mourners.

"I can assure you that the AG's office will not rest until the girl's killer is behind bars."

After the last mourner left, Norm followed Frip to the parking lot.

"How long do you think it will take to wrap this thing up?" Frip paused by a BMW, cupped his hands against the breeze, and lit a cigarette.

"Hard to say."

"Do you have a suspect?" Frip exhaled smoke.

"Several possibilities but I haven't narrowed them down yet." Norm summarised what he'd learned so far.

"Well, we need to come up with a plan forward. Why don't you write down your thoughts on how to proceed and we'll discuss them tomorrow?"

Instead of investigating the case, Norm spent the rest of the day writing a description of how to investigate it.

***

A phone call woke him at 5:00 AM.
"Deputy Sleater, Frip here. We caught a break. Meet me at 552 Saguaro Lane."

Norm told his wife to go back to sleep, shaved, and put on his uniform. He arrived at the modest house fifteen minutes later to find Frip and a half-dozen state troopers standing on the lawn beside a LETHEM, a Law Enforcement Tactical Hazard Elimination Module. The robot's titanium armor was a dull gray in the moonlight.

"I found out that the teacher, Walters, obtained birth control pills for the Runswatl girl." Frip held up a piece of paper. "Got a judge in Phoenix to fax a search warrant. Care to do the honors?"

"David Walters, this is the police," Norm said through the bullhorn. "Open up!"

The troopers didn't wait. They sent the LETHEM through the front door knocking it off its hinges. When the trooper operating the remote control gave the all clear, the rest flooded, guns drawn, into the teacher's house, dragged Walters from the bedroom in shorts and T-shirt, and brought him to the living room.

"David Walters, we have a warrant to search the premises." Frip handed him the document.

Walters sat on the threadbare couch while state troopers ransacked his home. The process lasted two hours with the police removing cardboard boxes and a computer to the evidence van.

"Mr. Walters, you're under arrest for violating the Prescription Drug Act." The trooper read Walters his rights, handcuffed him, and led him away.

"A technicality," Frip whispered to Norm, "but it'll keep him off the streets until we build our case."

The TV cameras were waiting when they arrived at the county courthouse. The troopers hustled Walters through the crowd of reporters while Frip stayed behind to mutter "No comment" for the evening news.

Norm sat in on the interrogation more as a spectator than a participant. The case was out of his hands.

"We know you bought the Runswatl girl birth control pills." Frip stared across the steel table at Walters and his lawyer.

"Have you seen these girls?" Walters asked. "I have. I've seen dozens get pregnant and drop out of school only to end up in poverty. I wanted to save Amy from that fate and give her a chance for a better life."

"You saved her all right," Frip said. "Here's what I think. She didn't take the pills and you got her pregnant. Then you killed her so no one would know you're a pedophile. Well, it's your lucky day. Plead guilty to murder one and I won't seek the death penalty. My offer's good for twenty-four hours."

***

The case was tied up in a neat little bow. The Neanders were happy, the governor was happy, and Norm was looking forward to his life getting back to normal. Everything was perfect except for one minor detail. The DNA tests came back saying that Amy's unborn baby had been fathered by a Neanderthal.

Neander civil rights leaders, including Pastor Donnatl, complained about police incompetence on the news. This stirred up the hate groups. Norm saw a bumper sticker on a pickup truck that said, "What do you call a dead ug? A good start!"

If it wasn't the teacher, it had to be the boy. Norm could have gotten a subpoena to test Eddie Treatl's DNA but the bureaucratic, paperwork approach hadn't worked so far. He knew a faster way. He simply parked down the street from the Treatl home and waited. When the silver-gray Mercedes pulled out of the driveway, he followed it for a few blocks and then hit the siren.

"Well, well, Eddie Treatl," Norm said after approaching the driver's window. "You have to be sixteen to drive in this state, son."? He sniffed. "I smell alcohol. I'm going to have to search your car."

The Treatl boy sat on the curb while Norm sprayed reagent on the carpeting inside the trunk. The liquid turned purple, indicating dried blood.

"Eddie Treatl, you're under arrest for the murder of Amy Runswatl. You have the right to remain silent…"

***

This time Norm led the interrogation. He would have preferred to question the boy alone but the parents had to be there since he was a minor.

"You're in a lot of trouble, Eddie." Norm aimed his words at the parents as much as their son. "If this had happened twenty years ago, you would have gone to juvenile hall and gotten out when you turned eighteen. But now we can charge you as an adult. We are going to charge him as an adult. Aren't we, Mr. Frip?"

"Absolutely! Neanderthals mature earlier," the assistant attorney general said. "As far as I'm concerned, if he's man enough to drive a car and father a child, he's man enough to take the punishment for his crime."

"You ever see an execution, Eddie?" Norm touched the boy's arm to make him look. "No, of course you haven't. I've seen three. They say the condemned doesn't feel any pain but I wonder about that. What must if feel like to be paralysed by the drugs while the poison bursts your heart and lungs? They make them wear diapers too for when they crap their pants.

"I don't want to see that happen to you, Eddie. I think you're a good kid and that things got a little out of hand but a girl died and someone has to pay. If you confess, we'll give you life. I'm not saying that prison's going to be easy but…"

"I did it!" Mrs. Treatl blurted. "That little skank thought she could trap Eddie and get her filthy hands on our money, money we sweated and bled for. What did she know about sucking up to rich farmers who think you're subhuman? So I invited her to dinner, said we needed to have a mother and daughter talk about the wedding ceremony, and after she ate, I did it." She looked at Eddie. "I did it for you."

Norm informed her she was under arrest. As he approached with the handcuffs, Mrs. Treatl spun and caught him in the eye socket with an elbow strike. By reflex Norm reached for his face giving Mrs. Treatl the split second she needed to draw his pistol from its holster.

"Vivian! No!"

Mrs. Treatl stuffed the barrel in her open mouth and jerked the trigger. The bullet tore through her skull splattering the walls with blood and gore.

***

Before informing the Runswatls about Mrs. Treatl's confession, Norm drove by the irrigation canal to pause where the sprinklers cast lazy arcs over fields of green. Despite all their differences, the Neanders proved all too human in their envy and fallibility. Norm hoped they would prove just as human in their capacity to love and forgive.

BORN ON A MONDAY

Julius Horne

They say that work is as good as anything for burying the pain that comes from loss. Especially on an anniversary. Today he would have been 35, and I ache without him, without his touch, his smile, his twinkling blue eyes, his ... but I doubt that my job will help. Not when I lost him to the ravages of the disease I've dedicated my life to fighting. I see him everywhere. In the stem cells that I grow, in the lab-grown organs that I blanch and prepare for transplantation – pig-grown but there to make a healthy replacement, to extend a life for someone luckier than he.

"One day," he said, "you'll cure cancer. I know you'll be the one. You don't think like the rest. For you there is no box. You even think outside of the hyperbox."

Hyperbox. He was always making up things like that. He meant a hypercube, a tesseract, but he always liked to add the personal touch. The little quirky things that set him apart. Oh god. I don't even know if I can do this today. Deep breaths. Focus.

The experiment. It's personal in another way. John and I were trying for a baby when they found the tumour. Trying to create a life the old fashioned way. Never mind genometrics and high tech turkey basters. We'd decided, after ten years together, that it was time.

So much for planning things. Yet here I am, project managing the most cutting edge conception and gestation since Dolly the Sheep. Test tube baby 2.0. All in the name of cancer research.

I wonder how ethics boards will treat me in the future? You cannot create human life, they say, not in a laboratory. Cloning is forbidden.

So. It's not human, and it's not a clone. To clone is to copy, and this is no biological Xerox. There is no *Homo neanderthalensis* to copy, so it — he — will be more of a reconstruction.

Loopholes.

I don't have the time for developing a foetus from scratch - you can't conceive and gestate a newborn in just a week. This calls for a fully grown specimen. Not even sure if its possible, but nothing ventured.

John, my love, I wish that you could see this. Maybe, if we're lucky, part of you will. Well, here goes.

Day One – Monday

The human body is made up on nearly 8,000 component parts. Bones, musculature, nervous system, circulatory system, digestive, excretory, endocrinal, integumentory, sensory, reproductive... all of these are here, donated, disassembled, bleached of host DNA, tested, reassembled, retested. Now, after weeks of preparation, the host body is finally complete. An empty shell ready to receive the designer genes that will grow into the spaces in between.

The adult human body has 37 trillion cells. The shell has fewer than a fifth of that. The remaining thirty trillion will be made up from stem cells, grown and harvested from a dozen of our non-human donors. Pan troglodytes. The common chimpanzee.

It's a contrived method, but that's ethics for you. Human organs, stripped of all but 5% their DNA, supplemented by a frankenstein genome that is 92% chimp and 3% neanderthal. To be fair, the chimp DNA is an exact match against the human and neanderthal genomes, and the 5% human DNA is an exact match against the neanderthal, so technically three per cent is enough to grow me a cave man.

The body is suspended in oxygenated amniotic fluid. Not donated. That we can simulate. It has been boosted with electrolytes and other additives which should help the new cells to do their job. When I say suspended, I mean that the body is held in place by around three thousand syringes, each of which contains a hundred billion cells, ready to adapt to the new host as they are injected. Cellular ingression is immediate. Accelerated organogenesis should take about an hour, with genome transcription happening at the same time.

Happy birthday, John. Miss you.

Day Two – Tuesday

Yesterday went well. The cells quickly settled into place and appear to have bonded well to the host frame. The life support system confirmed that the heart and brain were ready to function well before midnight, and

Dr Pfeiffer was on hand to initiate cardiac function. Sinus rhythm has been stable for eight hours, and there is brain function.

I wish I had been here, but I needed my sleep. Its hard enough being alone in my bed without the added complications of sleeplessness and work stress. Today we have two jobs. The first is to make full scans of the body - CT, ECG, MEG, MPI, MRI, ultrasound – followed by a regime of monitoring and recording over the next few days.

The second is to name our subject. I'm resisting the obvious temptation to name him after John, or perhaps after the child we never had, but the rules are pretty clear on the matter – the name cannot be something you get attached to. It has to be cold and clinical. Not something I find easy, especially with some of the ethical decisions I've had to make lately.

Looking at the subject, I can't but think of the donor body. Physically it still resembles him. There are superficial differences – the cranial ridge is already starting to protrude and bone density has shifted. The telltale features — the larger fingers, the denser muscle mass, the elongated tendon, the larger heel bone — similarly appear to be taking hold, which bodes well. One thing, however, I can't shake.

The eyes. It was necessary to stimulate consciousness for a moment to record the patterns of the iris and retina. The low level electrical charge we used had no other effect, but I couldn't help but feel a chill pass through my bones as they fluttered open. They were brilliant blue, full of the charm and charisma of the originals, but they were very different. The pigmentation may yet change, but that doesn't change what the Beatles would have called kaleidoscope eyes. They're like nothing I've ever seen before.

I presume they're the result of a recessive gene that's been reawakened, but if theories about the amount of interbreeding between *Homo sapiens* and *Homo neanderthalensis* is true, well, I'm surprised eyes like this have never been recorded. The effect appears to be due to a nictitating membrane—like that of a cat—which resembles a crazy-paved version of a compound eye. If I'm right it's a corrective lens, naturally occurring. Given that neanderthal evolution was for cold weather it might be some form of protection against wind chill or ultraviolet light, or possibly to adjust spectral perception. Night vision? Infra-red? It's a potentially groundbreaking discovery, just the sort of feature we've been looking for, but it makes me wonder why it became recessive.

The eyes are closed now. Thank goodness. While they were open, whatever name I gave him was irrelevant. All I could see was the donor body.

John.

I keep telling myself he wanted this. He donated his body to science and expressed his desire to be used as part of this programme, but it hasn't been easy. To be fair, the ethics board were more worried about me—about the impact of working with my husband's donated body; about my state of mind; about my capacity to see the experiment through to its inevitable conclusion.

Day Three – Wednesday

John. It's just you and me now. Here, in the laboratory. I know you're still in there. You can donate your body to science, but not your soul. The only spark of life in there is yours, and I feel you there, inside him. No psychological evaluation can deal with that.

They found me sound of mind. Hardly a surprise. I was married to a psychiatrist for ten years after all. I know that the brain inside that skull is brand new. None of the original synapses remain, but even without your memories and most of your genes, it's still you. Still my John. Still the love of my life.

I know I can't have you back. I know I have just a short time to get reacquainted; that you won't be able to speak, or to communicate, because you have no knowledge or education; just instinct. But our love was exactly that. Instinctive. We fell in love at first sight, and our time together was more than an accumulation of memories, it was a fusion of souls. The cancer brought it to an end, tainted it with grief and pain, but we were stronger than that. It's a cliché, but true love never dies. Certainly as long as one of us lives. I just wish...

I love you, John. I love you more than life itself.

Day Four – Thursday

Not happy. Pfeiffer has relieved me for the day. Told me to get my head straight. I was an emotional wreck first thing–I'd stayed up all night to be with J–the subject. Life signs were strong, no signs of infection or mutation. We weren't expecting such a smooth ride for our first attempt, which I confess made things worse. John was always a fighter.

But this was an experiment, not a long-term project. That's where the ethics has been so difficult. Creating a life for just a few days and then... terminating it. It's acceptable with animals, but not humans. Fortunately *Homo neanderthalensis* is no longer classified as human for the purposes of research. Yes, the *Homo* - prefix says they are exactly that, but that was more than a century ago. They used to be *homo sapiens neanderthalensis*, but the sapiens got dropped. Lucky for us. None of the laws or codes define them as human yet, and that's the loophole in which we operate. The only human involved— John—is legally dead. We've just brought his organs back to life for a while. Perfectly legitimate.

Which doesn't make killing him any easier. Especially when...when he's your husband.

I did my part. Between today and Saturday there will be almost two hundred biopsies carried out on his sleeping body. And then there will be the organ removals. Dissection whilst alive. It's—horrible. I hadn't seen it as anything but science until this week and now, now I'm a murderer.

I administered the first injections this morning. Put him into a coma. It's the first stage—he won't be waking from it—it's the beginning of the end. Moving him from tank to table was hard. I had to touch him. Even with amniotic fluid dripping from his sleeping body I could smell John. That was when Pfeiffer found me touching him, kissing him. I know it was inappropriate but, well I couldn't help myself. He was my husband.

That was when I lost it. Pfeiffer reported me, got me escorted from the premises, and stayed with him. I'm such an idiot. Deep down I knew this would happen. The Director called me this evening, reassured me that no action would be taken. No harm had been done, he said, and the project would conclude as planned. I'd still get full credit, and I can return to work on Monday when the job is done. Back to normal. Apparently it was always a contingency. They had confidence in me but, well, I crossed a line.

Day Five – Friday

Couldn't sleep. Knowing that today they'll be picking and prodding at him from dawn 'til dusk, it's been eating at me. My thoughts have been in overdrive, and my memories have been running rampant. The first meeting on campus. The first kiss. That weekend at Half Moon Lake. The first time we broke up. The passionate reunion. The whirlwind romance. The engagement. The six months we spent in Europe.

It was overwhelming. How can the most beautiful memories become an accumulation of anguish? How can so much happiness fuel so much pain? I had my grief, a year ago. It never went away but—losing him twice. I hadn't counted on that. I need to find a way to live with this pain. This ache. Worse than anything I expected. Worse even than the first time I lost him. At least ... at least his first death eased his pain. His suffering. This time — he may have been different, but he was in no pain. He could still live, have a lifespan of years even. Not days.

Day Six – Saturday (died)

One week. That's all he had. They called me this morning and confirmed that the brain was dead, and that the transplants had begun. By the end of today ... John will just be a collection of organs stored in jars. True, I'll be with them every day for the rest of this project, but I want more. Being with him should not mean staring at his pickled organs for the next three years. I need ... I want more.

I love you John. I always will.

Day Seven – Sunday

Another sleepless night. But I've decided. I know what to do. Today is the day John has a future.

They cremated his remains today, but all is not lost. I took a part of him — a souvenir — on Thursday. They'll never know. Not for a while. I hid three vials in my handbag when I left. Solomon Grundy, we called the subject, born on a Monday. Died on a Sunday. But there was one part of his life the rhyme didn't capture. The DNA may not be the same, but the semen I took is still John's. It may not be the most scientific method, but IVF is easy compared to what we achieved this week.

I may not have you in my life, John, but with any luck I'll end up having your twins.

A HARD MEAL

Matthew Wilson

ONE

She was asleep when it happened.

The small cave promised protection against cold and snapping animal teeth. The wolves on the hill howled at the moon and groggy, she woke, sat and checked her supplies.

In the mountain's shadow, everything ate anything. Dead or alive. Calla had not eaten in days. She distrusted her strained mental capabilities to see her safe through the cold so bunkered down for the night.

Not making fire was a cruel necessity but did not wish to attract passing carrion creatures.

In the puddle, she scooped a handful of rain water and washed herself sober when mercifully, most eye fizzle faded.

Men were here before her, scratching childish ideas of monsters in chalk like walls. Since her kind had banished her, she had been forced to eat rats and baby lizards, scooped from the ground and eaten raw. She had seen no creature such as this.

Men were prone to exaggeration and go near no water for fear of mighty dragons rising from and gulping them down in bloody teeth.

Calla touched the larger picture of a large brown woollen thing with blades for teeth poking out like lances either side its nose. Its height was close to tree tops and width near the cave mouth she reclined in.

Darn wolves. They became more excited with baying and Calla thought they must have come across death to feast upon. She envied their luck for her belly hurt.

Sleep would be nice but while up, supposed she should reward herself with nutrition before opening her eyes one morning and realised she lacked strength to raise her skinny, bone poking arms to defend against slobbering wolves.

Mother had warned her of demons here. Calla was wary only of things she saw. She believed in bears because she killed many and wore their furs to keep her warm. She believed in lizards as she had ate their innards and though Dragons may use this place for summer homes, she did not lose sleep over the idea of meeting one because she trusted her eyes. Not the idea of greater forces.

Yet mother had been so convincing. Before men burned her alive and exiled her daughter.

Calla looked up, the smell of guano annoyed her but food was food and even this pit kept out the chill.

"Uh," she challenged the things watching with angry red eyes in the ceiling. Bats. She had shrouded herself with furs to keep them off her neck while sleeping. Again, desperate for fire but mother said a little suffering was good for the soul.

The bats shrieked as she waved her arms. Day was coming and they were tired. Calla knew nothing of rabies. If the things upset her taste buds she might roast them over later fires. To soften the meat. She did not wish to live forever. Only not die today.

"Uh," she said again, squinting, taking better aim with rocks. Maybe she could stun one and catch it mid air to keep it from falling in the mess of its leavings. Snap its neck before it bit.

Before she had a chance, she felt the ground rumble and she squatted, changing her shape into that of a small target. She had heard thunder only once, thought the dragon came at last, blasting away dark clouds to swoop and take her away.

There was a rumble but no explosion. This was different. Something came.

Curious now, she found her dagger by familiarity as easy as a librarian would her favourite Dickens novel in a shelf of unlabelled hardbacks and walked into the cold.

The Wolves were coming, but not at her. She squatted again, feeling blessed the wind came at her rather than letting the devils know she was here. A dead end she realised now, to be massacred.

But the wolves gave no attention as they ran with fear in their eyes, snapping at each others tails in a bid to get away.

So there is something worse than wolves she thought and felt her heart catch like a rock dislodged by the quake had struck her breast. There was something coming down the hill toward her. Something large and brown.

Woollen with dragon like teeth either side of its trunk.

Sick, Calla looked back at the image on the wall. If the artist had more talent, the creature would have been a perfect match for the lumbering thing. Too large for speed but solid, a walking force aimed at her for reasons unknown.

Then giving her surroundings more attention, too tired to originally care, now alert and fearful, she saw spread out on the ground, several stretched hides.

All brown. Small.

Babies.

The fool who had used this cave as a temporary skinning base had sealed her fate by killing baby mammoths and moved on when his greed became so great he could carry no more. He had torn the last ones to shreds like cheap curtains rather than let anyone make off with his hard work and have something for themselves.

Wasn't me, Calla thought, but the mammoth did not stop as it threw itself at her, she hardly had time to break from her dumb wonder and dive back into the cave. As theorised, the mammoth did not fit. It tore an ear off, screaming hideously, more in rage than pain as again it threw its massive weight forward, trying to squeeze in, or more likely, bring the mountain down upon her.

Despite being mentally exhausted, Calla wondered why awful things happened to her. The things breath smelled fowl and Calla heard a click. She had been so scared her hands nearly snapped her bone dagger in two. She readied herself, needing to time it right before the roof did come down.

Shaken awake, the bats felt something was wrong, thought it the annoying woman trying to evict them again but with power behind the blows, realised one by one then suddenly in mass they had bigger problems and flew toward the door, shrieking.

The mammoth screamed as the furry devils filled its face and staggered back, eyes bleeding as rabid things found something to sink their teeth into. Calla ran forward, sliding on her belly as the mammoth raised its front paw, slicing open her belly button on a shard of rock.

She howled and this gave the creature something to lock onto as now, blinded, it came again and Calla threw herself aside, rolling, bruising her shoulder to the bone as the world turned once and drunkenly she stood.

"Ha!" She yelled at it, hoping to disorientate it and gain ground. She could climb no tree for the thing would knock it down, but she had advantage now. The air cold enough to clot the things nostrils for she could hardly smell anything herself. A snorting effort snapped some frozen moisture behind her sinus like a cavern icicle and bled freely. She hoped the thing had the same handicap.

At least she could see and threw a rock with all her might.

If the thing wished to leave that was fine. She could not believe she was fighting a thing of fantasy. If such creatures walked, then maybe Dragons lived too.

As it happened, the thing wanted to settle matters. Filled with maternal rage at the girl it considered had killed her children. She had walked miles to get here and though vegetarian, had killed bigger things than this child to protect herself.

With this pink, hairless thing in the world, the mammoths future children were not safe from extinction so for their good, stayed. Shook her head of the worst blood matting her furry caterpillar like eyebrows and waited.

Calla knew her game. The mad mother had ears large as boulders. Calla was amazed she could not hear her heartbeat how fast it boomed, but one premature action and the mammoth would know where she stood.

Calla stayed where she was and immediately realised its futility. She was cold, hungry and would soon turn to a statue in these conditions. The mad mother had enough meat on her to survive long after Callas blood froze.

Carefully, she raised the dagger above her head, not thinking the creatures sense of hearing that fine. In fact things went well till she reared back and clumsily overbalanced. Her shoulder still hurt her from where she rolled and cocking her arm back made it click.

She yelled and the mammoth came at her with hate in her eyes.

Calla shrieked in fear and threw. It whistled as it flew through the air, powered by desperation. The mammoth howled in mortal agony as though blind, the dagger punctured its eye and into its brain.

The mighty creature stopped mid step as if ran into a wall. It defecated and wet itself as if emptying all it had inside. Again, the ground rumbled as it fell to three knees. One paw still erect on the ground, defiant.

But something so big would not die quick. Gaining courage from seeing it hurt, Calla grabbed her dagger. It took effort working it free, wrenching it back and forth, but finally when she did, ignoring the pain of her shoulder and bought the finely made weapon down again.

And again, and again.

After many minutes, she did not know when the creature died, only when it stopped resisting. And gurgling lay down as if sleeping. Calla sat with a heavy thump. Tired, cold and close to puking but a sudden idea hit her.

One was she did not need a fire as the things innards would keep her warm against the cold. At least till she could make some furs from her coat. Something better than bear skin.

And the food.

Oh, the wonderful food. No more lizards, she had enough now to feed an army. She would eat well after she got her breath back and warmed her hands in its innards enough to get them working.

What she could not eat now would cut and carry in her pocket for later consumption. She would have to do something to keep the smell down, she did not wish to walk, smelling like a steak so another predator might pounce from trees.

From the hill, Wolves watched and licked their lips. Maybe there would be problems with them later. Smiling, Calla waved them on. If they wanted a mouthful they would have to work for it as hard as she.

TWO

Calla slept, dreaming of countries with no names. She heard the Lion before she smelt the wet fur in the rain.

She had been hungry a while, figured it her luck the first thing she killed all week attracted something meaner than her. Sniffing, she pulled the tiger toothed dagger out the Mammoths innards and moved to the mouth of the cave.

Lions had superior senses but trusted their eyes more than smell. The beast knew there was food in the cave, but mistrusted the dark. If it could not see it, he would not rush.

Calla thought he must be starving, for males of the species rely on the female for food. Faster, sleeker models of their mould covered bodies. Callas heart quickened so her chest hurt, forced her lungs to slow.

In, out.

Breathe was all that mattered, she refused to recognise her fear. It would grow claws and sink its wicked, withering teeth in her heart. Her mother had been killed in her cave at twenty two. Calla was determined to reach thirty at least.

The record of her family.

Gently she tapped the Tiger toothed dagger across the floor, chipping the edge.

Purring, the Lion tilted its head like a dog detecting a far off noise.

It found its source as she ran the tooth across the rocks. The Lion came forward, drooling now, all fear of the dark seemed forgotten.

Calla heard a tapping like hail against the mountain and she realised it was her hand knocking the floor. She was shaking. An insult to her nature worse than losing a limb. She had such little in life beside her name and pride.

And the dagger.

Calla did not know words. Her hunter life had no need of them beside shouts and bellows to scare birds from bushes she could take down with a well aimed rock.

Her hands were calloused and bloody after dragging the decapitated deer all the way home. She had no need of the spear for being practical, the dagger was enough to strip flesh off the deer.

Squinting, she wiped sunlight from her eyes and the Lion stopped.

Come on, you furry devil.

It's size seemed to stop her heart in her chest. Her adrenaline gave a loud kick and restarted her engine just when she felt she might fall.

She forced her legs to stand. Mom had shown her these things fed on fear. When small she marvelled at their co-ordination and killing methods. Ones she adapted and implemented in her own affairs.

A flinch might break its spell, make it feel this morsel was trying to run. Easily it would over take her. Break her legs with one mighty sweep of its paws and break her skull with a bite of its jaws.

But Calla was not running. She looked near the door. Her dagger had killed bigger beasts than the Lion. But all had been sleeping. In winter, their hides saved her from the cold. She could not afford chivalry.

Mother would be ashamed if she died of old age. She raised the dagger in one hand and a chicken sized egg in the other.

"Uh!" She shouted, and the lion sprang.

Immediately she stepped back, putting all her weight on her back foot, breaking into a pitchers stand. She threw the rock as if a baseball and ducked as the beasts head swung violently to one side.

She heard a crack and the thing staggered. Its thick tangled mane did nothing to soften the blow but the lion was not damaged, only stunned as it shook the dirt from its golden beard and stood.

Calla ran and picked up her spear. It felt reassuring, weighty like a drunken friend leaning against her. Singing and sweetening her heart. She felt immortal.

"Uh!" She said again, bloodied, the lion growled its hate. It's orange eyes burned like firelight and Calla did not feel the rains chill. She shook her sodden fringe of hair from her eyes and threw her dagger, still quivering, into the ground.

The chipped blade demanded total concentration.

"Uh! Uh!" She said again. Ordering action before her shakes got bad. If it was going to kill her, she would rather it hurried before her mental stubbornness completely broke down.

She refused to die easy. Mom would be appalled.

"Uh," she bellowed, and the thing came.

The explosion scared her as the lion raised itself up on its back legs like the shield of a distant prince and howled at the rain.

Click - click.

Calla heard the man snap the chamber of his rifle back and slot another shell in the breach. When he fired again, the Lion lost his brain, spattered across the floor and terrified, Calla darted away, running for the trees.

"Wait!" Shouted the hunter. The park ranger said there was no locals up here. He held up his hand for the gunsmoke to clear, then gave a signal to his son. Coast clear.

"What was that lady doing, daddy?"

The hunter snapped the rifle open, a blue shell spat out like an ejected torpedo, startling a ladybird snoring on dandelions at his feet. The hunter shrugged, noting, as predicted, his fluorescent red top felt two sizes too small.

"Dunno, son. Lady looked like a cave woman to me. Lot of nuts round here. Some hardly know who they are. Let alone what year it is."

THE PAST THAT YOU DON'T KNOW, CONTAINING ALIENS

Rebecca Fung

Scientists explore possibilities. They are obsessed with the future. What would the future be like? Apart from the rising taxes, overpopulation, flying cars and pizzas that cost one thousand dollars and taste like plastic, one thing that scientists often see in our future is aliens.

Alien contact. Alien invasions. Going to Mars and discovering aliens. One day, say the scientists, we will have the technology to build huge spaceships with fancy touchscreens and faster than light capacity, just like in television shows. Then we will go far out into space, and one day, some of us in the future will see real, live aliens.

Perhaps they will have bug eyes, or they will come from a watery planet and be covered in scales. Or perhaps they will talk in binary code. Perhaps they will be as small as ants or they will be like jelly and change shape every second as we talk to them. They will reflect a strange green light. It won't matter, the scientists say, the important thing is that we will have met aliens.

Scientists are always looking into the future for aliens. What would they think if the best place to look for aliens was in the past?

***

"Welcome, Mr Dantz," said Troy Vanker. "You are the Storyteller?" David Dantz winced. "I guess that's how we're known, though it's rather inaccurate. We collect stories; we know how to extract stories. The best stories."

"Names are unimportant. I just want what they say you can do, Mr Dantz," said Troy. David smiled. Troy Vanker owned several high-rises with his name plastered all over them. Thousands of Vanker Industries' employees wore the corporate T-shirt, "Vanker and Proud Of It". Troy Vanker was hardly a man who thought names were of no significance.

"Why is Vanker Industries participating in such an experiment?" asked David, as Troy led him to one door.

Troy smiled. "For the only reason. Because we can." He swiped a card, and pushed the door in. "I've got bucket-loads of money. I can do it and a lot of other people can't. I can do lot of things that other people can't. That's why people do many things, to do things first. Space travel, alien contact, invisibility. I've got labs testing those as we speak. But I do think the Neanderthals will be the next big thing. They're the project we've come the furthest on fastest. And we need to stay ahead. It's here."

David wasn't sure what he'd expected. He'd had visions of a crouching, hunched over, starving creature in a tiny cages, barely able to move, clutching at the bars begging for release.

The Neanderthal's cage was more like a cubicle. It was made of what seemed to be glass, framed with metal, floor-to-ceiling capsules with a bed and chair fitting comfortably in each. There was also a scattering of stones and other bits and pieces on the floor.

"We call him Ned," said Troy. He walked up to Ned's glass cubicle and tapped it. "Hey there, good boy, Ned. Say something, boy. See, he doesn't really communicate much. They'll be a bit of work, but it's why you're getting paid. You see, each Neanderthal we raise has been created out of DNA from someone who had real experiences, thousands of years ago. We believe they've retained their memories, if you can get to them."

David nodded. He had noticed the slight turning of Ned's head and the shrug of shoulder as Troy tapped at the glass. Troy might think they did not communicate, but they did as far as David was concerned.

"The cages are fully reinforced for security purposes but he can see and hear everything. We have a twenty-four hour surveillance system set up, with cameras over there, there, and there," explained Troy. "And lab researchers have been observing and taking notes. But we promised you some full sessions without disturbances. The cameras remain on, though. I want to capture the whole thing. Zenith Technologies are trying something similar, I heard from my sources. We've got to crack this before they do. I've got a lot of money in this. You're a man of the world, Mr Dantz. I don't need to tell you that information matters, and what matters more is who gets it first. We've tried everything else with this creature and we can't understand a damn thing. But the whole point in bringing back a human and not a cockroach is so you can talk to it, right?"

"I'll get to work," said David. He did not really like Troy's attitude, but he was intrigued by the Neanderthal. Like any good Storyteller, David put aside the client's motive. If it was a good story, he wanted to know it. Why the client wanted to know it – that was his business. "I can have something for you in twenty-four hours, I'm sure."

"Good," said Troy Vanker, and, thankfully, left.

David arranged his small pack on the bed and had a good look at Ned.

For the first hour he simply sat there and watched the Neanderthal. He did not write down a thing, but his mind was taking down the notes and David felt his body shift into Storytelling mode. His body began to acclimatise to the surroundings. Being a Storyteller was not an occupation you did a few years of a degree for, nor something, like Troy Vanker Industries, you gained a whole lot of money and simply "went for". It was something you started young and trained your whole mind and body for. Like a monk, he had been told. There was no occupation like Storyteller except maybe monk.

You had to adjust to their rhythm. It was a well-known fact that people said more without words than with them, everyone knew that, even Troy Vanker who had a book on body language and *Deciphering the Handshake: The Road to Corporate Success* in his office. But a Storyteller did much more than decide whether a person was trustworthy by whether his handshake was good or not good.

A Storyteller could feel whole stories from the muscle movements of a person, once they had been correctly calibrated. A Storyteller was sensitive to the sounds of the heart beating and blood flowing, they could smell sweat and watched hair twitching and understood the nuances.

And they coaxed out stories from people. The best stories.

David knew from experience that most people's expression rushed out in a jumbled stream of unordered unconsciousness, and it was part of the Storyteller's job to order the stories and make sense of them, without layering them with his (or her) own agenda of interpretation, taking out the clutter and sequencing the sense for the client. He had no idea how a caged Neanderthal would react or whether they would be easy to work with. But he was sure that it would not take long to work out whether Ned was cooperative or impenetrable.

The Neanderthal was a bigger, heavier man than most of the clients David worked with, but it was a mistake that many people made to think that such larger people would not have the same subtleties as smaller ones. It was a subconscious assumption you had to sweep out and try to feel the lighter nuances in the muscles.

Then David began to feel out the surroundings, sending out test communications and watching Ned respond. How did Ned react to this sound, to the way I shrugged this shoulder, to this little extra light? David expertly threw out hundreds of signals, memorising and interpreting responses. Very soon he began to build up a language he could use and he began to test it. Louder, softer.

Ned turned abruptly and looked at him, then sat hard on the floor. He began to pick up the stones and start to feel them in his hands. As he did, David felt a rush of new language, symbols. The rocks are important, he thought. He's comfortable with the stones. Let him be.

Ned sat for a long while. Rubbing one stone against the other, he shaped and chiselled the stone, and it relaxed him.

Good, good, thought David. He needed him relaxed. He watched the stones come to life as they changed shape. He first needed to gain trust, to calibrate. He would ask simple questions and let Ned talk to him as he felt comfortable.

"You are Ned?" asked David.

"That's what they call me," said Ned, or at least, as close to saying as David could hope for.

"May I call you Ned?"

Ned shrugged.

"Do you feel this is a strange way to live?" asked David.

"It is not what I am used to," said Ned. He worked away harder at the stone.

"Tell me what you are used to," said David. Then the deluge began.

***

There was a red strip on the horizon. Each morning. I liked to watch. That was my ritual.

The others didn't know this, or they didn't, before the Happening.

Then they knew, everyone knew. I couldn't hide.

But till then, I enjoyed the red strip with the bits of orange shooting out from it. It's where I sharpen my little stone axe. Everyone has a tool that they favour, this axe is mine, it feels heavy in my hand and I like it that way. Every day before the Happening, I would take it out and go with the others. But the Happening changed that. The Happening.

***

David's head began to throb a little. He hadn't been prepared for so many emotions, so soon, but perhaps he should have. How many thousands of years had this man had memories locked away in its cells before Vanker Industries had resurrected them? Now, Ned was pouring them forth like hot lava spewing forth from a volcano, a torrent uncaring of how its recipient might deal with it, just knowing it had to let loose.

"What Happening? What does Happening mean?" demanded Troy when David told him.

"That's what I'm finding out, but the process is slow. Ned needs to find time to dig into those thoughts, and I need to organise them. In the meantime, my head hurts."

"I'll get you a painkiller. So, something big? A huge Neanderthal War or something? If I'm the first to get this down …?"

"Whatever it is, it was important to Ned. Though remember what is important to him isn't what's important to us, necessarily. I've put together a good profile on Ned already. He has a strong attachment to this particular stone weapon, a small axe. I've got a very precise description of it. And he enjoys watching the dawn."

"Who gives a damn about that? Focus on the important stuff, Mr Dantz! Ned has got a story. Whoever knows the most about Neanderthals and gets it out fastest is going to make the money. There's media, there's awards, there's who gets the jump on the technology. It's everything, really."

David sighed. He had rather liked Ned's description of watching the dawn. Ned had humanity and the urge for aesthetic pleasure and tranquillity. "?I just need a vegetable shake to pick me up – no artificial painkillers, it messes with my concentration. I'll be back to work."

With him and Ned alone, he absorbed himself in Ned's presence. "You have a story to tell, Ned. Tell it to me."

"I have a story. It is a long one."

"We have as long as you need, Ned," said David. "Just talk. Tell me whichever way you want." Then he began and he let Ned's story wash over him. The story was what mattered.

***

It was dawn and I was watching the red strip, as I always did, as I wanted to do forever, when the Happening occurred and smashed my and my friends' lives to pieces.

Little black dots appeared on the red strip. One, two … five.

At first I thought they were on my eyes. I rubbed my eyes very hard, but they wouldn't come off.

So they must be on the red strip. Now that I thought about it, I had never known where the red strip came from each morning or why it disappeared. I simply enjoyed it.

The little black dots were growing bigger and the red strip was disappearing, as it always did in the morning, when the rays of golden sun exploded over the sky and introduced the morning. But the black dots did not disappear with the red strip. They hung in the sky and they grew bigger. And bigger.

"Insects in the sky! Insects in the sky!" I cried out, and woke everyone up.

"Why did you wake me up?" moaned Ada. (Here David began to insert names that seemed closest or the most similar to the signals he was receiving. Neanderthal names in reality were quite different from these.)

"How long have you been watching them?" demanded Raben.

"Since the red strip was here," I explained. We all watched as the bugs crawled towards us and took shape –? I had seen blurred black dots, now they appeared as dark ovals, and then again, the dark ovals took on a more definite shape. They had slightly pointier ends and some of them seemed to have two little things, like short and stumpy legs growing from their underbelly.

"Strange creatures from the sky," said Raben.

"Strange creatures from the stars," said Ada, and she was the first to give voice to the suspicions among us that would later prove to be correct. They were bugs soaring towards us from the stars, and we were all waiting for them to come at us and – well, what was it we expected a bug from the stars to do?

They stared for a long while, wondering at the strangeness of the situation, till Dylan broke their awed silence and suggested they go back to their homes and fetch their weapons – their axes, sticks, any rocks they could find.

"What are you talking about?" I asked. I had my little stone axe on me, anyhow.

"We have not been thinking about what these bugs are like," said Dylan. "What do we know of star-people or star-bugs? What do we know of why they are coming here? If they are hostile, we need to be prepared."

Dylan was a planner. We had been too caught up with how interesting and strange the day was to even think about what these bugs might mean to us. Soon we were standing in a large group, holding each to our favoured weapon in one hand, and a large stone in the other.

They no longer looked like little bugs. They had grown so large, they were larger than the sun, and then one seemed to drop out of the sky. Then another, and another, and another …

"That way!" yelled Raben.

The bugs-from-the-stars were huge. They were so large that if they had landed anywhere near us, just one bug would have squashed all our homes flat, and have had room leftover. But out here, past the hills were some open plains and five space-bugs had managed to fit. They were unmistakably our bugs. Black and shiny and only recently crashed here.

"How could something so big and heavy-looking come from the stars? How could they hang in the sky for so long? Surely something so heavy would fall?"

"Even large birds fly," Raben said.

"Large birds have wings," Ada reminded him. "And this has no wings, or … what is that?"

A hole was opening on the side of one bug. Later, I recognised it as a door, but at the time I remember thinking, the bug is growing a hole on its side! What is happening? All of us raised our weapons and held our rocks.

We did not dare say a thing.

Then, something green emerged from the hole. Something green and walking upright, like ourselves.

"It is a Being! It is an Alien from the Stars!" breathed Sadie. "It is green!"

"Hold onto your weapons," said Dylan. "Watch it carefully."

The tall, thin creature walked out of the side of the bug. Then another, and another until there were at least more than a hand of them –? that is, there were seven in all. They filed out and walked in a line towards us, like a row of ants, I thought, but far more elegant.

"Hold that stone axe ready, Ned," Dylan whispered. "We may have cause to use it soon!"

I did not know if I could do it. I had never hurt a person with my stone axe – hitting my finger accidentally once didn't count. The aliens walked like a very elegant human being, too close to humans to make me feel comfortable about striking them. I wished I could walk as they did, they were so very fine and erect and they strode towards us yet they did not seem to be walking so much as gliding. They were perfect. They were coming towards us.

"I am Jargtul, of the Yamul planet. You may lower your weapons. We have no intentions of harm," said one alien. He was the tallest. They were all so tall and bright green with shiny skin. Atop their skinny bodies, their bulging head showed just one eye. Jargtul was hypnotising. We lowered our weapons as he instructed.

"We have been observing this planet from afar for many hundreds of years," said Jargtul. "Our calculations say that this planet contains intelligent life like our own. Hello, fellow intelligent being! We salute you across the galaxy. For you know that while unintelligent beings are easy to come across, it's those with a flicker of intelligence that are so rare."

We stared. He peered at us closely. I am not sure he was convinced of our flickers of intelligence.

"We have sent you communications by radio pulses across the universe for years. Why have you not replied, my galactical friends? Do you not seek us out as we do you?"?

"Radio what?" repeated Raben. Jargtul seemed like a harmless enough creature, but he did not make a lot of sense.

"Food?" suggested Ada. "Water?"

Jargtul's eye blinked a few times, and he convened with his green cohort, gabbling on in some language we could not understand. Then he forced a smile.

"Indeed. Yes, thank you. We shall try the local cuisine."

We took Jargtul and his friends to our grounds and we put together a meal for them – freshly caught fish and skinned rabbit, toasted on the fire, water, and some plants. Raben is very good at collecting edible and plants and separating the ones to eat from the ones that taste bitter or are poisonous. Our alien friends ate well. Despite being so skinny, they could eat easily as much as we could. Dylan and Jargtul conversed and the rest of us entertained the other aliens.

While we were gathering the meal together, I noticed Mollitul. She caught my attention before we were formally introduced, with her gentle movements and the sweet gaze of her one eye. And she was looking at me too, I could feel that. Jargtul was the leader; she was the calming presence. She smiled at me and while the others busied around Jargtul and the other aliens, she spoke to me softly and held my hand.

They had come a long way from the stars to find us, she said. She had gazed up at the stars, like I did my red strip, and often wondered what was beyond there, so she had begged Jargtul to allow her to accompany them on this expedition. She had learned how to speak Earth language as competently as him, just to be allowed. I loved the dreamy look in her eye as she spoke, and the warmth of her hand pressed on mine.

Does it sound impossible for two to fall in love within an hour, especially an alien from Yamul and a Neanderthal from Earth? Then we did the impossible. It did not matter to me that she had green skin. It was silky to the touch and it began to feel natural. I heard in her voice someone who understood my dreams better than anyone else, even if she was born in a galaxy far, far away. She bit into a bit of rabbit and grimaced at first, but then she quickly got used to the strong taste. "So much more flavoursome than a synthetic nutrient triangle," she said. I didn't understand everything she said, but no matter, I did not feel I needed to. I just loved her.

Eventually Jargtul interrupted.

"This is a good place despite its shortcomings. We like it here. We have decided to present you with great gifts," said Jargtul. "We have brought them on our craft. We have spent years of perfecting the technology to create appropriate gifts for our Earth associates."

He looked at Mollitul and me, and I saw his mouth twitch a little.

"We have a great device that shall allow you to see Yamul from anywhere on Earth! We have beads that will create a powerful energy that will power any creation you please. You ask how our ships – you call them bugs – came to visit you. Our ships were powered by a single bead of this energy and brought us all the way to Earth. We present a great quantity of these to you. Then, the great Apramul, the three-headed beast, who can fly and wrestle and do mathematical equations with ease. And the machine that cures any sickness in humans.

Jargtul obviously expected us to be impressed but we were all bemused. Such gifts sounded wondrous, but what use were they to us? We would much rather have had some more fish or rabbit. Or in my case ...

Jargtul caught that look. "I add a final gift," he said. "Mollitul shall be your wife. May our planets live in peace together!"

Wife! I had not thought of it, but now that she had been presented to me, I was not averse to the idea. In fact, it was growing on me every second.

How could I be drawn so strongly to a green-skinned woman with just one eye? I thought to myself. This was not what I had been taught to admire, in fact it went against every manly instinct I had. Yet she seemed to me the most feminine and obvious choice for a wife I knew. She was the first woman I had loved.

"He has invited me to tour on the space-bugs and inspect the gifts before unloading," said Dylan. "I am excited –? Ned, I thought perhaps you should be the first, you saw them first …"

"You go," I said, and I meant it. Dylan was better at this sort of thing. "We'll stay here and … I think we should give them a gift too. What can we give them? They have given us so much!"

We put our heads together.

"I know," said Raben. "We can show them our dance. Nobody dances better than us! It will be a true treat."?

"Fantastic! Let's practice while they're gone and put on a display tonight," I said. "Dylan, we'll leave a role for you."

"You better," said Dylan. "This has turned out to be the most extraordinary day. Aliens, and Ned getting married!"?

So the aliens escorted Dylan to the bugs and we began to put together the finest display in the history of our dancing.

***

We had never danced better. Raben did not forget a single movement. Ada and Sadie were graceful in their duet. Even Dylan held his own.

This is for you, Mollitul, I thought, turning around in a circle and leaping in the air with a cry. Ada and Sadie threw up their hands and squealed appropriately.

Mollitul seemed rather baffled. I decided I would break the sequence we had decided on, and do another leap for her. It's like the rabbit, I thought, but she'll get used to it.

It was then that I noticed Jargtul's eye on me, cold and forbidding. Why had I not noticed before that not one of the aliens was enthralled? Did they dance better on Yamul?

Jargtul stood and roared. "Outrageous! We do not have to stand for this! How dare you!"

Unwisely, we continued playing our drums and Raben and I shook our bodies energetically before Jargtul.

"Grab them!" yelled Jargtul, and when two of his green lackeys rose, I saw it was no game. We stopped dancing.

"Didn't you enjoy the – I mean appreciate the – I mean we're good –" said Sadie.

Jargtul did not listen. "We have been insulted!" He began to bark orders I did not understand.

"What's happening?" asked Sadie and Raben, who were nearest me. "Don't they like the dancing? It was our best!"?

I approached Mollitul. She looked scared, her one eye darted and flickered and her green skin grew clammy as I tried to reach out to her. But she managed to stutter something, about our bodies, shaking, parading, it was a device used by lower beasts in touch with darker spirits. Beasts did this only when they wanted to cause great mischief to another. It was rumoured to be extremely effective, if you could harness the power correctly.

Jargtul had never seen it harnessed correctly. But he was as afraid as anyone of the man who could give it form and force. He did not like to admit it, to admit fear was a weakness and showed he was susceptible to superstition. Were we preying on him? Were we making fun of him? The green skin was good at hiding emotions, but not good enough. Jargtul's voice was terse with anxiety and his gestures were short and shaky.

"Jargtul," I cried. "Stop this! There is a misunderstanding …"

An alien ran from my home. Mine! Jargtul had sent him there. Now he held something in his hands, the little stone carvings I had made for Mollitul. The figures of her and Jargtul and of the alien cohort. I flattered myself they were decent representations, but Jargtul screamed in fury when he saw them and started to smash them. He grabbed each piece and threw it down savagely, and ground it into the floor with his foot, shrieking all the time. "Curses! Curses!"

"He's lost it," said Raben. "Those were Ned's carvings, you alien idiot! What are you doing? Landing on our planet, smashing things up? Who do you think you are?"

He ran at Jargtul, and one of the green cohort stepped in and hit Raben easily to the ground. Someone yelled, and threw a rock, and then another.

Well, that's how I remember it. I remember running to help Raben off the ground and looking up and everyone was throwing rocks and waving sticks, howling, yelling, pushing, slapping.

I had seen elegant, almost human beings before. No more. They were one-eyed slimy green aliens. My carvings! Mine!

"Fight!" said Raben, his eyes shining. "I would love to give Jargtul's nasty pompous face a big punch and slap!" He pulled himself to his feet. His ankle was bad but it wasn't stopping him going after Jargtul.

I looked for Mollitul in the crowd. She had joined in, but only half-heartedly, or at least so I convinced myself. She was bellowing and waving her arms about in a most theatrical manner, and she had taken a run at a few of us. She looked magnificent. Even when she was fighting against us, I couldn't help but think that.

Then a green brute did more than howl or yell at Sadie. It grabbed her and it would not let go as she screamed. It held her high then threw her down, hard.

Trickles of blood were coming out of her skull.

"Sadie! Sadie!" screamed Ada, forgetting the alien she was trying to intimidate by crossing her eyes and throwing pebbles at him. She gathered up Sadie's body in her arms and sobbed loudly.

Everyone else had stopped.

I did not know what to do except watch as Ada rocked Sadie in her arms and let the blood wash over her.

"This has to end," said Dylan.

"This has ended," said Jargtul. At least his voice had returned to normal.

***

So the aliens left. Not with a bang, not with an explosion or a great clash of bodies. We had been prepared for massive bloodshed since the aliens had landed, but I had never really been prepared for Sadie's passing. And it ended with a lecture.

I did not like being lectured.

Jargtul looked down at me – he really could do it very well, he had only one eye but I could feel its full force on me.

"This is hardly the planet for us," he said. "I do not see much hope for improvement, either, among your kind. We withdraw our gifts. You have the wrong sorts of values. I do not wish to plant the precious seeds of our Yamullion race on this land, overrun by beasts that have values such as what I have just been not-so-privileged to witness. We shall leave at once. All Yamullions, on board!"

"You can talk, you killed our Sadie," whispered Ada fiercely, but she didn't dare say it too loud.

They all boarded the main space bug. Mollitul was the last before Jargtul to board, and she turned slightly to meet my gaze. I'm sure she looked sorry but Dylan held me back.

Mollitul, you were almost my wife. My alien wife. Where are you going? Will you ever come back?

I was thinking this as I watched her green back disappear into the black bug and the door slide close. Dylan's grip was tight on mine and he said in a low voice, "?I wouldn't be surprised if they were watching us. They're crafty one-eyed little devils. So don't you run out or make a movement or even twitch your face until they've disappeared completely. Understand?"

I tried to keep my whole body as motionless as possible, but it was hard. I watched as the main space bug rose, then the other four, and they disappeared into the sky, the little blotches becoming smaller, till they were dots, then pin-pricks, then nothing.

"You can breathe," said Dylan, loosening his grip, and I fell to the ground, tired of trying to be strong.

"You really loved her, didn't you?" asked Ada.

"She was chosen for me for a reason. They came here for a reason," I muttered. That's what I'd thought when I'd met Mollitul. There was something special about her, and I felt I was supposed to be with her. Is it strange to feel that way about a one-eyed, green-skinned alien being from the stars.

"She left for a reason," said Dylan. "You have to forget her. We have to forget them." Then he moved away and started ordering everyone to clean up the mess of the ceremony and to wrap up Sadie's body. We would bury her in a ceremony that evening.

"It seems such a small reason to leave," I said. "Our ceremonial dance. We even did it because we thought it would please them. It was just a misunderstanding. But everything happened so fast and got blown out of proportion. I didn't want to fight. I got caught up."

Ada sat next to me. "How does any quarrel start? It's something small that gets blown out of proportion!"

"But this time I'll never see her again," I said.

***

"So that's that, then," said David. "Our Neanderthals saw the aliens long ago. That is Ned's story."

Troy Vanker's face grew red.

"But – but I just poured another seven hundred million into alien research!"

"Ned says he doubts they'll be back. But you never know. Either way, you won't be first," said David.

Troy snapped,

"My stock just went through the roof. I have to be first. Being first is what counts. Nobody will give a damn about aliens if some cavemen have already been partying with them. Aliens won't be original. We'll be a bloody laughing stock."

"Then what do you want to do about Ned? You wanted to be first with his story. I just tell stories, Mr Vanker."

Troy scowled.

"If it's a past no one knows about, maybe we can keep it that way. I'd dispose of him, but Neanderthals are the next big thing. I need a Neanderthal."

"So Ned's story gets squashed for all time?"

"It's not good for people to know too much, anyway. Or … maybe we can find that Dylan. Didn't he see those beads of energy or something? If we could figure out how to make those … I bet there's a hell of a lot of money in that!"

Troy looked excited again. "You can leave now, Mr Dantz. You'll be paid your full fee. We'll give you half an hour to pack up your things."

David packed up his few items.

"Goodbye, Ned," he said. Ned walked up to the glass wall and slipped something into the meal chute. David picked it up.

It was the figure of stone that Ned had been working on while he had been relaying his story. He hadn't had much in the way of implements. The sculpture was impressive. It was carved to show arms and a bulging head with one eye. David looked into the face, and he felt he saw traces of … well, something.

He held the figure in his hand as he left, tracing over the grooves with his fingers. He could feel images flowing towards him, tentative at first, but coming to him slowly and then flowing more freely as he left Vanker Industries.

***

We buried Sadie in the evening. It had been a very long day. I did not say anything as the sun set on our ceremony, except I looked up at the red strip of the sun falling behind the horizon as we all made our signals of respect to Sadie.

I wondered what Jargtul would have said about our ritual. Would he think it was strange, our ceremony for the dead?

There was nothing now, nothing on the red strip. They were gone forever. I had looked up at that strip, every morning, and I enjoyed it in the evening many times as well. Without the specks of black it had been the sky I loved. Now, it felt strange, and I thought, would I wake up each morning, not to enjoy the tranquillity of the rising redness and the first yellow streaks across the sky, but to search madly for any signs of their return. Mollitul's return.

They were not coming back.

It had not even been a full day and somehow Mollitul had affected in a way I had not thought possible. Her voice, her smile, the way her eye looked at me. I could not forget that. It was burned into my memory. I could feel her creeping into my skin and synthesising with my flesh and searing herself into my bones. No matter what other things happened to me, what other wife I would find, Mollitul would be a part of me.

I wondered if she was on the space bug, thinking that Ned Neanderthal would never be able to be separated from her, not even if someone used their sharpest knife and pared each bit of flesh from her skeleton (if she had one). Did her memories of me last as long?

I gave Sadie one last look, then we turned away and went back to our home area, and I tried to leave it all in the past. The past I could never forget, the past with aliens.

FIRST MAN, LAST TRIBE

Steve Graeme and Adrian Middleton

His name among the Sapients was Challenger—a literary joke drawn from the adventure stories of the early twentieth century. Like the fictional Challenger, he had seized the initiative and forged a career as an academic, the foremost anthropologist of his time—of all time.

His friends called him Ta'al—the Bringer of Light. It was the name he had earned on his first journey into the past, around 40,000 BC, on the day that he first set foot in the steep-walled valley of the then unnamed Düssel River, looking down upon the many cliff-dwellings dotted along its sides, their smoke-trails warding off newcomers in a show of strength that, perhaps, overstated the numbers of the valley folk that lay within.

Until that day he had been alone, an outsider revered as much for the sake of curiosity as for the breadth of his knowledge, a genetic experiment whose existence earned him certain rights—the spokesperson for an entire species that no longer existed, the celebrity rolled out to offer a different point of view, and the coveted professor of an ambitious university whose true purpose was to attract funds rather than to educate. Until that day he had been quite jaded, despite being mostly human like them. Only the tiniest change had been grafted on to his DNA, enough to make him Neanderthal in the eyes of the world. Enough to set him, irrevocably, apart.

There was an upside. Left alone to pursue his studies as he saw fit, his carousing overlooked by all but his doctor, Cusack, whose job was to keep him alive. It was a strained relationship, but one which kept him in touch with his human side—not that the Neanderthals weren't human too—but despite his belligerent, bearded exterior, on the inside he was more Ta'al than Challenger.

He missed Cusack—the doctor had been beside him on his many excursions, from Kripina in 130,000 BC to the Neander Valley to Lapedo Valley and Saint-Cesaire fifteen thousand years later—and together they had helped explode the myth that his ancestors had been ogrish protohumans whose lack of creativity had allowed them to be outsmarted by the more adaptive, innovative *Homo sapiens*. This, the last of his excursions, he was making on his own.

Drawing the white shroud-like veil across his face, Ta'al urged his camel forwards, pressing on through the sandstorm towards what would one day be the mountains of Edomite Mountains on the eastern side of the Jordan-Arabah valley. Here, ten thousand years before the birth of Christ, the Levant was the last province of the people of the valleys, withdrawing from the world of their more profligate cousins. This valley, a green oasis on the Eastern slopes, was unlike the more temperate hunting grounds he had seen at the other settlements, its barren unwelcoming approach well away from the migration paths eked out by the other humans.

From beneath his keffiyeh, Ta'al's glasses tracked the movement of the few animals and other life forms that crossed his path, zeroing in upon the hilltop watcher who stood, spear in hand, surveying the horizon. Auto-adjusting for the range, the lenses picked out his facial features—more Sapient than those he had seen at the other settlements, but still recognisably of the people. The spear-tip was sleek and polished—certainly of a better quality than any he had seen before—and the man's body was covered with a pale hessian-like fabric. He smiled. Perhaps the small trick he'd taught the members of an earlier tribe had taken hold, and evolved. To any other anthropologist knotted fibres in this time period would be seen as unusual, a sign of an advancing civilisation.

The watcher raised something above his head—a length of thread with something, a shell or horn perhaps—which he began to spin, generating a shrill sound similar to wailing wind, but of a higher and more recognisable pitch. A warning for the tribe below, and another sign of early adaptation. Change was happening, but perhaps a little too late.

***

Arriving at the foot of the mountain, Ta'al brought his steed up short as he entered the verdant zone that lay beneath its shadows. The familiar caves were present, but extended beyond the rocks, using sun-baked wooden structures which reminded him of the earliest human buildings. Perhaps there were Sapients here, or perhaps the innovations were another sign of progress.

Dismounting, the professor led his camel towards the settlement, his lenses picking out the faces of hidden tribesmen using scrub and other flora to conceal themselves. As he came closer to the village proper, he was amazed to see that a simple corral had been made from piles of stone and splintered wood. These had been set with hardened mud, and formed a low wall that he thought, at first, was defensive. His lenses, however, picked out several pigs and goats contained within their boundaries.

Farming? Ta'al was pleasantly surprised. Making his way forward as the tribesmen broke cover, their spears poised in warning that he go no further. Unhitching his veil, the scientist removed his glasses and exposed his head. The thick wiry facial hair, the prominent brow ridge and the projecting nose and jaw were immediately recognisable to the valley folk, whose spears lowered and whose elder came forwards to greet the stranger, hands extended to reach forward and stroke his face in the traditional manner. Again he saw evidence of development. His prior visits to such settlements had seen his approach revered, but this time they lacked the primitive awe he had expected.

Up close, he could see that his own features were more prominent and more Neanderthal than theirs. Despite the language barrier he was sure that this was what they were discussing among themselves as a guttural conversation started up among them. There were sounds that he recognised from the other settlements, but the consonants were longer and the vowels shorter. Unintelligible without translation, and he was loathe to impose the technology of his own time on these people. Not until he was certain about what he was going to do about them.

***

His fight with the Thing had cost Ta'al his position, his friendships, his credibility and three years of his life. It had started with a special delivery from one of the retrieval teams. Field scientists visiting the past used grandfather boxes to store any discovery or information that might be of interest in the future. These boxes used the energy generated by minor paradoxes to create a time differential between their interior and exterior dimensions, a lensing effect that rendered them invisible for the millions of years that they would lie buried underground, waiting for their timers to activate and for retrieval teams to find them.

This box contained something quite special.. It was a skull—the prominent mid-face, large brow, receding forehead and the large occipital bun needed no DNA confirmation, reflecting as they did the shape of his own head. This was clear evidence of a late period Neanderthal tribe, the very last known to exist. They were his people and now, just as the records of their history were about to be brought to a close, he saw his chance—to become their saviour.

Kurtén, his research assistant, had been less certain. "Its our job to record history, professor," he had argued, "not to change it."

"We use paradox as a fuel source, Björn," Challenger had explained. "We couldn't exist as a society without them, and the Thing makes whatever changes it needs to so that our existence is preserved."

"That's different. Engineered paradoxes happen far from human space. They're just cosmic events. They don't affect lives."

"Of course they do. Have you never wondered what sort of paradoxes we create? Anything that threatens Midgardr's existence—such as the appearance of primordial life on other worlds. It's nothing less than abortion on a cosmic scale, and we turn a blind eye because we never see the possibilities that we destroy. An anthropic universe, Björn, is one made to suit the needs of humanity."

Their home—an island suspended at the very end of time—was the anchor to which the history of human civilisation was pinned. From Midgardr they could see all of history, a vantage point which made humanity the dominant species within a strongly anthropic universe. The survival of a human civilisation was practically its mission statement.

He had easily convinced the boy, and was equally convinced that the simple request that he wished to make—to embark upon one last expedition with a new imperative—would pose no problems for the powers that be. The Sandvik University was the most respected institution in Midgardr, and its dreaming spire was one of the largest structures on the island.

When he presented his plans Per Magnusson had been keen to support him, and he too had expected approval to be a formality. Had the scale of the expedition not been so considerable, he would not even have moved the matter upstairs. The reality, however, failed to meet their expectations, and when Challenger was summoned to the Chancellor's office, it was a long-faced Magnusson who greeted him.

"The Thing has considered your request," he said, "but I'm afraid the State Ministry raised an objection. They turned you down."

"The Ministry of State?" It had been a simple enough refusal, but the consequences were far reaching and, Challenger had thought, unexpected. "What possible objection could they have raised?"

"Citizenship and Colonization are in their purview," said Magnusson, "and they believe that establishing a Neanderthal colony on a post-human world could pose a threat to the status quo. The Thing agreed."

"What possible threat could they envisage?"

"Humanity exists for only a short period in cosmological terms. What if your Neanderthal culture outlasts it?"

"What?" Your Neanderthal culture. Those words dealt a severe blow to Challenger, asserting that neither he, nor his ancestors, were considered to be human after all. "*Homo neanderthalensis* are human. Common ancestry, shared taxonomy. Their DNA was mixed with that of the earliest *Homo sapiens*. They're your ancestors as well as mine."

"William, I agree," said Per, trying hard to calm his friend. That name though, was one he had long since rejected. "I'm on your side."

"Are you? These species are closer than cousins—their universe and that of *Homo sapiens* are wholly compatible. My proposal even ensures that they would exist in a time where there are no *Homo sapiens* to compete with. What exactly is the council afraid of? And why did they make their decision without giving me the opportunity to speak?"

"I'm sorry. It's just not an issue they've had to consider before. You have to give this time."

"Time?" Challenger laughed. "They own time. They have all the time in the universe. There's no excuse."

"It will require a change in policy—they don't see any difference between your people and any other non-human species."

"It's completely different. Even their skin is as white as that of the old men you work for—even if the law does say that no man shall be discriminated against because of the colour of his skin..."

"It's not about skin, though. This is genetic."

"Genetic purity you mean? It isn't enough that humanity is dominant, now *Homo sapiens* must be the only member of the club. It's unconscionable."

"I'm sure they didn't mean it that way."

"I may be a minority of one, but I still exist, and I'm still entitled to exist, to belong, to multiply."

"You want us to create a mate? I'm sure..."

"What? Do you even know what you just said Per? I'm not Frankenstein's monster, I'm a human being. If I wanted to breed I would have done so. What I want is to give my people a chance. My people, apparently, not yours. The only way the Thing can enforce this is to redefine the taxonomy of the human race. To change science for political purposes. Are you going to stand by and allow that?"

Leaving his Chancellor speechless hadn't been the intention, but it gave the slammed door and the subsequent resignation letter a much bigger impact. Challenger trusted that Magnusson would take up his crusade—that's what friends are for, after all—but it was clear that such a lengthy dispute had no guarantees, and that he must take matters into his own hands. Of course, resigning one's affiliation had consequences. Everyone on the island worked in one of the Ministries—Justice, Science, State, Trade, War or Works, and it was rare for someone to move between them. Grímsey—as the island was known—was a tiny rock barely covering an area of two square miles. It's infrastructure—from the top of its miles-high skyscrapers to the tip of the needle-like underside that tapered for nearly two thousand miles beneath its surface—barely had the space to sustain its growing population, so unemployment was tantamount to exile.

Exile suited Challenger—or Ta'al as he now chose to call himself—and arranging passage into the past was a relatively easy proposition in a society of time travellers. The difficulty lay with the second part of his journey.

***

Months had passed, and during his time with the valley folk there had been no encounters with the Sapiens. The secluded location suited their survival, but only for so long as their cousins didn't come looking. Ta'al had learned the rudiments of their language and completed the first draft of the last chapters of his magnum opus, The Oral History of the Valley Folk. Not that there was an audience for such a book any more. Not in Midgardr.

As he had suspected, the later years of Neanderthal civilisation had involved much interbreeding, largely forced upon the valley folk by the Sapiens. Their mobility, fertility and urge to act individually had far outstripped the Neanderthals, whose preference had been to settle and survive in close-knit communities whose growth was determined by the environment in which they found themselves. Aa'mon, the community elder, had been keen to understand why Ta'al was a traveller like the 'breeders', as he called the Sapiens.

"I was brought up among them," he explained. "Or their descendants."

"They are so keen to fill the spaces of the world," said Aa'mon. "Wherever we go, they follow. We shared, we tolerated, but the day would come when we were hidden among them. Unhappy. Unsettled. We would have no choice but to leave and walk towards the sun."

"They forced you out?"

"We were so few they would not know that we were gone. Perhaps one day an old man might ask his grandchild 'what happened to the pale folk that used to live among us?'. We were of no concern to them."

"I had the same problem," Ta'al smiled. "As you moved away from them, so did I. I needed to be with my own people."

"You are much like us," the elder said, "purer, perhaps. They did not breed with you?"

"I did not breed with them," Ta'al corrected. "I was in no rush. My work was more important to me."

"Work, it is never finished. Children come only when we need them. To survive," Aa'mon sighed. "It is why we are the last of the valley folk."

"You don't have to be. That's why I'm here—to give you the chance of a new home."

"This is our home."

"But the Sapients will come, and they will breed with you again."

Aa'mon paused to consider Ta'al's words. They were, he knew, made simpler. The stranger's clothes and tools were difficult to comprehend, and his wisdom came from a higher place than the valley folk had ever known.

"I fear we must live through their eyes," he said. "All things must come to an end. This is our valley. We are settled."

Ta'al could barely contain his frustration. The elder's words may have been simple, but he was a philosopher at heart. Perhaps, he thought, a more philosophical argument will work.

"By 'here', do you mean this place, or this time?"

Aa'mon frowned. "There is a difference?"

"There can be," said Ta'al. He had had such conversations before. These people lived for the present—it was one thing that separated them from the Sapients, who were paranoid about the future. There were common beliefs though, and he dwelled on those. "Seasons change. People grow old and weak. They die. This place will still exist many, many seasons from now, long after the breeders are dead."

"Will it be the same? Do they not make their mark upon the land?"

"They do. This land will come to be known as the Levant, the Middle East; a place where they wage war upon each other, tearing the world apart as they covet each others' lands over different bloodlines, different beliefs, different customs..."

"It is ever thus," said Aa'mon, looking out across his valley. "We are happy here. Happier, perhaps, than we have been for many seasons. Happy and at peace."

"But for how long? This is your end time. That's why I chose it—"

"Chose?"

"I chose to come here from far away. You are the last of my people. The last of the valley folk, and within a few years the breeders will come. If you stay here their civilisation will rise from the death of your civilisation."

"Does it come so quickly?"

"Very quickly. They will wipe all trace of you from the earth, they will build great settlements from stone, and the black blood of the Earth itself shall bleed out onto the landscape."

Aa'mon shifted uneasily, looking around at the sky, and the land, and the mountain. "We have no wish to settle a spoiled landscape."

"It isn't spoiled after mankind. They come, they go, the rain falls, the trees grow, the wind blows, the dust settles and the world continues. It will be yours, to settle and to grow, as the need arises. The world will be yours."

"We don't want the world," Aa'mon smiled, "just this place. How will you change the seasons?"

"The seasons won't change," said Ta'al, pulling a small black remote from his pocket. It bore a single button and a small red light. Pressing the button, he watched as the air around them grew still and the outline of a large object appeared ahead of them. As they looked on, the air itself solidified into an opaque container the size of a small house.

"What is this? How can this be?"

"It's just a box, Aa'mon," said Ta'al. "We call it a grandfather box. I need you to help me bury it deep beneath the mountain. Then we must remove all trace of the settlement and step inside. First we will sleep, and then, after many seasons, we shall wake."

**

Within days the last traces of the colony were gone, with the exception of a familiar skull which Ta'al placed inside the caves. The tribe, which numbered no more than thirty, were happy to follow Aa'mon and Ta'al, whose advice they followed as they would that of a wise ancestor. Descending into the covered pit they had excavated, they passed into the grandfather box, and out of history.

It performed as expected, and many, many seasons passed. For fifteen million years the valley folk slept beneath the mountains of the Levant as, overhead, the Cenozoic Era—the Age of Mammals—drew to a close. *Homo sapiens* dominated the planet before abandoning their world in the great push towards the stars. The civilisations of those left behind rose and fell until, in the twilight years of the age, extinction overcame them. This final era—the Posthumic—saw a combination of tectonic rotations and solar storms transform of the planet, triggering a wave of extinctions and the dawn of hothouse Earth. Mountains rose, oceans fell, Africa rotated and the mountainous deserts of the Middle East became a verdant coastal paradise.

Inside the box the timer counted down as its occupants slept. Only seconds passed, but in those seconds its destination came closer, reaching forwards to its preset destination fifteen million years into the future. With *Homo sapiens* a distant memory only the retrieval teams of the future, time travellers scouring an otherwise natural globe, might pose a problem, but Ta'al had ensured that the retrieval window was hundreds of thousands of years behind them. This place, under the shadow of the same mountains, would be fresh, virgin territory, and a new history was about to begin.

***

Lights flickered, alarms sounded and ears popped as the grandfather box opened and the fresh air of a new dawn rushed inside. Four tightly packed rows of sleep chambers opened as the curious and slightly bewildered valley folk emerged from what, to them, had been very temporary confinement. Ta'al and the Neanderthals emerged into a small chamber—their original pit, eroded and fractured by the years of change—from which a small and unfamiliar passage stretched upwards.

Curious, the professor examined the opening, and discovered that the tunnel had been shored up quite recently. Certainly not millions, thousands or even tens of years ago. Telling Aa'mon and the other valley folk to wait, he set off alone, following the passage to its opening several metres further on.

Outside was brilliant daylight, broken by the striated shadows of the trees and other foliage that surrounded the entrance. Pushing the flora to one side, Ta'al stepped out, to be greeted by a small party of men led by his former research fellow, Kurtén. He was some years older, but still recognisable, as was the young woman who stood by his side. Challenger had never met her before, but the features were similar to his own. *Homo neanderthalensis*, but dressed in the clothes of his own time.

"Björn? What's going on?"

"I'm Naimh Challenger," said the woman, cutting Kurtén off before he could reply, "Professor Emeritus of the Institute of Chronoarchaeological Studies."

She paused. That had been Ta'al's title, and no doubt the DNA used to create her had been his own. Name and title. Was nobody unique or irreplaceable any more?

"Yes, that's right. I'm your successor. I'm also head of the Sandvik Cultural Resettlement Programme."

"Cultural..."

"Magnusson and I went back to the Thing," said Björn. "We—he—persuaded them to think again about your proposal. It took nearly ten years, and you weren't there to make it happen. Naimh took over because we refused to take responsibility without a proper spokesperson. You've got your wish, your people have a home."

Shocked, Ta'al looked around. The shadow of the mountain was vaguely familiar, but there was more. Beyond the trees he could see signs of a settlement, larger and more advanced than that of the valley folk. Adobe huts and palls of smoke were visible in the distance.

"How long have you been here?"

"The settlements are thirty years old," said Naimh. "Björn here established them according to your proposals, and we make periodic visits to monitor and observe. We've relocated a dozen scattered tribes, and we didn't know where you were until a retrieval alarm alerted us. They thought you were long gone."

"It's good to see you, Björn," said Ta'al. "How many are out there?"

"Enough to ensure a minimum viable population. When we started there were six thousand, and we've persuaded them that breeding is an imperative."

"Six thousand? I've never seen a settlement with those numbers. It makes them viable, yes, but it also means we may have fulfilled the needs of history. Instead of a paradox we might just be the ones that made these people extinct."

"It's possible," agreed Naimh, "but is that a bad thing? They were being marginalised, turned into outsiders, but here—without competition—they will be dominant. They can expand."

"Perhaps, but it feels wrong."

"Oh? And how many are in your grandfather box? Twenty? Thirty?"

"Thirty two. I estimated a 70% genetic survival probability, and with my knowledge I hoped to skew the cultural."

"That's too few," she said. "Think of the risks, the lack of diversity. So many things—from inbreeding depression to viral outbreaks or natural disasters—could wipe them out."

"It is too many," said Aa'mon, drawing attention to the fact that he and the valley folk had emerged from the darkness, clustering around the tunnel entrance. Each of them carried the few possessions they had gathered for their journey, and from their faces Ta'al could see a mixture of emotions. Uncertainty, fear, confusion. "This is not what you promised, Ta'al."

"Aa'mon, forgive me. This is not what I expected. But it is surely better. These are your people, certainly more than I. Surely you can—"

The elder's hand was raised in the halting gesture he had learned from Ta'al. In it, he held a short wooden rod aloft.

"I have the talking stick," he said, "and you must know that we feel betrayed. We are not settled. We are not happy."

"But this is the settlement," argued the professor, pointing to the outline of the mountain. "This is still your home."

"No." Aa'mon turned to his people, and in return the valley folk nodded in agreement with his sentiment. "We are not settled. We are not happy."

As one, the valley folk gathered themselves together, and walked towards the sun.

EXPERT HELP

Richard Freeman

The big cat crouched, motionless in the wan light of the Hyperborean shrine. Its fur was a golden brown in colour lightening to a sandy shade on the underside. It resembled no living cat known to man. The animal's longer forelegs and shorter back ones gave it a sloping, hyena-like profile. Its tail was short and stumpy like that of a lynx. But it was not the profile or tail that drew the observer's eye but the creature's spectacular dentition. Its canine teeth were vastly elongated, protruding down from the upper jaw like a brace of ivory scimitars. The amber eyes of the predator seemed fixed on some foe in an unblinking, pitiless stare.

This then was none other than *Smilodon fatalis* apex predator of the late Pleistocene epoch of North America. The silence of the scene was broken by the click of a camera taking a single shot. The great cat remained still.

A seemingly outsized hand reached down and moved the smilodon's paw a tiny fraction then the camera took another shot. The hand belonged to a tall, slim man with receding hair and intense, intelligent eyes. He mopped sweat from his brow with a handkerchief and looked down at the saber-toothed cat.

The beast was a moveable model. An articulated wore skeleton covered in latex and dyed fur. Fur, damned fur it never looked quite right. He was so much more at home animating monsters with scales or naked skin, even feathers. Fur could be a royal pain in the backside. The way it could rumple up from shot to shot making the final animation look as if the subject was being assailed by a giant, invisible hair dryer. He had animated many creatures, dinosaurs, dragons, mythical monsters but this saber-cat was the most difficult since the hydra. He just couldn't seem to get a handle on it. . He was beginning to wish he had stuck with his original idea of animating an *Arsinoitherium andrewsii*, a horned, superficially rhinoceros-like prehistoric mammal for the scene instead of the smilodon. Its bare skin would have been much less trouble.

Moreover the cat's movement didn't seem to be right. It looked clunky and awkward. Not at all realistic or smooth like his other creations.

Stop-motion animation was time consuming. In a full day's work in his studio he was lucky to get five seconds of finished film. The live action sequences had already been filmed in Malta, Madrid and Jordan. The production was now awaiting the stop motion monster sequences and he was beginning to fall behind. He hoped the visitor he was expecting that afternoon could help him.

There was a knock and the co-writer and producer of the film Charles H Schneer put his head around the studio door.

"Ray, how's it going?"

"Not too well I'm afraid."

"Trouble with that darn sabre tooth still?"

Ray stood up and stretched his back aching after hours of crouching over his creation.

"Smilodon blues Charlie. It's the single most difficult thing I've ever tried to animate. The giant octopus on the Golden Gate Bridge was a walk in the park next to this."

"Remember I told you I'd got hold off a guy who could help?" said Charles beaming.

"A paleontologist?"

"Oh no my friend, someone far more qualified than that. Won't you come on in Mr. Oop?"

Another figure appeared behind Charles and walked into the studio. He was the strangest looking man Ray had ever seen. The fellow was not a tall man, about five feet four inches, but he was massively broad. The man's shoulders put the largest American football player to shame. His barrel chest strained the buttons of his ill fitting shirt. The muscles that played beneath dwarfed those of an Olympic weight lifter. His jacket seemed to barley fit him and his hands protruded from his shirt sleeves to their wrists. Ray noted how hairy the back of the man's hands were.

As he moved closer Ray saw he had shortish, somewhat bandy legs but they too were powerfully muscled. His feet, in brogues seemed wider than normal. Yet the oddness of his body was not what drew the viewer's attention. It was the man's face. A mane of auburn hair fell down to his titan shoulders. He had no facial hair. His skull had a thick, gorilla-like brow ridge above large, brown eyes. His nose was both large and broad, the nostrils huge. He had wide mouth with narrow lips that revealed large, square, white teeth as he smiled. Despite his massive jaw the man had little chin to speak on, the face flowing into the short, bull neck.

The man strode over, took Ray's hand in a powerful grip and shook it.

"Mr. Harryhausen, I'm very glad to meet you. Your work is inspirational." His voice had a slight Russian accent.

"Er ... thank you Mr. Oop" answered Ray trying not to wince from the strange man's bone scrunching hand shake.

"Please call me Alley."

"Well thank you Alley, call me Ray. I think you may be able to help me. I understand you have some knowledge of sabre-toothed cats?"

The man nodded his woolly head.

"Yes indeed but not this particular species. *Smilodon* was native to North America; my people never crossed the ocean. The ones I dealt with were *Homotherium latidens*. They had shorter canines but they hunted and moved in much the same way."

Ray was puzzled. "You mean you have studied their fossils of these things?"

"Oh no I dealt with them in the flesh, in tooth and claw."

Alley unbuttoned his shirt revealing a massive chest almost as hairy as a gorilla's. Four lines of scar tissue ran across his chest at an angle.

"Feisty little buggers I can tell you."

"But sabre-cats died out..."

"Approximately ten thousand years ago along with scimitar cats like my *Homotherium*."

Ray's puzzled stare confirmed that he wasn't following Alley at all.

"Then how could you possibly..."

"Don't you think I look a little odd Ray?"

The animator blushed slightly.

"Well you are extraordinarily muscular."

"And hairy. And you won't see another skull like this one outside of a natural history museum."

"I'm still in the dark here Alley."

"Ray, I am a surviving Neanderthal. As far as I know the only one."

Alley moved closer allowing Ray to get a better look at his features.

"I'm used to folk staring so don't be shy."

Indeed Alley looked very like reconstructions of Neanderthals painted by the Czech artist Zdeněk Burian.

"How did you survive?" Ray was still not sure he was believing his own eyes.

"Quite a story. I lived with a small tribe in the mountains of what is now called Kazakhstan. I was out hunting Ibex in the late Autumn and the weather was beginning to get nasty. I was separated from the other men in a blizzard and hid in a cave over night. It was no big deal. We Neanderthals are cold adapted. Look at the snozz for example; it heats up the cold air as we breathe it in."

Alley paused to point to his large, wide nose.

"Anyhow the blizzard passed and I began down hill again. The out of the forest comes a cave bear. Well they should have been going into hibernation at this time of year but there had been a poor crop of fruits in the woods that year and many of them were staying awake longer and eating more meat, including people!

"The cave bear was a huge thing, bigger than a polar bear or a Kodiak and mean as a sack full of wolverines. He came at me all teeth and claws. My spear was smashed like a twig and I thought my number was up. I ran like hell but a cave bear can really shift despite its size. I've seen them run down elk so what chance did I have?

"I was feeling his breath on my neck then *bam*, the ground just seemed to open up and I was falling. Next thing I knew I was having bright likes shone into my eyes and three skinny men with tiny noses and almost no hair there looking at me. I thought I was with the gods. I was strapped to a table, though I didn't know what a table was back then; I just thought it was some kind of odd rock in a very well lit cave.

"As it turned out they were Soviet scientists on a zoological expedition. Apparently I had been frozen for 45,000 years! Talk about oversleeping."

"Didn't being frozen kill you?" asked Ray.

"If it had been pure ice that preserved then I was. I got luck. I fell into a crevasse full of frozen mud. Apparently there were chemicals that had leeched down from the rocks that helped preserve me. I never did fully grasp quite how it happened. I don't think the scientists did either.

"At first I was terrified. They kept me locked up in a cell passing food and water through a hole in the wall. But us Neanderthals have great memories and we are very adaptable. That's why we lasted so long. I picked up modern Russian very quickly. It soon became clear to them that I was an intelligent human being. They started treating me a bit better after that."

"How come you ended up in England?"

"I got bored. Day after day endless rounds of question on Ice age animals, every aspect of Neanderthal life and culture, the climate, the vegetation. On top of that all the tests comparing me with you Cro-Magnons. I got a bit ticked off in the end.

"Because they had got to thinking of me as one of them they trusted me. I was in some government laboratories secreted in the Urals. It was one of those secret places, cold war and all that tummy rot. It was a piece of cake for me to shoot up a tree and drop down over the wall. I was off into the forest before they knew what was happening. I survived in the mountains with ease. After living in the Ice Age the Urals were a walk in the park.

"I wandered across Russia for months living off the land. I finally do to Moscow and made some money on the underground fighting ring. I'm about eight times as strong as a modern man and my bone structure is a lot thicker. When you've tangled with mega-fauna a few old Cossacks aren't much threat.

"Anyhow I made a fair bit of cash in these punch ups so I got myself a fake ID and passport. I thought I'd head to Britain."

"Why Britain of all places?"

"Well we used to get quite a bit of UK telly in Russia. I really like David Attenborough he seemed much nicer than the Russian scientists. I'd learned the basics of English off the box so I wandered down through Scandinavia (where I was mistaken for a troll a couple of times) then got on a ship to England.

"I got a job as a bouncer in a London night club. That's were your friend Charlie met me. We got talking and I'm a big fan of your work. I loved *Animal World* and *Valley of Gwangi*. Damn glad the dinosaurs had gone by my time though. Mammoths and woolly rhino are one thing but even I would blanch at a *Tyrannosaurus rex*!

"Charlie said you were having trouble with the old Smilodon and I was happy to come along and help."

Ray was still agog. "That is quite a story; you really have to write a book some day."

"I think I might just do that."

"What became of your race, why did the Neanderthals die out?"

"I haven't a clue Ray. They were doing fine when I was around. We lasted at least another 15,000 years after I fell down that crevasse.

Ray shook himself out of his dazed state. "Where are my manners? You come all the way from Russia and 45,000 years through time and I haven't even offered you a cup of tea!"

After consuming a large pot of chai and a plate of macaroons Alley clapped his scoop sized hands together and said "Now let's have a look at this sabre-tooth of yours."

Alley strolled over to the model and smiled.

"Not bad, not half bad."

"I just can't seem to get its movements right" mused Ray.

"Have you been watching big cats and trying to emulate their movements?"

Ray nodded. "Yes I've been watching lions and tigers in London Zoo and on wildlife films."

"That's where you're going wrong my friend. Sabre-toothed and scimitar-toothed cats didn't move or hunt like modern big cats. They specialised in taking down large cumbersome prey like bison and musk ox. They sacrificed speed for power. A sabre-cat would ambush its prey then grapple with it, pulling it down with the claws and its muscular front legs. Sabre-cats did not leap down upon their prey to stab at it with the long canines. They were far too fragile and would have snapped. Once the prey was down the sabre-teeth would be used to slash at the neck and windpipe. They had a far larger gape than modern cats and that allowed them to get those exaggerated teeth around the necks of the victims."

***

Over the next few weeks Alley helped Ray to animate the smilodon. He often posed himself in attitudes like those he had seen the big cats in. He suggested a light spray of water to slick down the fur and make it more manageable. With Alley's advice Ray managed to animate a life-like sequence with the smilodon battling Sinbad the Sailor and troglodyte. The latter creature amused Alley no end as it was a fictional 'cave man' depicted as being twelve feet tall and with a rhino-like horn atop its head, completely unlike any real species of hominin.

"Don't get me started on cave man horns," laughed Alley, "us male Neanderthals have priapism!"

The sequence was filmed on time and Columbia Pictures was delighted with the result. *Sinbad and the Eye of the Tiger* went on to be a very successful film. Alley and Ray became good friends over the weeks they worked together.

Ray asked Alley to stay on and help him animate monsters in his future projects. Alley declined and when Ray asked why Alley told him.

"Did you ever hear of the *almasty* Ray? They are supposed to be some kind of wildman living in the Caucasus. Apparently back in the 1950s there was even a Soviet Government commission to study them. They are not like the Himalayan yeti. They're smaller and more man-like than ape like. The theory is that they are surviving Neanderthals. Not ones frozen in time like me but ones that have survived naturally by hiding in the forests and mountains far from the reach of modern man. I thought I was all alone in the world, my kind long gone. Now it seems that there is a small change some of my people may still be alive I have to try and seek them out. I'm leaving for Russia at the weekend. I hope you understand."

***

Of course Ray did understand, though he was sad to see his unique friend go. Ray never did Alley again but about a year later he received a parcel by air mail. It had come from a post office in Nalchik in the Karbadino-Balkaria region of the Caucasus. Inside was a necklace of bears' teeth, shells and semi-precious stones and a letter written on rough paper that read...

"Dear Ray,

Your old Pal Alley here. Sorry for not writing for so long but I have been rather busy. I'm living in the Russian Caucasus now. The almasty were real and they are living Neanderthals! At first we had a few language problems as their tongue is different to that used by my tribe 45,000 years ago. But they accepted me into there society and I picked up the language pretty quickly.

I have taken a mate, Ooola and gone through the pair bonding ritual. She is expecting our first child. I do not plan to return to modern society. Life here is so much more simple and rewarding. I miss the mammoths and woolly rhino but you can't have it all.

I'd deem it a favour if you keep this a secret. My Neanderthal society meeting modern man is not a good idea. As well as transmitting modern diseases I think it would mean an end to our culture. Just look what happened to the American Indians. Look at what is happening to native people all over the world.

I'm happy here but I will never forget the week I spent working with you, the greatest monster maker of them all. You would make a fine shaman.

Yours with Love,
Alley Oop.

Dedicated with much affection to the memory of Ray Harryhausen June 29, 1920 – May 7, 2013

A BRIEF HISTORY OF NEANDERTHALS IN SPECULATIVE FICTION

David Willard

Of all the hominid species uncovered in modern times, none has been more inspirational than Neanderthal man. Since its 1850 discovery by a local schoolteacher, Carl Fuhrott, in the limestone caves of the Neander Valley, through to the complete DNA sequencing of the Neanderthal genome in December 2013 there have been more questions posed about our nearest cousin than about any other.

The obvious reason for such curiosity is that they were—having coexisted on the planet with *Homo sapiens* for around three hundred thousand years—our last contemporaries. Their extinction, but for the grace of God, was ours (the grace of God is used here as a euphemism for random chance). Of the many theories as to why *Homo sapiens* proliferated and *Homo neanderthalensis* died out, most dwell on our superiority—a classic misrepresentation that has resonances with modern racism. In his book, Outline of History, H G Wells said:

"...we know very little of the appearance of the Neanderthal man, but this... seems to suggest an extreme hairiness, an ugliness, or a repulsive strangeness in his appearance over and above his low forehead, his beetle brows, his ape neck, and his inferior stature". This view, reinforced by a quote about "gorilla-like monsters with cunning brains, shambling gait, hairy bodies, strong teeth, and possibly cannibalistic tendencies" being "the germ of the ogre in folklore".

This attitude established the idea that the Neanderthals were ape-like sub-humans given little credibility as competitors for the vastly more advanced *Homo sapiens*. Racial superiority seems an unlikely reason for their extinction. It took so many millenia for us to outcompete the Neanderthals that the difference may just have been a half a percentage difference in birthrate, so whatever saw the shift in our favour was the sum of many factors.

Perhaps we were slightly more fertile or had a slightly shorter gestation period. Perhaps our diet was more suited to the climate changes of the last 100,000 years. Perhaps we were more flexible in our lifestyles and our migratory patterns. Perhaps we just made a key discovery first—clothes, agriculture, the domestication of dogs—certainly we have been painted as a more innovative people when compared to the stagnant Neanderthals, but is that really true? We have been blinded by our bias towards our own people, and our own flaws could be the cause of their undoing. Were we the more aggressive species, or were we just the more communal, forcing ourselves upon them wherever they were discovered? We know there was interbreeding, but we cannot tell if it was voluntary. In the last five thousand years of their existence, we lived alongside the Neanderthal. Maybe there was not just some early interbreeding, but also a period of cohabitation. Then again, the incoming *Homo sapiens* may have taken Neanderthal women in much the same way as Vikings took Celtic or Pictish women in their raids, or perhaps we simply assimilated them into our society until they disappeared, right under our noses.

One clear reason for the enduring popularity of the Neanderthal—especially in literature—lies with the timing of their discovery. It was in 1864, just five years after Charles Darwin published On the Origin of Species, that *Homo neanderthalensis* was classified as a related but distinct form of human being—seeing off the much less subtle name of *Homo stupidus* in the process. It was the poster child of evolutionary theory, begging the question "is this our ancestor or our cousin?" While some cried blasphemy, the curious wanted to know, were these people 'the missing link' between apes and men?

The fiction followed, with thinly veiled Neanderthals appearing as Morlocks in H G Wells' The Time Machine (1895), and as ape-men in both Conan Doyle's The Lost World (1912) and Edgar Rice Burroughs' The Land that Time Forgot (1916). The first true Neanderthal story, J H Rosny's Quest for Fire (1911) took the known facts of the time and turned them into a speculative novella about primitive simpletons. This approach would not happen again until Clan of the Cave Bear, the year before Rosny's story was committed to film. When Wells openly referenced them in The Grisly Folk (1921), he set the precedent of promoting flawed speculation and bad science. This and later stories reinforced society's superiority complex towards the primitive, both in the real world—where microcephalic freaks were sometimes called Neantherthal 'throwbacks' to the literary trend of portraying certain primitive cultures as 'sub-human', giving the racist attitudes of the interwar years free reign. Lovecraft's Deep Ones and the primitive Tcho-Tcho people are classic examples of using such tropes to draw thinly-veiled allusions to position white Caucasians as a master race while relegating other forms of *Homo sapiens* to the fantasy realm of 'racial inferiority'.

The Second World War brought with it the rejection of such concepts as genocide and eugenic preselection. Postcolonial cultures began, quite rightly, to revile the idea of using cavemen as a racist metaphor, and a new form of literature slowly emerged.

William Golding, who had already explored the darker side of human nature in his seminal book The Lord of the Flies (1954) returned again to the subject with his tale of two people, The Inheritors (1955). This took the sympathetic view of introducing Neanderthals as viewpoint characters before shifting the perspective to that of *Homo sapiens*, but its use of simplistic names and motivations helped perpetuate the portrayal of primitive humans as stupid, and this writer certainly sees the inspirations for a Doctor Who story (The Tribe of Gum, 1963) within its pages. The latter helped open up the possibilities of using Neanderthals in an SF context, and there have been many examples in which surviving or recreated Neanderthals, or telepaths, or time travellers, have been included as an alternative to aliens or early *Homo sapiens*.

In the wake of this more enlightened approach to storytelling, a new genre—that of prehistorical fiction—has emerged. Spearheaded by Jean M Auel's Clan of the Cave Bear (1980) and Björn Kurtén's Dance of the Tiger (1980) this has taken the portrayal of the Neanderthal away from its racist roots (although there remain some links between the appearance of the Neanderthal and some of their physical similarities to Australia's aboriginal culture), although the use of Neanderthal culture as a thinly veiled metaphor to emphasise the darker side of modern man's nature has become a powerful theme. These changes have similarly been reflected in the evolution of the artistic form. The brutish, microcephalic dioramas of the twenties and thirties inspired by the work of Marcellin Boulle (whose theories were not dismissed until 1957) gave way to softer, more humanlike representations which, while retaining key features, have done away with many inaccurate assumptions. In fine art, meanwhile, the rendering of the Neanderthal has moved away from emphasising the differences in favour of emphasising the similarities.

Neanderthals in literature - a reading list:

A Story of the Stone Age, H G Wells, 1897;
Quest for Fire, J H Rosny, (novella) 1911;
The Grisly Folk, H G Wells (short story), 1921
Og, Son of Fire, Irving Crump, 1922
Og, Boy of Battle, Irving Crump, 1925
Three Go Back, James Leslie Mitchell, 1932
Og of the Cave People, Irving Crump, 1935
Dian of the Lost Land, Edison Marshall, 1935
The Gnarly Man, L Sprague de Camp, 1939
The Sentinel, Arthur C Clarke, 1948
The Inheritors, William Golding, 1955
The Ugly Little Boy, Isaac Asimov (short story), 1958
The Alley Man, Philip Jose Farmer (short story), 1959
The Bull from the Sea, Mary Renault, 1962
The Simulacra, Philip K Dick, 1964
Og, Son of Og, Irving Crump, 1965
The Goblin Reservation, Clifford D Simak, 1968
Neanderthal Planet, Brian W Aldiss (short story), 1969
To Your Scattered Bodies Go, Philip Jose Farmer, 1972
Eaters of the Dead, Michael Crichton, 1976
The Clan of the Cave Bear, Jean M Auel, 1980
Dance of the Tiger: A Novel of the Ice Age, Björn Kurtén, 1980
The Valley of Horses, Jean M Auel, 1982
The Nest, Poul Anderson (short story), 1984
The Man Whose Teeth Were All Exactly Alike, Philip K Dick, 1984
The Mammoth Hunters, Jean M Auel, 1985
Singletusk: A Novel of the Ice Age, Björn Kurtén, 1986
Ghost Light. Marc Platt (novelisation), 1990
The Plains of Passage, Jean M Auel, 1990
Hunting the Ghost Dancer, A A Attanasio, 1991
Timewyrm:Genesys, John Peel, 1991
The Ugly Little Boy, Isaac Asimov & Robert Silverberg (novel), 1992
Down in the Bottomlands, Harry Turtledove (novella), 1993
Ember from the Sun, Mark Canter, 1995
Neanderthal, John Darnton, 1996
Circles of Stone, Joan Dahr Lambert, 1997

Frameshift, Robert J Sawyer, 1997
Waiting, Frank M Robinson, 1999
The Silk Code, Paul Levinson, 1999
Manifold: Space, Stephen Baxter, 2000
Manifold: Origin, Stephen Baxter, 2001
Evolution, Stephen Baxter, 2002
The Shelters of Stone, Jean M Auel, 2002
Neanderthal Parallax: Hominids, Robert J Sawyer, 2002
Neanderthal Parallax: Humans, Robert J Sawyer, 2003
Neanderthal Parallax: Hybrids, Robert J Sawyer, 2003
Raising Abel, W Michael Gear and Kathleen O'Neal Gear, 2003
Darwin's Radio, Greg Bear, 2003
Heaven, Ian Stewart & Jack Kohn, 2004
The Sky People, S M Stirling, 2006
Heal Thyself, Orson Scott Card (short story), 2008
The Neanderthal Correlation, Jeff Hecht (short story) 2008
N-Words, Ted Kosmata (short story), 2008
The Land of Painted Caves, Jean M Auel, 2011
Shaman, Kim Stanley Robinson, 2013

CONTRIBUTORS

Matthew Sylvester lives in Exeter and describes himself as a 'father, author and martial artist.' Matthew has been reading and writing fantasy and science fiction since he first read the Hobbit at the age of 7. Currently he is working on the worlds of Shattered Lands and Faraway, adult steamfantasy and child's steamfantasy. The latter is a co-operative project with his eldest daughter.

Anne Henderson is currently an academic administrator, associate provost and dean for the sciences at the Graduate Center of the City University of New York. As a professor, she was a geneticist and has published over 100 scientific articles in peer-reviewed journals and books. She also writes short stories.

Christer Van is the master of the unfinished story, which he claims is because he lives close to an airport which provides constant interruptions. He loves the works of Jack Kirby, anything in a mask, and privacy. He lives in the vicinity of Dayton, Ohio, but shoots trespassers.

Eric Stein is a journalist and editor who writes fiction in his spare time. He lives outside of San Francisco, California, with his wife and their two children.

Andrew Freudenberg is a creator of dark fiction. He has always loved words. He returned to writing seriously after a long period of musical distraction. As well as running his own label, making records and playing live, he also promoted club nights including London's notorious 'Club Alien'. Although his DJ appearances were few he did once play for Russian gangsters in Moscow. He'd never admit it though. His short stories can currently be found haunting the pages of numerous anthologies. These include 'Kizuna: Fiction for Japan' and releases from KnightWatch, MayDecember Publications, JWK Fiction, RainStorm and Angelic Knight Press. He lives in the South-West of England and is working on a variety of projects as well as raising three young sons.

Derek Muk is a writer and social worker from California. His short stories have appeared in various online and small press magazines, including "Diabolic Tales 3," "Both Barrels of Legends of the Monster Hunter I and II," "The Trigger Reflex: Legends of the Monster Hunter II" (anthology), "Suffer the Little Children" (anthology), "Splatter: An Anthology of Horror," "Death Rattle," "Dark Things II" (Anthology), and many others. He has three chapbooks published: "Three Parts," "The Sacrifice and Other Stories," and "Sin after Sin." In addition to writing, he enjoys reading, traveling, museums, art, dining out, and meeting new people. He has a bachelors and masters degree in social work. "The Occult Files of Albert Taylor" is his first full length collection of short stories. His website address is: http://theoccultfilesofalberttaylor.wordpress.com/

Christine Morgan works the overnight shift in a psychiatric facility, which plays havoc with her sleep schedule but allows her a lot of writing time. A lifelong reader, she also reviews, beta-reads, occasionally edits and dabbles in self-publishing. Her other interests include gaming, history, superheroes, crafts, cheesy disaster movies and training to be a crazy cat lady. She can be found online at www.christine-morgan.org.

Vince Liberato was a finalist in the Amazing Stories Gernsback Writing Contest 2015. He will be featured in an upcoming anthology via Amazing Stories, and his other work can be found in the Demonic Visions series, Redshifted: Martian Stories and Master Minds (via Third Flatiron Press), and several other science fiction anthologies which are linked to his Amazon profile. He lives in Texas.

Chris Amies was born in South London. He is a Languages graduate and taught English as a Foreign Language in Greece before working for the British Civil Service. He moved to Birmingham in 2011. He has had several stories published in magazines and anthologies including several Fringeworks titles; his novel *Dead Ground* was reissued in 2013 and is soon to be followed by a sequel. He is translating Arthur Bernede's 1927 novel *Belphegor* for Fringeworks.

Andrew Miller lives in Los Angeles. He has stories forthcoming in *Asimov's Science Fiction* and *Kaleidotrope*.

Jon Wesick is host of the Gelato Poetry Series, instigator of the San Diego Poetry Un-Slam, and an editor of the *San Diego Poetry Annual.* He has published over seventy short stories in journals such as *The Berkeley Fiction Review, Space and Time, Zahir, Tales of the Talisman, Blazing Adventures,* and *Metal Scratches.* He has also published over three hundred poems. Jon has a Ph.D. in physics and is a longtime student of Buddhism and the martial arts. One of his poems won second place in the 2007 African American Writers and Artists contest.

Julius Horne (1906-2006) was a Staffordshire storyteller whose works went unpublished during his lifetime. A raconteur, a practising white magician, a collector of folk tales and other arcane stories, he claimed that many of his tales were drawn from real life, and that truth will always be stranger than fiction.

Matthew Wilson has had over 150 appearances in such places as *Horror Zine, Star*Line, Spellbound, Illumen, Apokrupha Press, Hazardous Press, Gaslight Press, Sorcerers Signal* and many more. He is currently editing his first novel

Rebecca Fung is a legal editor from Sydney, Australia. She spends her days watching others being published - and by night, she writes and hopes to join them. She has previously had her short published in Midnight Echo and Eclecticism magazines and is a regular contributor to the "Demonic Visions" anthology series.

She has also been published in various anthologies, including several other Fringeworks anthologies - "Potatoes!", "Her Dark Voice", and "Grimm and Grimmer". Her ebook "Dead Lucky" will be published by Perpetual Motion Machine Publishing in their "One Night Stands" series in late 2014.

Steve Graeme is the pen name of Steve Jones, a long time SF fan whose name gets him mistaken for others all the time. Most famous as the mobile green room at various conventions, Steve was the inspiration for Terry Pratchett's bursar, and occasionally gets published in anthologies alongside famous people. He lives in an invisible tower with his feline companion, Captain Fang.

Adrian Middleton is a former civil servant and policy adviser who got bored and set up a small press called Fringeworks. Yo-Yoing between poverty and prosperity, he sometimes regrets his decision, but damn, he's obsessed.

Richard Freeman is a full time cryptozoologist and searches for and writes about unknown animals. He has hunted for creatures such as the yeti, the Mongolian deathworm, the giant anaconda, the almasty, orang-pendek, the naga and the Tasmanian wolf. He is Zoological Director at the Centre for Fortean Zoology, the world's only full time mystery animal research organization. It is based in North Devon. He writes mainly non-fiction books about cryptozoology, folklore and monsters including *Dragons: More Than a Myth?*, *Explore Dragons*, *The Great Yokai Encyclopaedia: An A to Z of Japanese Monsters* and *Orang-Pendek: Sumatra's Forgotten Ape*. He has recently branched out into horror and weird fantasy with *Green Unpleasant Land: 18 Tales of British Horror* and *Hyakumonagatari: Tales of Japanese Horror Book One*. His influences include E.F Benson, M.R James, William Hope Hodgson, Manley Wade Wellman, H.H Munro, Edward Lucas White, H.P Lovecraft, Clark Aston Smith, Alan Moore and classic TV horror and SF such as Dr Who, The Prisoner, Quatermass, Ace of Wands, Kolchak the Night Stalker, The Outer Limits and Sapphire and Steel.

Darrel Bevan: Colour-blind, Darrel is a portrait and figure illustrator who, due to colour blindness, specialises in graphite illustration—mainly on black and white images. When he isn't producing photorealistic pencil drawings, he teaches.

FIND OUT MORE ABOUT FRINGEWORKS BY SCANNING THE QR CODE BELOW

WWW.FRINGEWORKS.CO.UK

www.ingramcontent.com/pod-product-compliance
Lightning Source LLC
Chambersburg PA
CBHW061133200626
46817CB00016B/1382